ANN WILLIAMS
What Lindsey Knew

Silhouette Sensation

*First published in Great Britain in 1993
by Silhouette Books, Eton House, 18-24 Paradise Road,
Richmond, Surrey TW9 1SR*

© Peggy A. Myers 1991

Silhouette, Silhouette Sensation and Colophon are
Trade Marks of Harlequin Enterprises B.V.

ISBN 0 373 58799 6

18-9305

Made and printed in Great Britain

Other novels by Ann Williams

Silhouette Sensation

Devil in Disguise
Haunted by the Past
Angel On My Shoulder

To Pat Hall,
my best friend.
Remember that one special
lunch at the Lotus?

Prologue

"Damn it! What do you mean you're not sure about your end of things?" The tall, rawboned man, dressed all in black, half rose from his chair. The table shook as he spread large, hairy hands flat on its shiny surface and fixed his companion with hard, angry black eyes.

"We been planning this heist for over a month. Don't start jerkin' me around now." He started to sit down, then hesitated. "And don't think you're gonna weasel out of your end of things, either."

Shaking a finger under his cringing companion's nose, he added, "I'm the one who says whether we go ahead with it or not. And if the only reason you got for wantin' to put it off is 'cause you suddenly discovered you got a yellow streak where your backbone ought to be—well, that's just too bad," he snarled.

"It makes me real nervous when you start hedgin' like this—and you know how I get when I'm nervous." The threat was obvious, even though he sat down, picked up the menu and began to scan it.

"Now, let's just forget all about your worries." He let the plastic-covered menu fall back and looked across at his companion. "You got any objections to that?"

The smaller man swallowed tightly and nodded in anxious agreement, then saw his companion's swarthy face darken and quickly shook his head instead.

"Good." The bigger man adjusted the menu for a closer look in the dimly lighted room and added, "I'm starved. Let's order. We can go over the details while we eat."

Debra Foley released the pent-up breath she'd been holding and blinked startled blue eyes. Was that for real? Had she really sat here and listened to two criminals planning an actual *heist?* It sounded too bizarre to be taken seriously. Surely men intent on such a criminal undertaking would have been smart enough to have picked a place where they were less likely to be overheard.

Debra gazed around at the other diners to see if anyone else had overheard the men. But everyone appeared to be totally engrossed in their own little world, unaware of the dark plot being hatched in the secluded alcove only a few feet behind where she now sat.

What should she do? Should she tell someone? The waiter? The restaurant manager? Or should she call the police?

Where was Lindsey? Debra glanced up the narrow aisle, searching for the familiar figure of her best friend. The other woman had excused herself to go to the ladies' room a few minutes earlier and should have been on her way back by now.

At that precise moment she spotted her friend's familiar figure as she turned the corner and glided smoothly down the small walkway between tables, heading in her direction. Good, now someone else would be witness to what was taking place at the hidden table behind her, and she could stop feeling as though she had somehow stumbled onto the set of some grade B thriller.

Debra barely restrained herself from motioning for her friend to hurry.

Lindsey Hamilton slid gracefully onto the chair across from Debra and fixed her crystal-green eyes on the other woman's face. "You look flushed. Is anything wrong?" Her voice, naturally low and husky, was barely audible above the noise from the other diners.

"No—that is, I don't know." Debra straightened, looped a stray blond curl behind one ear and shot her friend an agitated glance. By now she was having serious second thoughts about what she had—or thought she had—overheard. "In any case," she added, "you won't believe me."

"Believe what?" Lindsey asked, familiar with her friend's nervous gesture and knowing, too, that it was brought on by feelings of discomfort or suppressed excitement. Which of those, she wondered, was responsible this time?

Debra indicated the room divider behind her with a flutter of one hand and motioned for the other woman to draw closer. "Back there," she whispered.

Slightly exasperated, but nonetheless curious about what her friend had come up with now, Lindsey played along with her.

"What?" she asked in a low tone. She'd been unable to make out anything above the usual sounds in a restaurant full of hungry people intent on sharing loud, hurried conversation along with a quick meal.

"I—I'm not certain exactly. But I think I heard two men plotting a crime."

Lindsey gave Debra a dubious glance and settled back in her chair. "Crime?" she asked.

"Yes, crime, as in heist. You know—the theft of someone's property. One man sounded very angry because the other one didn't want to go through with it."

"You heard all that just now?"

Debra was always seeing some sort of intrigue in the most innocuous situations. She could pass a stranger on the street and come up with a whole repertoire of mystery and romance from the expression on his face.

Lindsey had always secretly thought the other woman should have taken up writing or acting as a career, instead of going into secretarial training. Such ordinary work was too mundane for as fertile an imagination as Debra possessed.

Even as an adolescent, Lindsey had recognized that Debra was a dreamer, someone who would no doubt spend her whole life chasing one rainbow after another, looking for the pot of gold reputed to be waiting at the end.

Sometimes she envied her friend the bright, optimistic outlook she had on life and the future. But she was wise enough to know that in today's world a person had to be cool-thinking and shrewd, less susceptible to frivolity of any nature, if she expected to survive.

However, despite their differences, they shared a rare bond of friendship closer than most sisters. And that, Lindsey reflected, was perhaps why their friendship had lasted for so long. It was said opposites attract, and they were as different as night from day.

"I know it sounds improbable—crazy, even," Debra said, defending her position. "But, Lin, I swear I heard two men planning something illegal."

Hearing the stubborn yet almost pleading note creep into Debra's voice, Lindsey sharpened her gaze. Was this for real, and not a romantic embellishment of a half-heard conversation?

All at once both women were startled by the abrupt noise of a chair being scraped across the tile floor. Lindsey glanced around, expecting others to have been disturbed by it, but none of the others showed even the slightest interest in anything outside their own table.

"I don't give a tinker's damn what you're afraid of!"

The two women glanced at each other in surprise before focusing their attention on the conversation taking place behind them.

"We made a deal, and damn it, you're not backin' out at the last minute. Either you live up to your end or I'm gonna see that a certain person gets the word on that little matter we discussed the last time we got together.''

"You wouldn't do that,'' a second, weaker voice protested in faint, alarmed tones.

"Wouldn't I?''

"We're pals—'' the second man began, only to be interrupted.

"We used to be. But that was a long time ago.''

A taut silence followed. And then, "You really think it'll come off just like we planned?''

"I do.''

"But if he should guess it was me—''

"How's he gonna know? Did he suspect about the other? And I'll be in and outta there in the blink of an eye. I'm good, and you know it.

"Besides,'' the stronger voice continued, "everybody's gonna be out of town, right? So you're worryin' for nothin'. And when they get back, we'll be long gone.''

"You mean you'll be gone. I'll still be here—''

"Come on, don't start whinin'.'' The placating tone disappeared, and the voice took on a dangerous edge. "Nobody's gonna tumble to your part in this. And besides, you're gettin' paid real good for the little you're doin'.''

"A lotta good money will do me in the joint,'' the second man muttered. And then, "What do you want that stuff for, anyway? I sure never figured you for a art collector.''

"No? Well, there's a lot you don't know about me. Just 'cause we grew up on the same street, that don't make you no expert on what I like.''

"I know you don't know a Remnant from a—a Picasso.'' The other voice sounded a little belligerent now.

"That's Rembrandt, dummy, and it's none of your business.''

"Well, I know that you ain't fenced nothin' since the accident. So what's the deal? What are you gonna do with a bunch of fancy snuff boxes?''

"They're valuable antiques, ain't they? And they got jewels and things on 'em, ain't they? So where's the mystery?"

"Since when do *you* know anything about antiques?" the second voice sneered.

By now both women were practically glued to the partition. And though they tried, neither was able to see through the thick foliage and intricate latticework to the men's faces on the other side.

A slight scuffle ensued, and the next time the second man spoke it was in a choked whisper. "Okay, okay, I can take a hint. No questions. Now, let me go."

"The only thing you need to know is that the door had better be left unlocked and the alarm turned off. You got that? I'll take care of the rest."

"Yeah, yeah."

"And play dumb. You don't know nothin' about nothin'," the gravelly voice emphasized. "You keep your yap shut, or I'll shut it for you—permanent."

In the next alcove, Debra eyed Lindsey with wide blue eyes. "There, you see? I told you so," she mouthed all but silently. "They're thieves. We've got to do something."

"Don't be ridiculous," Lindsey protested when she'd recovered from the shock of hearing the men's conversation.

She could have used a stiff drink under the circumstances, but she didn't want Debra to know how unsettled she was feeling, so she scanned the immediate vicinity for their waiter. It was time to order and add a more normal note to the atmosphere.

"Lindsey!" Debra protested, realizing her friend wasn't taking the men seriously.

"You don't know what that was all about—not really." Catching sight of their waiter, Lindsey signaled for him. "For all you know they're simply two actors rehearsing their parts in a play," she added, refusing to acknowledge her own concern about what she'd heard. Things like this just didn't happen in the real world. Not in her world. Not anymore.

"You don't believe that for a moment," Debra chided her.

"Don't I? Well, whatever I believe, I'm not going to call the police and make a fool of myself because of something I overheard at lunch. Be sensible."

"Sensible? Isn't it sensible to want to stop a crime from being committed?" Debra picked up her napkin and shook it out before placing it across her lap. "And besides, who mentioned the police, anyway?" She met the startled glance from her friend's green eyes defiantly.

"Good day, Miss Hamilton." The waiter had arrived to take their order.

"Hello, Rob, how are you?" Lindsey asked quickly.

"Fine, but I don't much like the snow."

His deep voice rumbled as he spoke, taking on an intimate note as his dark eyes caressed Lindsey's face. Debra watched the interchange with interest.

"No?" Lindsey said. "Well, take heart. I heard on the radio a little while ago that we were in for a warming trend in the next few days."

She glanced across the table at the other woman and felt her face grow warm at the sight of the speculative glance Debra was giving the young waiter. She knew the expression on her friend's face only too well.

"That sounds good to me," Rob answered, apparently unaware of the scrutiny he was getting from Debra. "Now, what can I get for you today? Our special is shrimp fried rice, and for you, I'll add a bowl of wonton."

Wonton soup was her all-time favorite, and at any other time the offer would have been welcomed with a smile of thanks. But with Debra shooting narrow-eyed glances at the two of them, she felt uncomfortable with his offer.

"No soup today, Rob. Just the fried rice."

"Whatever you say, Miss Hamilton."

"He's very good-looking," Debra commented with a grin when Rob left to place their order. "And he likes you."

"Oh, come on." Lindsey shifted uneasily on her chair. "He must be all of twenty-two. I'm not into cradle snatching. Anyway, it's the tips he likes, not me."

"Don't sell yourself short. You're only twenty-eight yourself, not forty." Debra eyed the other woman's glossy mass of mahogany hair pulled artfully back from cheekbones that had been exquisitely sculpted by nature's fine hand, and with a smile observed cheekily, "Scraping your hair back that way only shows off your gorgeous bone structure, it doesn't make you look any older."

Lindsey put a self-conscious hand to her face. "I'm not trying to look older, and I'm certainly not looking for a man. Remember Brian?" she added as an afterthought.

"No." Debra made a face. "I don't want to remember him."

"Debra..."

"All right." She raised a hand. "I'll leave the ever-precious Brian out of my conversation. But just let me say one thing. He's a cold, egotistical, self-interested, manipulative, arrogant, son of a—"

"Debra!"

"—gun. Okay, okay," she added, seeing the mounting distress in the other woman's pale face. "I won't say anything more about him. At the moment," she qualified under her breath.

The waiter arrived with their order, and for a little while they enjoyed the food without conversation, each thinking her own thoughts.

The first one finished, Debra put down her chopsticks and wiped her mouth on her napkin. "So, what are we going to do about what we overheard back there?"

"Do?" Lindsey shrugged. "Why, nothing."

"But we heard two men plotting a crime. You heard them, they're planning to steal antiques covered in jewels—they could be worth a fortune." Her eyes had grown round with excitement. "We have to do something."

"What?" Lindsey put down her fork. "Call the police? And tell them what? That we overheard two men whom we don't know, didn't actually see and cannot identify talk about stealing *snuff boxes?*''

She leaned over the table and gripped the other woman's hand. "Debra, they'll put us away. They'll have the little men in white coats coming after us."

Dropping her friend's hand, she abruptly sat back. "If— and I'm only saying a great big *if,* mind you—what we heard is for real, do you have any idea how the police could twist it, perhaps even make it appear as though we were a part of it? And you know I can't afford to have something like that get into the newspapers. Too many wealthy people trust me with their money, lots of money. Can you imagine anyone taking my advice about their finances if they read in the paper that I was undergoing psychiatric evaluation for coming up with something like this little story?''

Debra stared at her friend's solemn face. "They wouldn't do that, would they? The police wouldn't—''

Lindsey couldn't contain the smile twitching at the corners of her perfectly shaped mouth.

Debra saw it and frowned. "Oh, you—you carrot top!'' she muttered. That name had never failed to raise Lindsey's ire when they were children and there was more red than brown in her long, wavy tresses. And then *she* grinned, too.

"Seriously, it could happen. We could get caught up in something neither one of us is expecting. It could even get ugly. And I can't—won't—become a part of something like that...." Her voice trailed off as her gaze turned inward, focused on some distant memory.

Debra looked at her, really looked at her, for the first time that day, and noticed a drastic change in her friend's appearance. Fine lines were etched at the corners of the green eyes ringed by dark smudges. There was a brittle, drawn look to her face, and she appeared almost on the point of exhaustion. Wasn't she sleeping—again?

"What is it, Lin? Is something bothering you?''

Keeping her eyes on her hands, the other woman shrugged without comment.

"Is it . . . the nightmare again?" Debra asked hesitantly.

"Yes," Lindsey answered after a long pause. Debra had to strain to hear her reply. "I don't know what brought it on. . . ." Again her words trailed off. She'd never really told Debra, or anyone, about the details of the nightmare. She couldn't. It was shrouded in too much fear, too much blackness, too much guilt.

Debra knew nothing at all about the period of defiance Lindsey had gone through the summer of her twentieth year, following her mother's death late in the spring. Debra had gone to Europe to spend some time alone coping in her own way with the loss of her own parent a few months earlier in an air disaster. When she returned, Lindsey was in Europe with her father, and it was a long time before they returned to the States.

And in all the years since, Lindsey had been unable to bring herself to tell her friend what wild and crazy things she had gotten up to that summer—her summer of rebellion.

The nightmare—the one she was still having—had begun for Lindsey while she and her father were staying in Switzerland, after the Derek episode had taken place in the States. Derek. How had she ever allowed herself to become mixed up with someone like him?

Could it be *his* face, *his* eyes, that stared at her in her dreams?

No, it couldn't be. Those eyes were gentle, kind, concerned, and she had never seen kindness or concern for anyone in Derek's eyes. And the color was all wrong; Derek's eyes had been brown, but these eyes were the most beautiful shade of turquoise she had ever seen, and she saw them only at night—in her nightmare.

A shiver passed over her, one she couldn't hide from her friend's discerning glance. But she simply pulled the sleeves of her silk blouse more closely about her wrists and pretended it was a draft in the restaurant that had caused it. Only she knew the real cause—the memory of the horror, the feeling of helplessness, the intense, all-pervading fear she always experienced during and after the dream.

Swallowing tightly, she attempted to push aside the visions that began to crowd her mind. This was a public place; she couldn't afford to make a spectacle of herself. And normally she was able to put the memories behind her in the light of day. Maybe Debra was right in what she was always saying. Maybe she *was* pushing herself too hard. Maybe she did need a rest. God, she needed something, some way to shake the dream.... The blood drained from her cheeks at the memory.

"Lin, Lin honey, are you all right? Lin..." Debra reached over and touched the other woman's hand.

Lindsey gave a slight jerk and looked up with wide, startled eyes. For a moment there wasn't so much as a trace of recognition on her face.

"Are you all right? Is something wrong?" Debra asked, concern creating a deep vertical line between her eyes.

"No." Lindsey shook her head. "Nothing's wrong." She released her grip on the table and relaxed in her seat. Taking a deep breath, she repeated, "There's nothing wrong—nothing at all." She attempted a smile.

Debra wanted to refute her denial and ask questions, but she maintained her silence. Sometimes she felt as though she knew her best friend not at all, and never would.

One thing she did know: Lindsey worked too hard and played too little, trying to follow in the footsteps of her father.

As an adolescent, Lindsey had once, in a burst of girlish confidence, confessed that she found it hard to love the man she called Father. She had admitted that she felt guilty about it, because he provided her with nice clothes, spending money, piano lessons, vacations—everything.

She should love him, she had whispered, her voice husky with unshed tears as she stared at Debra in guilt. She wanted to. She tried, really tried, but he made it so hard. He was so strict, so distant, so unfatherlike. And so different from her warm, loving, extroverted mother.

Lindsey had ended up crying that night, a night she had been sleeping over at Debra's house. And Debra remem-

bered she had done her best to comfort her. It had been one
of the few times Debra had played the stronger role in the
girls' friendship. Even as a child, Lindsey had been more
self-possessed than the other girls her age.

And that was another thing. Histrionics—nightmares—
didn't seem to fit her friend's cool, controlled personality.
Debra knew the other woman to be warm, sensitive and
loving, but those emotions were kept under wraps, well
hidden from the general public.

Obviously, something really terrible must have happened
to upset Lindsey's equilibrium so drastically, but what? The
nightmare was the one thing Lindsey consistently refused to
discuss with her.

Was it only stress from being constantly under her father's tutelage, in order to be properly groomed to take over
the business from him at the right time, that had initiated
the dark dream in Lindsey's life?

It seemed to have started, from what Debra could gather,
about the same time Mr. Hamilton had taken her out of
college and kept her locked tightly under his own wing.
Debra had been gone for the summer that year, and when
she and Lindsey had finally met again, Lindsey had been
different, more brittle, living on her nerves. It had been
months before the other woman had admitted to even having a problem sleeping. And she had totally refused Debra's attempts to get her to see a doctor, a psychologist, for
help.

Debra realized, even if Lindsey refused to admit it, that
her friend needed more relaxation, more free time to pursue other interests besides her career. She needed freedom
from the burden of running the company her father had left
her in charge of when he died a few years ago. She needed a
life of her own, not merely an extension of the one her father had lived.

If Lindsey didn't slow down soon, Debra was afraid that
her friend would end up a physical and emotional wreck.
She had noticed that Lindsey was looking fragile today, way
too fragile. One of these days she was going to crack from
all the pressure.

Debra decided to cut her some slack and referred back to the other woman's desire to forget the conversation between the two men. "Maybe you're right. We should just finish our lunch and forget all about that silly conversation. I won't mention it again if you won't." She put on a cheerful face and gave a careless shrug, as though it didn't matter in the least. "It was probably a gag, anyway. They're no doubt sitting behind us right now, laughing up their sleeves, wondering if they managed to fool any unsuspecting listeners.

"Or, perhaps like you suggested, they were only two actors rehearsing their parts over a meal."

But Lindsey wasn't really listening. Her eyes were on the red tablecloth. She was trying hard to force her thoughts away from the painful memories. Sometimes she wondered if she would ever forget, and sometimes she longed to remember—all of it.

"Lindsey? Lindsey!"

She glanced up into Debra's concerned eyes.

"Are you certain you're feeling all right? Is there anything, anything at all, you need to talk about? I'm not being nosy, but you know you can always talk to me."

Perhaps this time, Lindsey thought, she would tell Debra what frightened her so badly that in the past she had showed up at her friend's door at three in the morning shaking, needing to spend the rest of the night with the only person she really felt close to.

"I'm fine," Lindsey answered slowly. Then, seeing the skepticism Debra tried her best to hide, she quickly added, "But I would like to ask how you'd like to spend a weekend in Florida when I get back from this business trip."

Debra hesitated before answering. She didn't like to accept the plush holidays Lindsey infrequently planned at her own expense. She wasn't in a position to afford such luxuries for herself, and though accepting them weighed heavily on her conscience, she agreed now and again, knowing Lindsey wouldn't go alone. But she always insisted on accepting only the ticket, refusing to allow Lindsey to pay for everything.

"How long are you going to be gone this time?"

"Two days. I should be back late Wednesday afternoon."

Debra toyed with her teacup. "Does this weekend getaway to a warmer climate include Brian?" The one trip all three of them had made together had been a disaster from start to finish. "Because if so—" she met the other woman's glance head-on "—count me out. And let me warn you, nothing, nothing at all, is *ever* going to thaw out that cold fish."

"Debra..."

"Well, it's true." On this she would not budge an inch. "I don't know what you see in him. He's never going to love *anyone* as much as he loves himself. And what you need is a real, live, flesh-and-blood man."

Lindsey gazed discreetly around her, hoping no one else was overhearing them.

"Someone," Debra continued, "who leaves you in a puddle of desire every time he gazes into your eyes. Someone who wants to get you into *bed*. And that certainly leaves Brian Kingston out, if nothing else does. The only thing *he's* interested in getting into is your bank account."

"I don't want to discuss this again, not here, and not now."

"You never want to discuss it. But I'm right, and you know it. And the only reason you refuse to do anything about it is because for some reason you're scared."

"Scared?" Lindsey repeated with haughtily raised brows, but her whole upper body tensed.

"Yes, scared," Debra insisted stubbornly. "Of men."

Lindsey flushed with angry color. "Let's leave this for another time."

"Another time may be too late when it comes to the subject of Brian Kingston and his self-serving attitude."

And then all at once Debra took note of her friend's flushed cheeks and overbright eyes and relented. She was only adding to Lindsey's strain.

Besides, she knew it would take more than her opinion to make Lindsey see Brian Kingston for what he really was. Debra suspected that Lindsey felt "safe" with the man. He might be a womanizer, among other things, but he wasn't really a very strong personality, not like Lindsey herself. And if *she* knew that, then Lindsey certainly did.

Lindsey could be very stubborn when it came to some things. And Debra suspected her friend had her own closely guarded reasons for seeing Brian Kingston to the exclusion of other men.

"Oh, all right, I'll drop the subject for now. But only if you promise to leave him out of your plans for this weekend trip."

For a moment Lindsey's shoulders remained stiff; then all at once she relaxed. She could never stay mad at Debra for long. "No Brian," she promised with a grin. "Just the two of us, with all that warm sand and beautiful water. We'll both need new bathing suits—"

"No suit for me. My old one is fine," Debra insisted. A fancy new suit was beyond her budget right now, and she wasn't about to let Lindsey spring for one.

Lindsey wanted to protest, but she saw the glint in her friend's eye and knew she would be going too far. "No Brian, and we both wear our old bathing suits," she agreed.

"Great." Debra laughed. "Then I'll see you Friday, with my bags packed, ready for fun in the sun."

Lindsey glanced up past Debra's shoulder and waved. "There's Mac. Gotta go before I miss my flight." She signaled for the check, added a substantial tip for Rob and gathered her things. "I'll call the minute I arrive in Chicago."

"You had better. You know how I feel about you flying around the country so much. Call me as soon as you touch down. I should be home by then."

"I won't forget." Lindsey started to turn away, paused, then turned back to give the other woman a sudden, brief, hard hug.

Debra squeezed Lindsey's arm, swallowed tightly and brushed a hand across misty eyes. After a moment she turned to watch her friend shrug into the coat Mac, her chauffeur, held for her, and then they were both gone.

Debra swiveled slowly in her chair and stared down at the empty table. She would miss her. She always missed Lindsey when she was gone on one of her business trips. It seemed as though a vital part of her own life went missing whenever Lindsey was away.

And just for a moment that thought bothered her. She should have more of a life of her own; she couldn't be forever hanging on to Lindsey's skirttail simply because she had her own fears to contend with. Who was she to tell Lindsey to face her fears, see a psychologist, when she herself was afraid to face her own future?

One of these days life was going to come up and hit her right in the face, and then where would she be?

Oh, bother, she didn't want to deal with that right now. She needed something to take her mind off her friend's departure and her own problems.

But what? There was only work. She wasn't dating anyone at the moment. And there was no one she'd met lately whom she wanted to get to know any better.

A sudden light sprang into her eyes.

What had become of the two men who had lunched in the alcove behind?

Chapter 1

Jonas stood back against the wall, one hand holding the blinds apart, the other thrust into the pocket of his black wool slacks, and stared down onto the street below.

He was tired, tired of following one middle-aged man after another, each one trying to recapture his lost youth in a fling with a younger woman. Tired of reporting to men past their prime on the affairs their much younger wives were having with men their own age. He was tired of the whole business of being a private detective.

This was not how he had envisioned applying the modern techniques of police detection he'd learned all those years ago in law school and while going through training at the police academy. Oh, he'd wanted to be a detective, all right—a police detective. But that avenue, he reflected bitterly, was closed to him and had been for over eight years now.

Movement at the end of the street caught his attention. A long, shiny black limousine turned the corner and drove slowly down the street, stopping at the curb in front of the building that housed his office. A portly black man in a gray chauffeur's uniform climbed out, opened the back door and bent to assist his passenger to the sidewalk.

Brown high-heeled pumps and then long, shapely legs came into view as a tall woman wearing mink glided gracefully to her feet. She paused to have a few words with the chauffeur, then turned to stare up at the building for a long, silent moment.

The hand holding the blind tightened as Jonas leveled a narrow, penetrating glance on the upturned face of the woman below. Hair the same mink brown as the coat she wore was swept back from pale features and knotted smoothly at the back of her head. It was impossible to make out the color or expression in the widely spaced eyes that appeared to be glued on the window behind which he stood, but he could make a good guess.

Something raw twisted in his gut. *This* was the prospective new client he was waiting for? The woman whom he'd thought never to lay eyes on again? The woman whose father had practically destroyed him eight years ago?

Lindsey entered the building and stepped into the elevator with misgivings. Was she making a mistake by being here? The police had been no help, but what about Ryan Dennison? He was the mayor of the city and had been her father's best friend as far back as she could remember before her father's death. Should she have put aside her pride after all and gone to him?

The elevator arrived on the fifth floor, and she stepped off and into the hallway. It was too late now for second thoughts. The decision was made, and she was here. For better or for worse, she was within seconds of meeting Brian Kingston's brother—a private detective.

With her gloved hand knotted into a tight fist, she struck the door panel sharply, once, twice, and waited. After what seemed to her an inordinate amount of time, a voice from inside told her to enter.

"Good afternoon." She spoke in a low, controlled tone, trying to hide the nervousness she was feeling—and the shock of meeting his eyes. "I'm Lindsey Hamilton," she managed coolly, wishing he would say something and not simply stand there watching her with those eyes—eyes straight out of her nightmare. "Are you Jonas Kingston?"

Her eyes were catlike, green, sharp and clear as crystals—just as he'd known they would be.

"I am," he answered in a carefully neutral tone. But Lindsey noticed something flicker far back in his startlingly beautiful turquoise eyes.

"I'm glad to meet you." She held out a gloved hand. "Your brother has spoken highly of you."

Jonas's gaze roved from the ivory beauty of her face over narrow, mink-covered shoulders to her outstretched hand. He stared at the brown leather palm without moving. She was breathtaking. With all the beauty aids money could buy at her disposal, nothing had been spared to create an expensively beautiful woman, but in her case artifice was unnecessary. Even without the makeup and carefully crafted hairstyle, the expensive designer suit and mink, she would have been a knockout. He knew that for a fact.

The one thing all that money hadn't been able to buy for her was a sense of calm, a way to mask her state of distress from his discerning eyes. Not that she wasn't attempting to hide it from him. She was, but Jonas had learned over the years to look deeper, beyond conventional displays of surface emotion to what lay hidden beneath.

It wasn't difficult for him to read the tension in the stiffly erect carriage, brittle tone of voice and solemn expression. He could almost smell her fear.

Jonas accepted her hand with reluctance—he would have preferred not to touch her—and released it almost instantly. He was laboring under some pretty heavily disturbed feelings of his own. He had never expected to see her again after so long a time, and especially not like this, without warning, in his office.

He felt a bit as though the enemy had managed to sneak through his perimeter and launch a surprise attack. All at once he needed to put some distance between them, so he went to stand behind his desk. What was she doing here, looking at him as though she had never seen him before in her life?

"Have a seat." He gestured toward the straight-backed wooden chair directly across from him.

He sounded abrupt, and he knew it, but her appearance in his office, sent here by his own brother, had thrown him off balance. He didn't know how to react. He wasn't certain what he was feeling, how he should feel about *her,* as he stood trying not to stare at her lovely face. A face that had become all too familiar to him over the years—a face that haunted his dreams. And even though she looked very different now, he knew he would have recognized her anywhere.

The question was, did she recognize him? And if so, why didn't she admit it?

Lindsey felt disturbing fissures in her outward show of serenity. She felt off balance looking up at him. Even though she was standing, too, he was taller by a good six inches. She wished he would sit down before she got a crick in her neck. Her stomach was churning, and there was a sharp, almost waiting quality in the air that she couldn't account for.

Wondering if perhaps it was her own anxiety creating the tension, she sat down and crossed one silky knee over the other, totally unaware that a wide expanse of creamy thigh was now on display for Jonas Kingston's perusal. She rested her purse on her lap and lifted her eyes to meet his—and felt an unreasoning wave of blind panic.

Just for a second she was hurled back to a time she couldn't account for and to a vision of those eyes—those eyes that, in her dream, were so kind—directed at her with that very same censorious expression in them.

But that was impossible. She'd never been in this building until today, and she was quite certain she'd never met this man before now. Without appearing to, she studied his rugged features more closely.

It must be nothing more than one of those inexplicable moments of déjà vu, which no one could ever reasonably explain to anyone's satisfaction, and the strange coincidence that this man's unusually beautiful eyes were the exact color of those in her nightmare.

Her nervousness increased at the realization, but her worry over Debra's welfare overrode her own personal fears. She was here on behalf of her friend, her *missing* friend, and she must not lose sight of that fact for a moment.

"I know you must be wondering why I insisted on seeing you at such short notice," she began. "And without an appointment...."

She felt impaled by his steady, unblinking gaze, and found it rough going when he refused to make any sort of comment.

"I do appreciate your agreeing to see me under the circumstances."

The brittle silence continued. "Have I come at an inopportune time?" she asked with a slight catch in her voice, the first outward sign of her true state of mind.

Jonas turned away without immediately answering and went to stand at the window. He refused to acknowledge, even to himself, how the hesitant words, spoken in the deep, husky tones from his dreams, rippled down his spine. He could have put her at ease with a few simple words, but at the moment he couldn't seem to make himself speak them.

"It's my job to listen to people's problems," he finally managed with a glance back at her over his shoulder. His eyes shifted all at once toward the clock on the wall. He'd only been in her presence for a few minutes, yet it felt like hours since he'd looked down in to her upturned face as she stood on the street below and found himself hurled back to a time he'd been trying for the past eight years to forget.

"Am I keeping you from something important?" She had followed his glance to the clock.

"I do have an appointment with a client in fifteen minutes," he improvised on the spur of the moment.

Lindsey felt unaccustomed color stain her cheeks. He was letting her know she'd all but forced her way into his office, taking up his valuable time. He probably thought she was one of those people who demanded things of others as their right. But she wasn't. And if it hadn't been for her worry about Debra's safety, she would have stood up and marched from his office.

However, she couldn't afford the luxury of such balm for her wounded dignity. The police had been less than helpful when she had gone to them, and she knew that, if he chose, this man could help her. According to his brother, he was the very best man for the job. He specialized in finding missing persons.

Even though her dander was up at his rudeness, she decided to brave it out. Perhaps he was upset at the high-handed method she'd used to get a meeting with him. It might have been better to go through setting up an appointment herself, rather than letting Brian do it for her that morning. Even though he'd assured her that his brother wouldn't mind in the least how short the notice was, she suspected now that he'd been lying.

"I came," she said, twisting her hands in her lap, "because my best friend is missing, and I think she's been kidnapped."

Jonas turned, his sharp glance going to her face. "Did you say kidnapped?"

Lindsey nodded. "Yes, that's what I believe has happened."

"On what evidence are you basing that assumption? Have you been contacted by the kidnappers? Have you received a ransom note? Have you been to the police?"

Lindsey let the other questions slip by and answered only the last. "Yes, but all they did was have me fill out a missing person's report. The desk sergeant showed me a thick folder overflowing with similar reports. He said they were swamped with them. He's the one," she confessed, "who suggested that I hire a private investigator."

"I see. Did you tell him about your...theory...of a kidnapping?"

"Yes," she admitted somewhat reluctantly, then raised bold eyes to his. "He didn't put much stock in it. But," she added quickly, "perhaps if I start from the beginning and explain it all to you, you'll understand my concern."

He gave a slight nod. Not much encouragement, she thought, but nevertheless she continued. "It all started exactly a week ago, on Monday, at lunch. Debra, that's my friend, and I met for lunch at the Oriental Palace. It was a kind of goodbye lunch, because I was leaving on a short business trip directly afterward.

"We ate, and I left as planned, but Debra never returned to work, and no one has seen her since."

"And what, exactly, has led you to reach the conclusion that she's been abducted?" It didn't sound like all that desperate a situation to him. The young woman had no doubt simply taken off for a few days by herself.

"Several things," Lindsey answered. "For instance, Debra insisted I call her when I got to Chicago. I tried, but she wasn't home. Then, when I tried to contact her at work on my return, her boss told me a very strange story. He said Debra had called him on Monday afternoon and said she was going to stay with a sick relative for a few days."

Her troubled glance rested on his austere features as though she was expecting him to understand her anxiety.

"Perhaps she did go to visit a sick relative," Jonas offered in a dry voice.

"No." Lindsey shook her dark head. "How could she have, when she has no family? There were only her parents, and they've been dead since our college days."

"Perhaps someone you didn't know existed—"

Again she shook her head in quick denial. "I can assure you, there is no one. But let me continue. Then you'll better understand my suspicions."

She shifted on the narrow, comfortless chair, inadvertently drawing his attention to her creamy thighs. His eyes hardened imperceptibly before he glanced steadfastly away.

Unaware of that aborted glance, Lindsey hunched slightly forward and, with her hands gripping each other tightly, continued.

"As I've already said, my friend and I met for lunch. And it was there, at the restaurant, that the...incident...occurred that has led me to believe Debra has been abducted—to silence her."

"Silence her?" he echoed dubiously, raising an arched brow as he moved to his desk and took a seat.

"Yes, silence her, to keep her from repeating what she—what we both—overheard."

"And what was that?"

Lindsey didn't like his tone, but she continued with her story. He would believe her by the time she was through, she vowed silently. "We heard two men plotting to steal some valuable antiques."

"You heard this...plot...in a restaurant? And that's what you went to the police with?" He was hard put not to laugh out loud. He would have loved eavesdropping on *that* conversation.

"Yes, we both heard it." Lindsey met his eyes, read the skepticism and amusement he was hardly attempting to disguise, and looked hurriedly away.

She understood his reluctance to believe her. Hadn't she reacted in the same manner when Debra had first apprised her of what she'd overheard? But, all the same, the amusement was hard to take.

"It's true, every word I've told you, I swear it." She gripped the edge of her coat in taut fingers. He *had* to believe her.

"Who were these men? Did you get a look at them? Can you identify them? Can you identify their voices? Who was the intended victim?" He fired the questions at her.

"I don't know. We didn't actually *see* them. And I don't think I could swear to the sound of their voices."

She couldn't look at him. She was ashamed for Debra's sake that she hadn't paid more attention to the men and what they'd had to say.

"I should have listened more closely, and I should have realized Debra wouldn't be swayed so easily when I asked her to forget all about it. Not when it concerned something as exciting as a real plot to commit an actual crime." Her voice dropped to a bare whisper. "I just . . . didn't want to become involved."

"Why not?" he asked harshly, drawing her eyes like a magnet to his steely gaze. A few years ago, he recalled, her father hadn't wanted to become *involved* in what might have turned into a public scandal, and, as a result, Jonas's life had been changed forever.

"I was going on a business trip," she explained haltingly. Somehow her eyes had become focused on his hands. She almost forgot what she was saying as she became fascinated by the way he picked up a pencil with long, tapered fingers and held it balanced between them, testing its strength.

"I didn't want to—"

The pencil snapped, sounding like a pistol shot in the quiet room.

Lindsey jumped and darted an astonished look at his face. He was watching her.

"Call the police?" he finished for her.

"W-what?"

"You didn't want to call the police," he repeated.

"Oh, no. Debra didn't want to call the police, but I—I should have listened to her, let her explain what she did have in mind."

Lindsey stood, drew the mink around her like a shield and paced to the window. She hadn't wanted to call the police, either, as she recalled, hadn't wanted to become involved.

"I put her off. I said something to the effect that the two men probably were no more larcenous than two actors rehearsing for a play."

She moved from the window to the desk and stood behind the chair on which she had previously sat. She couldn't seem to light in any one spot for very long. She'd been like that since she'd begun to suspect Debra had disappeared at the hands of the two men from the restaurant.

"And she believed that?" Jonas asked, referring to the statement she'd just made, speaking from directly behind her.

Lindsey gave a start and shied away from the feeling that he was breathing down her neck. She wasn't proud of her part in the events that had led to Debra's apparent abduction, but she didn't need him to beat her over the head with it. He was making her feel as though she, and she alone, was responsible for Debra's disappearance.

"Your friend allowed you to persuade her that the two men were only actors rehearsing a part?" he repeated insistently.

"I don't know!" she shouted.

Lindsey felt hunted. When she moved, he moved, as though she were an animal and he was stalking her around the room. She stopped all at once, determined to confront him—and found that he was standing across the room, in front of the window.

"I don't know if she believed me or not," she continued in a quieter tone, "but she seemed to at the time."

She felt like a fool for yelling at him and for thinking that he'd been attacking her in some way. Her nerves were shot because of this situation, and that was all there was to it. She couldn't even concentrate at work. Twice in one afternoon she'd forgotten important business appointments.

"What happened next?"

"Next? I left the restaurant. Mac, my chauffeur, had arrived, and I had to leave or miss my flight to Chicago."

"It was time to go." He shrugged wide shoulders nonchalantly. "So you left. Weren't you worried that your friend might go ahead without your support and try to make contact with the two men?"

Lindsey bristled instantly. There it was, that tone that she instinctively resented. Was he implying that she'd been negligent of her friend's safety?

Holding her purse across her chest with both hands, she faced him defiantly. She searched the irregular planes of his handsome face, dived into the depths of those amazingly beautiful eyes, and found nothing. His thoughts were his own, a closely guarded secret.

Perhaps in her anxiety over Debra she was only reading obscure meanings where there were none. It was possible. She had never felt so panic-stricken, so unable to handle a situation, so *helpless,* as she did right now.

Her shoulders sagged. "Yes," she answered unnecessarily. "I left." There was no denying the truth of what she'd done. "I left Debra there, alone."

"And now you think she was kidnapped. What I don't understand fully is why."

"I think it's obvious," she answered tiredly. "She's gone—no one knows where. I can't find her, the police don't believe me, but I know those men must have somehow discovered what she overheard."

"I see. Now *you* believe in the credibility of their conversation," he said, his eyes probing her pale, drawn features. Yes, he answered his own question silently, if her state of nerves was an indication, she did indeed believe her friend was in peril.

"Yes, I do."

"A little late, isn't it?" he couldn't help whispering softly. "Where's your proof?" he asked before she could sort out her thoughts and answer what had not really been a question but instead an observation.

"I—"

"The police didn't put much stock in your story, so how can you expect me to?"

"But that's different. They needed more proof—"

"Exactly," he agreed. "You're wasting my time. I think she probably went off to spend some time alone."

In a few words he dismissed everything she had just told him as invalid. "She'll no doubt get in touch with you in her own good time."

His gaze, like cold steel, sliced through her renewed reserve, behind which she was hiding her confusion. She was disoriented by his abrupt switch from accuser to skeptic. And, too, she felt a renewal of the uneasy tension she had sensed in him earlier, when their interview had first begun.

What had she said? Had she offended him in some way? And was this his way of getting back at her? But why? There seemed almost to be something personal in his attitude toward her.

Lindsey's glance slid from his face to the powerful thrust of his shoulders and on down to the knotted muscles of his forearms, visible beneath the rolled sleeves of his white sweater. He didn't look or dress much like a private detective, not the ones she had read about, or seen in movies. He looked more like a construction worker, only a bit less brawny.

She noted that his hands were held at waist level, and in each fist he still clenched a jagged half of the broken pencil. Lindsey couldn't seem to take her eyes off those sinewy forearms and rigid fingers. A thrill of fear raced down her spine. She was unable to hide the resulting shiver from his discerning gaze.

"How did you choose me, Miss Hamilton?" he asked in a low voice. "Of all the detectives listed in the Yellow Pages, how did you come up with *my* name?"

"Your brother," she whispered, dry mouthed. "I'm a friend of your brother's. He's the one who suggested you to me. He called you."

"Ah, yes." He turned away. For a moment he'd forgotten the true nature of this visit and his brother's part in it. "When I see him again, I'll have to thank him for that."

Lindsey felt a ripple of unease pass down her body. This man disturbed her on a level that no one had been able to reach for a very long time. And she didn't like it.

"You and your brother don't appear to have a lot in common," she observed abruptly, hoping to gain time to allow her to get her emotional equilibrium back. Perhaps then she would be able to come up with some fact that would gain his interest and make him take her worries seriously. She wasn't used to being unbalanced so easily by another person, nor to having her words discounted.

"And how is that?"

"Well, the obvious, I guess. You try to help people—the innocent, one supposes." She earned a narrow-eyed glance for that and continued, "While your brother, being an assistant district attorney, deals with punishing the guilty.

"And then there's your appearance," she added when no comment was forthcoming from him. "You don't in the least look like brothers.

"But that's deceptive, isn't it?" she added abruptly in a silky tone, once more in control. "In actual fact, the two of you are very much alike."

She had his attention now, and she knew it, even though he kept his back to her. "You don't believe me any more than your brother—or the police, for that matter—did. And none of you cares that a woman's life might be at stake here."

Jonas glanced back over his shoulder, watching the play of emotions on her face, the most prevalent one being anger. She was an undeniably attractive woman, and the green fire sparking in her eyes, the heightened color in her pale cheeks, only made that beauty come more hauntingly alive. It was all he could do not to give in to his instincts—and to her—and accept the case.

"Let me tell you something about missing people, Miss Hamilton." Perhaps reason would help him as much as it would help her. "Most of the people reported missing each year aren't really missing at all. Not, in any case, as you or I would think of being missing. On the contrary, they are people who have simply chosen not to be in a certain place any longer.

"Maybe," he said, shrugging, "it's because they need time alone, time to work out some problem or other for themselves. Or perhaps they just want to leave, to get away from a situation they can no longer handle, or a person they don't want to see anymore."

He twisted around to stare with unseeing eyes at the dark clouds visible outside the window. He knew what that was like—trying to run from an intolerable situation, trying to run from your own conscience, with nowhere to go except round and round in circles.

"Whatever the reason," he took up his observations, "those who want to *will* be found. And those who don't, stay lost forever. Maybe your friend just needed to get away, and maybe we should respect her wishes."

"You mean leave her among the lost?" Lindsey asked in scathing tones.

He shrugged.

"That's a very strange attitude for a man in your profession to take. Isn't this supposed to be how you make your living, by finding missing people?"

She saw the muscles of his back stiffen. "Look." She tried one last time. "Debra wouldn't have just left on her own. Not without speaking to me first. Why don't you believe me? Why won't anyone believe me? What must I do to get all of you to listen?" she asked despairingly.

Why couldn't she accept the fact that he was telling her no and simply leave? he wondered. He was finding this interview every bit as hard as she was, but for very different reasons.

"You have no motive for a kidnapping." He was getting angry, caught up in memories of a past he'd thought he'd come to terms with—or almost come to terms with, he amended, thinking of the dreams he still had—and all but forgotten.

"So what if these...thieves were overheard? Stealing is one thing." He swiveled to face her. "Kidnapping is a lot more serious. Why would they risk that for a few thousand dollars?

"And who is going to believe a wild story some lunatic broad says she heard in a restaurant, anyway?"

Lindsey opened her mouth to refute the term "lunatic broad," then closed it again without speaking. Her eyes darted around the room, seeking some means of getting through to him, and came to rest on the dented filing cabinet, moved to the scarred desktop and then on to the hard, wooden chair on which she'd sat not long ago.

"Name your price," she said succinctly. "I'll pay you anything. Just name your price."

"Save your money," he answered through tight lips, his nostrils flaring with barely restrained anger. "I don't want it. I *choose* who I go to work for. I'm not for sale. I never was."

There was no denying this time that she'd offended him. She realized that no argument she could have put forth would have put a dent in his firm resolve against taking the case.

Lindsey was unaccustomed to having to explain herself to people. She was used to receiving respect from employees and colleagues alike. And never in her life had she had to resort to attempting to bribe another individual. Her father had been a past master at the art of greasing the right palms, and she had always found that knowledge unpalatable. She felt deeply ashamed of having attempted to emulate a man she had found it hard to love and even harder to respect.

Without another word, or a glance in Jonas Kingston's direction, Lindsey headed for the door. There she paused without turning around.

"I just want you to know two things. First, I'm not in the habit of trying to *buy* my way into anything.

"And second, if anything happens to Debra, I shall hold you, more than anyone else, personally responsible. You could have helped, and you refused."

The glass in the door rattled as she left his office. She should have known that coming to Brian Kingston's brother for help would be an unqualified disaster. Brian Kingston was a man who curried favors; he didn't do them. And it appeared that his brother was a man without sympathy for others. He lived by fact, and fact alone, with no room for the human element in his life.

As she rode down in the elevator, a suspicion darted into her mind. Could Brian have said something to his brother that had predisposed him against taking the case?

She stared at the closed elevator doors, feeling despair sweep through her. How could he have turned her down? How could he in all good conscience refuse to help find a missing woman? She had expected so much more of him when she'd first seen him and stared into those extraordinary eyes. Despite her nervousness, after seeing those eyes— for a short while, at least—she'd been confident she'd come to the right person for help.

Lindsey left the building and crossed the sidewalk to the waiting limousine. Once inside, she leaned back and closed gritty eyes. Her mind kept going over the time she'd spent in Jonas's office. She could understand the police having to follow certain rules in handling a missing person case, but Kingston was a man for hire. Why had he refused her?

Surely he had dealt with similar cases, where the evidence was more intuitive than factual. Where were his powers of deduction? Didn't he understand the worry and fear that had driven her to seek him out?

If for no other reason, he should have agreed because of the money she would pay him. The furnishings in his office attested to the fact that he wasn't independently wealthy and could use some new clients—paying clients.

Whatever his reasons, he'd left her once more with all her fears intact and nowhere to turn. What was she going to do? She was the only person that Debra had to depend on for help. Unless she went to the mayor. Ryan Dennison would help her. No, she wouldn't resort to asking favors just yet.

All at once she straightened in the seat, a new gleam in her green eyes. If she couldn't get anyone to help her, then she would do what she'd always done in similar situations: she would rely on herself. She didn't need anyone's approval for that, and it couldn't be that hard.

But where did she start? Her brain reeled with thoughts, but no concrete ideas. And a small voice she couldn't help but acknowledge asked, *What if the others are right? What if you are seeing bogeymen where none exist? What if Debra has only gone off for a few days alone? Shouldn't you wait a few days to make certain?*

Her eyes narrowed and her chin shot up as she denied the small voice. Not by a long shot, not when she felt certain Debra had not left of her own accord, not when she knew how desperate her friend's plight might become. And not when she was feeling so guilty for her part in the whole mess.

It shouldn't be too difficult to track her down. Jonas Kingston was in the business of finding missing people, and she hadn't been overly impressed with his abilities a short while ago. She was the much-respected head of a chain of investment brokerage houses; several hundred people looked to her for employment. She had traveled and taught people all over the world how to manage their capital to their best advantage. Surely she could find her own friend in a city that had been her home all her life.

Her father had begun grooming her at an early age to take over the business he'd built up during his lifetime. And after her mother had died, after the fiasco of that horrible summer when she had become involved with Derek . . . No, she wouldn't think about that now.

She was stubborn and she was intelligent and there wasn't anything she couldn't do if she put her mind to it.

She had put herself in her father's hands and allowed him to teach her the job of running the company exactly as he would have done. He'd often told her jokingly that he'd made a better man out of her than many of the men he'd been doing business with for years.

Despite what she felt emotionally for her father, she had always known that he was a brilliant businessman and nobody's fool. And he had assured her many times in the years before his death that she had his head for the business. Surely that meant she could handle a task as simple as finding out what had happened to her best friend.

She had to! Partly to assuage the guilt she felt at not realizing Debra might get herself in trouble, but mostly be-

cause the thought of what might be happening to her friend
froze her heart with fear. The thought of having to live the
rest of her days without her friend filled her with sadness.

Lindsey leaned forward eagerly and tapped on the glass
partition separating her from her driver.

Mac lowered the window a few inches and glanced up at
her face in the mirror. "Yes, Miss Hamilton?"

"Take me to Debra's apartment, Mac."

Chapter 2

Lindsey relaxed against the leather seat, listened to the low murmur of the car's engine and felt her spirits rise. At last she was doing something constructive to find Debra.

Her reflection in the darkened window captured her attention, and for some reason that made her think about Jonas Kingston and his magnificent eyes. She considered the puzzle of his eyes matching those in her dream.

Could the eyes in her dream, which always appeared at the end of her nightmare, be a premonition, a sign from a realm outside her imagination telling her that everything was going to be all right? Or a sign foretelling that she would one day meet a man, when she was desperate for help, who would come to her rescue?

The thought, the very idea, of believing in something so outside the realm of possibility was preposterous, yet . . .

Lindsey turned her eyes determinedly away from her eerie reflection and such imaginative thoughts. Her mind became busy with thoughts of the differences in the two brothers.

Brian was without a doubt the more classically handsome of the two, his features more finely drawn and his jaw
less pugnaciously square. His hair was black, not dark blond
and his eyes were dark brown, the color of raisins.

He was always dressed with impeccable taste and would,
she was certain, rather be dead than caught dressed in ca-
sual wool slacks without a knifelike crease and a loose
sweater like the one his brother had been wearing.

And Brian was never less than charming, even when he
was cutting someone to the quick. He somehow managed to
do it with the air of telling the person for that person's own
good.

The only time she had seen him lose his urbanity was
when he had glared at poor Debra the night she had spilled
a Bloody Mary down the jacket and pants of his white
summer suit on their ill-fated vacation together. He had of
course apologized quite handsomely later, but Lindsey had
never forgotten the cold fury of his cutting remarks about
her friend's clumsiness.

She had come close to refusing to see him again after that
incident, but once he had apologized to Debra, he'd gotten
her alone and apologized profusely to her, too. And he'd
done it so charmingly, been so abjectly sincere, almost
comic in his remorse, deliberately turning the whole unfortunate incident into a huge joke at his own expense, that
he'd had her laughing after a few minutes. And she had,
naturally, relented.

She continued to see him for many reasons. They shared
many of the same interests and many of the same friends.
Ryan Dennison, her father's best friend, the man who had
been more like a father to her than her own father, seemed
to admire Brian's drive and ambition. He always spoke
highly of Brian's abilities as an assistant district attorney and
frequently issued joint invitations to the two of them to city
functions as well as private parties in his home.

Even though there continued to be some friction between Debra and Brian, Lindsey had always put it down to
a bit of jealousy on both their parts.

Debra should have realized that no one, no man—and certainly not Brian, a man Lindsey held in affection but was not in love with—would ever come between them. And Debra had never before been as outspoken about her dislike of the man as she had on Monday at lunch.

As for Brian, most of his remarks about Debra were of the catty variety and easily dismissed. From the beginning of their relationship, his remarks had been easily overlooked because Lindsey was familiar with the nature of his personality. And, too, he was always so apologetic afterward, asking her to put it down to a bad day at work.

Lindsey, knowing the daily pressures under which he worked, accepted the excuse. She'd finally come to the conclusion that the two would never like each other and, liking them both herself, settled on keeping them apart as much as possible.

The car hit a pothole jarring Lindsey from her reflections. She glanced at the window and was once more met with her own reflection, her eyes appearing wide and startled at the unexpected jolt.

She recalled other eyes—Jonas Kingston's eyes. There had been something about them, about the expression in them, when she'd first entered his office and glanced into their depths. Had it been stunned surprise, or a kind of vulnerability, or perhaps a mixture of both?

Neither emotion quite went with the cool, brisk personality he'd evidenced when questioning her about Debra and the conversation in the restaurant. Still, she could have sworn that when she first entered his office, for the briefest of moments as his glance had rested on hers, it had been unguarded, filled with some indefinable emotion.

The car lurched to a stop, bringing Lindsey to the present with a jerk. She glanced out the window and realized that it was almost dark outside. Snow was falling in large, fluffy white flakes, and there was already a light covering on the ground.

Telling Mac to stay where he was, she climbed from the vehicle unassisted. On the street she pulled the collar of her coat more firmly about her in an attempt to shut out the bitter wind and hurried toward the building.

Lindsey used the key Debra had given her, pushed hard against the door and found herself inside the warm entry hall. The apartment house was a nice one, with lush, rose carpet in the hallway and walls painted an attractive, soothing shade of pale green.

But Debra could have lived in more sumptuous surroundings had she wanted. She could have shared the penthouse suite with Lindsey. There was plenty of room, and they would never have had to run into each other if they had wanted it that way.

How many times had she asked her friend to come live with her? To accept a position in one of the company offices?

Debra's answer had always been the same. There was no way, she'd told Lindsey, that she would take advantage of their friendship by working for or living off her. She didn't need to live in a penthouse suite, nor did she need some high-powered job that would only end up giving her prematurely gray hair and ulcers.

She'd laughed and said that if she ever did feel the need to wallow in the lap of luxury, all she had to do was to visit Lindsey for a few days until the feeling went away.

Lindsey stepped off the elevator into the hallway directly across from Debra's apartment door. She wished now that she'd forced Debra to listen to reason. If she had, perhaps she wouldn't be here now, searching for evidence that her friend had been kidnapped.

Or would she? Debra had the kind of nature that cried out for adventure, even though most times Lindsey knew her friend suppressed it. Something told Lindsey that this—or something quite like it—was bound to have happened at one time or another in her friend's life.

She put her fears and speculation behind her as she entered the apartment. It was time to focus all her concentration on the task at hand. She was going to try to figure out whether Debra had taken anything with her when she'd left—or been forced into leaving.

Minutes later she stood in the center of the living room, looking around her in dismay. Should she be glad or upset that nothing appeared to be missing? At least nothing she could identify, except the clothes Debra had worn to lunch on Monday.

Didn't this reaffirm her conviction that, wherever Debra was, she hadn't gone there of her own accord? What woman left on a trip without her makeup bag or her curling iron?

Her spirits soared. Surely this was positive proof that Debra had been taken against her will. Wouldn't this make a difference to the police and their attitude toward her story of a kidnapping?

Then she recalled the thick, overflowing file she'd been shown by the desk sergeant, and her spirits plummeted. This new evidence would in no way change that.

But what about Jonas Kingston? Would this be enough to get him to reconsider his position?

She doubted that, too. He was going to need something more concrete than the fact that Debra had left without her favorite lipstick to convince him that a crime had been committed.

Or should she simply go to another private detective agency? For a moment she toyed with the idea of picking up the Yellow Pages and doing that very thing. But something stopped her.

His eyes—the color of Jonas Kingston's eyes. She didn't quite understand her reaction to them, despite the fantasy she'd concocted in the car about a premonition. But his eyes made her want to trust him, and while she'd been in his office they had given her the feeling that somehow she would make him believe her, believe the desperate state of mind she was in and the desperate situation her friend might be in, too.

Except that hadn't been the case.

She was all alone in her search for clues to her missing friend's whereabouts. She was certain that to find Debra's trail there were questions that needed to be asked, but what questions? And to whom did she voice them? There must be clues that were only waiting to be taken note of, but where did she look?

She walked over to the desk and picked up Debra's day-to-day appointment calendar. She flipped through the pages looking for she didn't know what. There was a dental appointment scheduled for next Friday at nine in the morning, and she'd taken some clothes to the cleaners that she needed to pick up the day after tomorrow. There were birthdays marked, but nothing Lindsey could see that would help her to understand what had happened to her friend.

She put the calendar down and reached toward a small figurine, a bright, delicate, hand-painted porcelain clown about six inches high. It was very beautiful and very expensive. She knew, because she had one at home exactly like it.

She smoothed it in her fingers, thinking back to the thirteenth birthday party she and Debra had shared. That had been her mother's idea. And for some reason her father had gone along with it. He had even bought presents for both girls.

The presents had, of course, reflected the fact that one child was his daughter and the other nearly a stranger. All except one package, the one containing the clowns; they were a matched pair. He'd given one to Lindsey and the other to Debra. It had been the first time—and the last—that he'd ever in any way acknowledged the girls' deep friendship.

Instead of replacing the clown where she'd gotten it, Lindsey found a tissue and carefully wrapped the delicate figurine, then placed it in her purse. She would take it home with her and put it alongside the one she had in her bedroom. It would make Debra seem closer, and might in some way help her to find her friend.

She wiped a tear from her eye with another tissue and smiled just a little. It was a silly notion, thinking that would make any difference in finding Debra, but she couldn't bring herself to change her mind and replace the figurine where she'd found it.

Picking up a picture of a smiling Debra, taken this past summer on a beach in the Bahamas, she asked it almost angrily, "Damn it, where are you? What happened to you after I left you on Monday? Why didn't you let well enough alone? What kind of mess have you gotten yourself into now?"

But Debra's likeness stared silently back at her, a twinkle in the bright blue eyes, leaving Lindsey to experience the same feeling of helplessness she had in the police station, and again in Jonas Kingston's office.

Was Debra still alive? Or was she at this very moment lying dead in some as-yet-undiscovered grave? The question followed her from the apartment.

She was locking up, thinking how eerie the place felt without Debra's cheerful presence to give it life, when the doors to the elevator banged open. She gave a startled yelp and glanced up as a big man, dressed in a dark overcoat, with a black felt hat tipped low on his forehead, stepped into view.

His glance touched hers briefly. He held the elevator doors as she nodded in reply to his silent question, then stood back to allow her to pass. The strong odor of cigar smoke caused her to cough lightly as she passed within a few inches of him.

The doors had all but closed when she looked up to see him move slowly, haltingly, down the hall, a brown leather suitcase banging against his left leg.

"Well, did she keep the appointment?"

Jonas turned slowly to face his unexpected visitor. "Ever hear of knocking?"

The younger man shrugged, removed his topcoat, hung it on the coat tree behind the door and crossed the room to join Jonas at the window. It was past six, and the streetlights below had winked on, turning the snow-covered street into a scene from a Christmas card.

"What's gotten stuck in your craw?" Brian finally asked when the other man let the silence between them drag out. "It doesn't have anything to do with a visit from a certain young woman, does it?"

Jonas kept his face turned aside as he answered, "Yes, I do have you to thank for that, don't I? You didn't tell me her name."

"You sound upset," Brian commented in surprise.

"You know, that friend of hers could actually be in trouble." Jonas faced him challengingly. "So why, exactly, did you want me to turn down the case? Admittedly, her story about the restaurant scenario is a bit farfetched, but—"

"Hey, what is this?" Brian interjected swiftly. "I didn't think you'd mind doing your only brother a small favor. And you did agree to do it," he pointed out softly.

"True, but I should have known better. If I hadn't been in such a lousy frame of mind when you called, I would have gotten the facts—all the facts."

He pulled a string, elevating the window blinds, and rested his hot forehead against the cool glass. He could still see her eyes, those clear green eyes gazing at him so reproachfully before she'd left. He hadn't treated her very well, and he was ashamed of it.

Brian leaned his shoulder against the edge of the wall near the window, watching his brother with a frown. "You sound as though you wish you'd agreed to help her. Why is that? Considering your opinion of the upper class in general, I figured you'd get a real charge out of telling her no."

Without changing position, Jonas turned so he could look into his brother's cool brown eyes. "I thought she was a friend of yours. Don't you want to help her find this friend of *hers?*"

Jonas knew that Brian was always looking for a shortcut to what he wanted. It followed that if he wanted the woman, helping her to find her friend was a surefire way to get into her good graces, yet he wasn't trying to help; he was putting a stumbling block in her way.

The younger man broke eye contact and slid his glance casually around the contents of the room before answering, "Not particularly."

"Why not?" Jonas asked in a sharp tone, earning himself a deeper frown from his brother.

"Lindsey is a very beautiful woman," Brian remarked softly, carefully examining the other man's face.

"Is she?" Jonas asked without expression.

"You didn't notice?"

"All right." Jonas straightened and moved across the room. "I noticed. How could I not? But that has nothing to do with my question."

"Then what does it have to do with?"

Brian wasn't totally convinced of his brother's lack of interest. Over the past six months, he'd seen men as solitary and emotionally impervious as his brother fall under her spell.

Not that she encouraged them, from what he had seen, or even appeared to take note of their interest. Lindsey Hamilton had something of a reputation as an ice maiden. And that was another reason he wanted her for himself. Not only did being her escort assure him of a place among the city's socially elite, but she was a challenge that, once met and defeated, would show others, those in high-ranking places in city government, that he had the ability to meet and overcome seemingly insurmountable odds where others before him had failed.

"Is she that important to you?" Jonas asked.

"Yes."

The room reverberated with silence. Jonas turned away, walked to the desk and removed a small black rectangular object from the top drawer. He held it for a moment before turning to offer it to his brother. He hadn't ever intended to tell Brian what had taken place eight years ago.

But it had been quite a shock to him to learn that his brother knew—was dating—Horace Hamilton's daughter. He wondered if what he was about to reveal would make a difference in the younger man's attitude toward her.

He didn't stop to check his motives for suddenly deciding to reveal the true facts behind his leaving the police force after only a short tour as a rookie.

Brian stepped up to take the leather wallet from him and flipped it open. The face of a young man, dressed in a dark blue uniform, gazed up at him from beneath the clear plastic. Across from the picture, pinned to the opposite compartment, was a badge. Brian glanced up at his brother with a puzzled frown.

"It's been eight years since he died and I quit the force."

Brian read the name below the picture. "I didn't know Hank Wilson was a part of why you left."

"Not left," Jonas almost snarled. "Was forced out! By a man with no conscience, but a whole hell of a lot of power, political power, and money."

Surprised at his vehemence, Brian stared at him for a moment in silence before asking, "What does this—" he nodded toward the picture "—have to do with Lindsey's visit here today?"

"You asked what was stuck in my craw. There." He pointed to the badge. "That's your answer."

Jonas twisted away to hide the emotion clouding his face. There were some things about that night, the night Lindsey Hamilton had entered his life for a brief but cataclysmic time, that he couldn't tell Brian, things he hadn't been able to talk to the police psychologist about, either. Thoughts and feelings he didn't understand but found easier to ignore than try to explain.

Every officer involved in a homicide, whether it was a criminal's or a fellow officer's, saw a police psychologist. It hadn't helped him. Not then and not now. He still had nightmares as a result of that night's events. And just recently they had become a nightly occurrence.

"All these years I've wondered—would Hank be alive today if I'd done what I should have and followed him into the park that night?" Jonas whispered almost to himself.

"I still don't see what this has to do with Lindsey's visit." Brian spoke impatiently, his eyes on his watch.

"Why don't you want her to find her friend?" Jonas asked softly, realizing that his brother hadn't made the connection.

Friends. It was all about friends, losing friends. And most especially, about the loss of *one* in particular. He'd lost his closest friend by the worst possible method—*murder*—and it had happened on the night he'd met Lindsey Hamilton for the first time.

And now he was faced with the unwelcome suspicion that his brother, whom he knew could be ruthless, might be involved in the disappearance of a young woman, the friend of Lindsey Hamilton.

Somehow, possibly because of the missing young woman's relationship with Lindsey as well as his brother's interest in her, Jonas felt involved. It was confusing, even to himself. He should have been glad to do as his brother had requested. He should have been able to refuse to help a Hamilton and then put the whole situation out of his mind.

But down deep inside, he knew that he wanted to take the case, wanted to find the woman. Not for Lindsey Hamilton's sake, but for his own lost friend, for Hank. "Why don't you want her to find her friend?" he repeated.

"What did you say?" Brian asked stiffly, his glance flying to his brother's accusing face.

"You heard me." Jonas could be ruthless himself in the pursuit of the truth, a fact many of those he'd worked for in the past could attest to.

"How did you get the idea...?" Brian hesitated. He knew his brother was far from being a fool. Jonas wouldn't be put off with a play of innocence. "It isn't that I don't want Debra to be found," he hedged.

"Then what?"

"She—Debra—has been trying to make trouble between Lindsey and me since the beginning of our relationship."

Brian kept his face out of his brother's line of vision until he felt he'd mastered the right expression, playing the injured, misunderstood party for all he was worth.

"Naturally I don't want anything bad to happen to her, but—" he raised militant eyes to meet his brother's glance "—I can't in all honesty say I'm sorry she's out of the picture for a while."

Jonas took a threatening step in his direction. "Did you have anything to do with this woman's disappearance?"

"What? No!" Brian answered indignantly. "Of course not."

Jonas searched his brother's face keenly. When they were children, he'd been able to tell whenever his brother was lying to him. But it had been a long time since he'd been put in the position of having to determine the truth in his brother's words.

Brian realized that by admitting his dislike of the woman he'd lost valuable ground where his brother was concerned. He decided it would be prudent to repair the damage as well as to get Jonas's thoughts fixed on something other than himself.

Brian knew better than to burn his bridges behind him. You never knew when someone you considered of no importance, even a failure like his brother, might be able to lend you valuable assistance at an opportune moment.

"Tell me about what happened to Hank. I never really knew how he died, only that he was killed in the line of duty and that shortly thereafter you quit the force."

"I haven't spoken about it to anyone." Jonas took the badge from Brian's hand. "Not since Annie, Hank's wife, gave me this before going to live with her parents after his funeral."

"Perhaps it's time you did."

"It all happened so long ago. It almost seems like another lifetime." Jonas gripped the wallet holding Hank's badge and reconsidered what he was about to reveal. "Maybe it's better left forgotten."

"Apparently *you* haven't forgotten it." At his brother's show of reluctance, Brian's interest had been sparked, but he didn't want to show it.

Jonas stared down at Hank's face in continued silence, seeing it as it had looked that night just before they'd heard the call—the one Jonas had insisted on answering, the one that had resulted in Hank's death.

He and Hank had been friends since their youth and had planned to become policemen together. But Jonas's aunt, who had taken over the task of raising Brian and him when their parents were killed in an accident, had had her heart set on his becoming a lawyer like his father, so Hank went to the police academy alone, while Jonas went to law school.

It wasn't until his aunt's death that Jonas left law school and began to fulfill a lifelong dream to become a policeman. By then Hank was already on the force, and when Jonas graduated from the academy, somehow he managed to draw Hank as his partner.

He'd done his best not to think about this these past few weeks, when the dreams had become so bad. But it had become impossible to shut out the memories. And today, when Lindsey Hamilton had showed up so unexpectedly to relate the story of her friend's disappearance, it had all come hurtling down around him. All the memories, all the pain, all the guilt....

Brian fidgeted. He had never been one to wait patiently for what he wanted. And he wanted an explanation for his brother's strange mood as much as he wanted to remove any questions from Jonas's mind about the purity of his motives where Debra Foley was concerned. He should have known that Jonas, being the straitlaced type that he was, would require an explanation for being asked to turn Lindsey away.

He reached inside his pocket, withdrew a silver cigarette case and placed a cigarette between his lips. Keeping his attention focused on his brother, he held a flame to its tip and took a long drag.

Jonas smelled the smoke and looked up. "Must you?" he asked in disgust.

He waved a hand in front of his face, moved across the room and asked a question he'd wondered about for a long time. "Do you resent me, Bri?"

Brian stared down at the toe of his black boot without answering. Resent him? Hell yes. He'd had to work his way through college and law school, while Jonas had had his way paid by their aunt. Jonas had been the old lady's favorite. She had died suddenly while Brian was in his last year of high school, and the annuity that had helped pay for Jonas's college had died with her.

"No," he answered, shifting his eyes to the tip of his cigarette. "Of course I don't."

"I know it wasn't easy for you, working and going to law school at the same time. I helped as much as I could—"

"Is that why you quit law school and went into the police academy?" Brian asked curiously.

"No, the truth is that it was Aunt Lucy's idea for me to become a lawyer like Dad. I never really wanted that, but I felt I owed her something—" He broke off.

"You mean that when she died and you quit to go to the academy," Brian asked, unable to hide his incredulity, "that's what you really wanted all along?"

"I always wanted to be a cop. Does that surprise you?"

"If that's what you wanted so bad, how could you give it up so easily?"

"It wasn't easy. I didn't want to quit. I had to."

Brian ground out the cigarette and dropped it into the wastebasket beside the desk where he was perched. "Okay, so you had to leave. Why?"

Jonas didn't answer.

Brian pulled back the sleeve of his blue pin-striped suit and glanced at his watch. "Look, I don't want to sound as though I'm not interested, but I have an appointment—" It wasn't true, but he was never comfortable for long in his brother's company.

"With Miss Hamilton?" Jonas asked in a hard voice.

Brian glanced up. "Well, as a matter of fact, yes."

"Maybe you're right. Maybe it is time I told you what went on eight years ago, who was responsible for Hank's death—and ruining my career. Does the name Horace Tipton Hamilton ring a bell?"

Brian flashed a narrow-eyed glance at his brother's face. "That's Lindsey's father's name."

"That's right," Jonas agreed in a rigid tone. "Lindsey Hamilton's illustrious father. He bought his daughter out of a prison sentence, and me out of a job."

Lindsey, fresh from the shower and a change of clothing, was in the process of trying to decide how best to go about tracing Debra's last movements when the buzzer on her door sounded abruptly. Wondering why Willy, the security guard, hadn't announced whoever it was, she peered through the peephole and found herself staring into Brian Kingston's smiling dark eyes.

"What are you doing here?" she asked testily as she swung the door back.

She hadn't quite forgotten her suspicion that Brian might have in some way prejudiced his brother against helping her to find Debra. She didn't want to believe it, had even talked herself out of the notion at least twice. After all, what would it gain him? But traces of the thought lingered around the edges of her mind, making her reception of him less than cordial.

"I came to invite you to dinner."

He gestured expansively, making a sweeping bow as he stepped across the threshold into the apartment, allowing her a brief glimpse of the charcoal-gray suit, pale pink shirt and deep maroon tie beneath the dark overcoat.

"I know it's short notice, but I've been invited to a small dinner party at the mayor's house. I was told point-blank to bring you along. It seems Mayor Dennison feels as though you're not getting out enough socially."

His smile held something triumphant in it. It was the first time *he'd* been invited to dinner at the mayor's home and asked to bring Lindsey along. People—the right people—were beginning to pair them together.

"Dinner?" she asked softly, holding on to the edge of the door with white-knuckled fingers. She could hardly believe her ears. "You came to ask me to dinner? How can you even consider making such an invitation under the circumstances?"

"You have to eat," he answered in a reasonable tone.

"But a party! Do you honestly think I want to be surrounded by people bent on having a good time, forced through good manners to appear as though I, too, am enjoying myself, when in reality I'm eaten up with concern about Debra?"

"I know you are, baby. That's why I'm here, to take your mind off it."

"I don't feel like company," she protested with a frown.

"I'm not company, I'm . . . a friend."

Lindsey stared at him in silence for a long moment. She didn't like being called *baby*. Her first thought was to show him the door, but as she met the sincere expression in his dark eyes, she slowly relented.

To the Brians of this world, the disappearance of a friend would no doubt be taken in stride. She shouldn't be surprised by his attitude. She had known from the first that his was a shallow personality, but she'd gone out with him anyway because he was charming and she couldn't help liking him, even when she knew he was being an ass.

And he *had* tried to help her. He'd sent her to his brother. If her trace of suspicion that he'd had something to do with his brother's refusal to help her was incorrect, she was being very unfair to the man. And right about now, she could really use a friend.

"I'm warning you, I'm not leaving my apartment this evening. I'm not in a party mood. And I'm sick with worry over Debra."

Lindsey slammed the door and marched past him into the living room, caring little whether he followed her or not.

He followed her, determined to make her see reason. "Look, the mayor is *your* friend. And besides, there's nothing you can do tonight about whatever fix Debra has gotten herself into. I fail to see how your staying holed up in this apartment will help her."

"What if the kidnappers call?"

"Kidnappers? You don't know that there are any kidnappers," he answered reasonably, hiding his growing exasperation.

"Then where is she?"

"I don't know, maybe she—"

Lindsey whirled to face him. "If you dare to suggest one more time that she's taken off with some man, I'll—" she searched for something horrifying, but could only come up with "—I'll scream!"

Brian moved to stand directly in her path and, placing a finger beneath her chin, he lifted it so their eyes were on a level. "I wasn't about to suggest anything of the sort. I'm as much in the dark about her whereabouts as you are. And I'm sorry if I offended you earlier today when I made that stupid remark about her having a boyfriend you knew nothing about."

Lindsey's angry gaze softened. She was being hard on him. After all, he didn't share her affection for Debra, and that wasn't exactly a crime.

"Okay, apology accepted." She gave in. "But I still refuse to budge from this place tonight."

"You know, Mayor Dennison is a very powerful man and your good friend. If you're so worried about Debra, why haven't you told him about her disappearance?"

Lindsey freed her face from his hand and looked away. She'd thought about it, even picked up the phone several times to call him in the past few hours, but something had held her back. She'd told herself it had to do with how busy the man was and that she didn't want to bother him with this, that she could find Debra on her own.

But in reality she was torn by the idea of using her relationship and influence with a man of such stature to gain personal favors. The police had rejected her plea to find Debra because there was no real evidence of a crime having been committed. She would be asking him to overstep the police's authority, and she couldn't bring herself to do that, not when there were still steps she could take herself.

She kept thinking about her father and how he had never hesitated to use his influence and money whenever he wanted something. As much as she loved Debra, as badly as she wanted to find her, she couldn't bring herself to ask Ryan Dennison to intercede with the authorities on her behalf. It smacked too much of what she'd been so strongly opposed to in her father.

She knew the option was always there if worse came to worst. And if it came down to the fact that she couldn't manage this on her own, if she suspected that Debra would remain lost to her without doing so, she would put aside her pride and ask Ryan to intercede.

Moving away from Brian, she turned toward the bar along one wall. "Can I fix you something to drink?" She glanced up into the mirror, barely missing the look of frustrated anger chasing across his face.

Lindsey, he had discovered, was one of those women who kept things to herself—too much so, for his taste. He'd been trying to get behind her guard, breach her defenses, for months now, but to no avail. He wanted a closer, more intimate relationship but, so far, she had continued to keep him at arm's length.

He'd finally come to realize that his unflattering references about her best friend, far from removing the other woman from the scene, merely served to irritate Lindsey, so he'd stopped doing that and even suggested that the three of them spend more time together.

That hadn't worked out very well, either. He'd felt left out of things, hard put to hide his feelings of jealousy at the closeness between the two women. And then later, during dinner at the resort where they'd all gone, when Debra had accidentally knocked over her drink, spilling it down his new suit, he hadn't been able to hide his anger. The evening had been a total disaster, and all three had been relieved to part.

It had taken all his guile, all his charm, to get himself out of that one. And though he'd managed, he knew Debra hadn't been fooled for a moment by his profuse apology. And things had never been quite the same between him and Lindsey since then, either.

But now, secretly glad Debra was out of the picture, he was planning to use her absence and Lindsey's unsettled emotions to make his move.

So far, she wasn't cooperating. Perhaps he was taking the wrong approach.

When Lindsey met his eyes in the mirror over the bar, he was smiling gently. "I'll take a Scotch. Make it neat."

Lindsey poured his drink and made one for herself. As she splashed in a hefty portion of liquor over the ice cubes, Brian came to stand beside her and picked up his glass.

"That's a pretty stiff drink." He nodded toward the tall glass of Scotch she was pouring for herself. She was normally almost a teetotaler.

"I need it," she whispered huskily, taking up the glass and going to sit on the sofa.

Brian removed his coat and placed it on the back of a chair, then picked up his drink again and moved to sit close beside her.

"Sorry," Lindsey said after taking a long pull from her glass. "I should have taken your coat when you arrived."

Placing his drink on the glass-topped coffee table, Brian twisted toward her, laid a gentle hand on her knee and said, "I understand. We've traveled beyond the necessity of such politeness between us, haven't we?"

Lindsey's eyes jerked to his face. What exactly was he saying? Her eyes darted toward his hand placed so intimately on her leg and glanced away. She took a hurried gulp from her glass, looked back and found her eyes locked with his.

What was wrong with her? Why didn't she simply tell him to get his hand off her? She wanted to, but her tongue seemed to be stuck to the roof of her mouth.

Brian, sensing her panic, eased off a bit. He removed his hand casually, stood and leisurely removed his jacket, loosened the knot of his tie and then sat down again—closer to her.

Lindsey didn't say anything, but watched as he leaned forward to pick up his drink in one hand. When he sat back, his other arm was somehow along the back of the sofa, resting lightly against her back and shoulders.

What was he doing? If she didn't know better, she would think he was planning a seduction. Shallow he might be, but surely he knew better than to try something like that at a time like this.

She took a hurried gulp of her drink and slid to her feet. All at once she needed to put some space between them. When Brian had first arrived she'd been inclined to be angry with him, but he'd offered her friendship at a time when she needed someone badly. Now she didn't know what to think. All she knew was that he was making her feel even more on edge than she already was.

"It isn't like you to be so jumpy." He spoke softly from directly behind her, causing her to start and spill some of her drink on the front of her sweater.

"I told you, I'm worried." She dabbed at the wet spot with an empty hand, keeping an eye on him at the same time.

"I know, I know," he muttered in a soothing tone. He took the glass from her unsteady fingers and placed it on the window ledge behind her, then withdrew a snow-white handkerchief from his pocket.

Lindsey's eyes grew wary as he applied the clean cloth to the damp spot on her gray sweater.

"But I'm here now, and there's no need to look for comfort at the bottom of a glass." He stepped closer, and Lindsey held her breath.

All at once she felt as though he was surrounding her, crowding her with his nearness into a small tight space. She felt flushed, light-headed, as though little by little he was withdrawing all the air in the room until she couldn't breathe.

She took a step back and felt the solid ridge of the wooden window ledge at her back.

"W-what are you doing, Brian? What are you t-talking about?" she asked jerkily.

"I'm only offering you what you so badly need—comfort." His voice had dropped to an intimate level. "You were right, we don't need to go to another party."

He dropped the wet handkerchief alongside the glass on the narrow window ledge and placed his hands on her shoulders. "What we need—" he dipped his head "—is some time alone with each other." His breath filled her mouth. "Time for me to help take your mind off this terrible shock you've had."

Lindsey strained back, refusing to allow him to make contact with her lips. "W-what are you doing? Stop this at once!"

Brian drew back slightly. "But I'm only offering what you need, a little... comfort," he replied softly.

"Comfort? Is that what you call it?" The nervous stutter was gone from her voice as she pulled determinedly out of his arms.

"What do *you* call it?" he asked with a dangerous light springing into his dark eyes. She had been "touch-me-not" for too long. He had decided that now was the time to push their relationship to its next stage.

By offering her the shoulder she needed to cry on, he planned to cement their relationship and be well on the way to getting what he wanted from her, both short-term via the bedroom and long-term for his career. But for some reason the lady was being uncooperative.

"Sex! That's what I call it!" she threw at him. "How could you? I know you aren't the most sensitive man in the world, but I thought even you had more sensitivity than that.''

''Oh, come on, what's this act you're putting on? We both know where we're headed. Every relationship ends up in the bedroom some time or other, and we're long overdue.''

He was losing his cool, a dangerous thing to do with a woman like Lindsey, but he couldn't seem to stop himself from continuing.

''We both need this. You need someone to get close to, someone to offer you a shoulder to cry on, and me—well, you know what I need.''

He moved to within a few inches of her. ''Come on, let's let our friendship take its natural course.'' His eyes pleaded with her, and a small coaxing smile played around the corners of his finely drawn mouth.

''I'm a fool,'' Lindsey whispered, keeping her distance from him.

''No, you aren't, baby, it's okay, I understand.'' Brian smiled. She was finally getting the picture.

''Don't call me that!'' she shouted, and whirled away from him, moving so that the sofa and coffee table stood between them. ''I'm a fool for letting you in here this evening. I'm a fool for thinking I could have a relationship with someone like you.

''You're too much like my father, too hard, too self-oriented, too ambitious. But I thought we were friends,'' she ended on a sad, almost plaintive wail.

The smile on his face froze. And if brown eyes could ever be termed cold, his turned to chips of black ice.

''You can't be as naive as all that. Friends? You and I? Don't be ridiculous! Friendship is something you have with someone like what's-her-name. Let me tell you about friendship.'' He took a threatening step in Lindsey's direction, and she backed up a couple of feet.

''Friendship is merely a device used by one person to get another into the position whereby he, or she, can get what they want. And the one being used either wants something in return, knows and doesn't mind, or is too stupid to realize that they're being suckered. Take what's-her-name—''

"Debra!" Lindsey broke in angrily, her hands knotted into fists at her side. "Her name is Debra, as you very well know."

"So I do," he answered, turning aside. "Little Debra, the hanger-on, the poor little mouse, your shadow."

"My friend!" she disputed loudly. "And your example of what being a friend means is disgusting!"

Brian knew he was blowing it. If he said half of the things he was thinking, wanted to say, he would be kissing Lindsey goodbye for good. And along with her would go his chance at being the new district attorney.

Because if Mayor Ryan Dennison got wind of their parting, if he had an inkling that Brian had hurt Lindsey in any way, he would forget he'd ever heard the name Kingston. Brian knew he'd better repair the damage, if he could. It might already be too late.

He clamped down on his anger, tried to smooth it over with smiles and soft words.

"You're right, of course, forgive me," he said with a little-boy pout on his handsome face. "And I didn't really mean it—it was only sour grapes. I'm jealous of you. Can't you see that?" And in that, at least he was being honest.

"Debra is a nice girl and your very dear friend. I shouldn't have called her those things. And I didn't mean what I said about friendship. I'm sorry."

"Are you?" Lindsey asked without any change of expression. "I thought you rather enjoyed saying it."

"I'm not myself. There's a lot of pressure at work just now. And of course I'm worried about you—and Debra, as well." His patience was fast waning, but he tried to maintain an outward show of calm.

"Oh, don't feed me that bull!" Lindsey all but shouted, throwing her hands into the air. "You have never worried about anyone but yourself in your entire life.

"Did you know your brother refused to work for me?" she asked abruptly. "Did you have anything to do with that?"

"What? Of course not! Didn't I make the appointment for you?"

Damn Debra for creating a furor and causing dissension between them at such a crucial time in his career. With things heating up in the D.A.'s office the way they were and his boss losing support from the mayor, he couldn't afford to have Lindsey angry with him. Not when success was within his grasp.

He was next in line for D.A. if he could only manage to keep Lindsey on his side. Mayor Dennison was a longtime family friend of hers and if—when—the present D.A. was ousted, he was a shoo-in. He wanted that so badly he could already taste it like the sweetest of honey on his tongue.

He couldn't *afford* to have Lindsey angry with him! This was all Debra Foley's fault. She was the proverbial thorn in his side. She didn't like him, and no matter what he tried, she still refused to cave in to his charm and accept him in Lindsey's life.

And then there was that little matter of the innocent offer he'd made her once when Lindsey was out of town on a business trip. He was certain she could make it sound like a whole lot more than what it was—a simple night out on the town, a treat for someone like her....

"Darling..." Brian took Lindsey by the shoulders and squeezed, at the same time attempting to draw her closer. "You know I'll do anything I can to help you in this."

But she shrugged him off; his touch only served to irritate her all the more. And she knew instinctively that he was lying.

"Go home, Brian, or go to your dinner party with someone else. I want to be alone to think."

"Lindsey—"

"Get out!"

When he failed to make a move but only stood looking at her affrontedly, she pointed back toward the door. She could see his mask of good humor was beginning to slip.

"Go on, go before you make me say something both of us will regret. I refuse to discuss Debra with you, and I won't go out with you. So go away and leave me alone."

His fists, hidden from view, knotted in frustration, yet he managed to maintain control of his mounting anger. Who was *she* to speak to him in that tone of voice? He knew things about her now, since listening to his brother's tale of woe, that she would no doubt *pay* to keep hidden. But he continued to play the game.

"I understand, darling," he murmured in a soothing tone guaranteed to smooth the most ruffled of feathers.

But his effect on Lindsey was just the opposite. She became so angry, in fact, that she would have thrown him bodily from her apartment if at all possible. Suddenly all the sly innuendos he had ever made regarding Debra came fully to mind.

"Hypocrite!" She turned on him like a virago. "You don't understand anything! You are without a doubt the most egotistical, manipulative, underhanded boor I have ever had the misfortune to meet. You're immature, jealous, insensitive—a fraud from the word go.

"I used to think that someone who shared the same interests I had, someone who had ambition and drive, someone who had the polish and charm you possess, someone a man like Ryan Dennison finds merit in, couldn't be all bad. But I was wrong!

"Debra is not your champion, that's true, but she never said a word against you until you made it quite evident you didn't like her. And still I let myself be fooled by you, making excuses for you, because I didn't want to believe you were as cold and unfeeling as you really are.

"I don't know how I let myself be fooled for even an instant by your brand of smooth, false charm." Her eyes shot bolts of green fire. "Yes, yes I do." She met his eyes head-on. "I allowed it because I knew you couldn't touch me."

She placed a closed fist against the pearl-gray sweater, feeling its dampness near her left breast. "Not in here," she continued. "Not where it counts."

She took a step closer, until she was all but touching him. "But you weren't after my heart, were you? Not that I'd have given it to you, in any case. You only wanted my *name,* my *influence!*

"You're a cold fish, Brian Kingston. Your only thought these past few months has been to use me. You said it yourself when you defined your idea of friendship. You intended to use me in whatever fashion you could to further your own interests.

"And I would have let you—because it didn't matter." The hot fury began to die out of her voice, though her eyes continued to burn like green flame. "I thought it was because I liked you, because you were a friend, but I was wrong—about a lot of things. It was because *you* didn't matter, not enough for me to put a stop to it.

"I realize now that I didn't stop seeing you or let your obvious dislike of Debra color my opinion of you because down deep inside I must have known all along that you weren't that important to me."

The anger was gone now from both her face and her voice. Debra had been right all along in her assessment of Brian's character, as well as about Lindsey's reasons for continuing to see him.

She knew now that she had been using him as a buffer against other men, men who might have gotten past her defenses, made her face her fears, those fears inspired as a rebellious twenty-year-old, seeking affection, trusting the wrong man and ending up as his victim.

Brian drew himself up to his full height and backed away from her, offended. His offense quickly turned to a fierce, burning anger. An anger such as he hadn't felt since his law school days, when he'd decided he would never wash another dish or cook another hamburger in some fast-food joint ever again, as long as he lived.

"Your *friend,* Debra, is nothing but a leech. She latched on to you a long time ago." He thrust a finger in her direction. "And you were too stupid to know it! She's had a free ride for years."

"Her? And what about you? Are your motives so pure?" Lindsey asked coldly. "Why are you hanging around if not because of what you think I can do for you?"

Maybe there was still a chance, slim though it might be, that he could turn this situation around. "I love you."

"Oh, please, not that!" She turned away from him in disgust. "The free ride, as far as you are concerned, is over as of now."

His future, the only one that would be left to him once Lindsey had spread the word, doing a thorough character assassination on him, passed before his eyes like a death sentence. It never occurred to him that she would simply say goodbye and that would be that as far as their relationship was concerned. In her place he would have extracted his revenge, and he expected that she would do the same.

"You don't know what you're saying." Just for a moment he considered groveling at her feet.

His mind grappled with the present state of affairs. How could this have happened? *Gone!* a voice inside his head screamed. *The money, the power, the trips, the expense accounts, the luxurious style of living he had craved as long as he could remember.*

No, it couldn't be gone, not like this, not in the time it took to snap a finger, blink an eye, not after all his hard work.

Summoning up a tone of humility when what he really wanted was to strangle her, he went to stand behind her, close, but not quite touching her. She had to listen to him, she had to change her mind about him before any damage could be done to his plans, his career.

"You were right when you called me insensitive. I should have known this wasn't the right time for a change in our relationship." One hand hovered inches away from the sleeve of her sweater. "Forgive me—please. My only excuse is that I've missed the advantage most men have to learn about tenderness from a mother's gentle love.''

But Lindsey wasn't listening; she was reaching for the phone. ''Willy? This is Miss Hamilton. Would you please call Mr. Kingston a cab? He's leaving immediately.''

She was sure that Brian had been expecting Mac to drive them to the party. She knew he liked being seen arriving in a limo.

Her eyes met Brian's furious glance before adding, ''Oh, and, Willy, don't allow Mr. Kingston to arrive unannounced in the future.''

She noted with satisfaction that the brown eyes had turned black with anger again, a more believable expression than the one of piety he'd just tried on her.

''What? No, I'm not angry with you, Willy. Just see that I'm not surprised again, that's all.''

Brian was at the door before she had replaced the receiver. He paused only long enough to slash a fulminating glance in her direction and whisper in barely leashed fury, ''You are going to live to regret this night's decision, I can assure you.''

There were things about her that she had no idea he knew, and he was certain they would come in useful when he gave her a dose of her own medicine sometime in the near future.

And then he was gone.

The door closed softly behind him, sounding louder in the silence than any angry slam would have done. Lindsey stared at the white-painted surface and gave a sudden shiver.

Would she? Would she live to regret giving Brian Kingston the boot?

Shaking off the feeling of dread his words had instilled for a brief moment, Lindsey turned back into the room. That question was as ridiculous as the threat had been. What could he possibly do to her? He was merely venting his vitriolic rage at her expense, hoping to give her a few moments of unease.

Debra would be pleased to learn she had finally come to her senses and literally shown him the door.

And then she remembered.

Debra—where are you?

Chapter 3

"Lindsey, you have a call on line one. It's your pharmacist. Should I put him through?"

Lindsey frowned in momentary confusion. She'd been miles away, her thoughts fixed on something other than the job at hand. She'd been worrying about Debra. Her mind had been busily dredging up various forms of brutality to kidnap victims that she'd read about in newspapers or heard about on TV. She'd been terrifying herself by wondering which one her friend might be experiencing right at this moment.

"Pharmacist?" she repeated questioningly. She hadn't spoken with Wayne Riddell for several weeks, not since she and Debra had attended his and his wife's anniversary dinner.

"Put him through, Pam."

Jonas slipped the last paper into the manila folder and thrust it into place, then gave the file drawer a shove. It clanged shut while he was taking a set of keys from his pocket. He inserted the smallest one and turned the lock.

There, that was the last of the "Case of the Misunderstood Husband." And one more satisfied customer, he thought wryly.

Every now and then, when he was feeling particularly low, he gave the case he was currently working on a title, just like the detective stories on television and in books. It gave him a chuckle when he really needed one.

This case had turned out well, leaving him feeling good about the check he'd accepted a short while ago.

An elderly woman had hired him to tail her husband to his regular Saturday night poker game. He had begun losing a considerable amount of money in the past month. She suspected that he was seeing another woman after nearly forty years of marriage.

It turned out the old guy was playing poker with matchsticks. The large sums of money his wife thought he was losing he was putting aside for a special fortieth wedding anniversary surprise. He'd been visiting travel agencies trying to decide what cruise to take her on. The travel agency he'd settled on was run by a younger woman eager to help him find exactly the right cruise, and that accounted for the smell of perfume.

Jonas had sat down behind his desk, preparing to tackle the hefty stack of mail he hadn't bothered with for the past week, when the telephone rang.

"Please, not a husband wanting his wife trailed to her weekly bingo game," he groaned. It never failed to amaze him how distrustful people who had lived together for years could be of each other.

"Hello?"

"Mr. Kingston? This is Lindsey Hamilton."

Jonas's jaw clenched. There had been no need for her to identify herself; the whiskey-soft tones purring in his right ear sounded far more familiar than he wanted to admit.

When he'd told his brother about the events leading up to his resignation from the police force so long ago, he'd purged himself of some of the pent-up anger he'd kept hidden for so long. Now all that remained was the guilt. He hadn't quite rid himself of that—nor his aversion to the Hamilton name.

"Hello? Are you there?"

"I'm here," he answered shortly.

"I need to talk to you, Mr. Kingston, but I would prefer not to do so over the telephone. Could you meet me for lunch?"

Jonas gripped the phone tighter. Lunch? No way. "I don't think—"

Sensing his intention to decline, Lindsey added hurriedly, "I have new evidence to support my theory that Debra is missing due to...foul play."

Foul play? Even she knew that the dramatic words dredged up from some movie sounded farcical in the extreme, but she hoped they would capture his attention.

Apparently they did. "Evidence of foul play?" he repeated despite himself, the detective's instinct for trouble coming into play. "What kind of evidence?"

Lindsey's husky voice dropped an octave lower. "Please, meet me for lunch."

She wanted to get him to the restaurant where Debra had last been seen, let him see just how easily what had taken place on Monday could occur, and see his face when she told him her news.

Jonas forced himself to sit back in his chair in a false pose of relaxation, even though there was no one there to see it.

"I'm sorry, Miss Hamilton, but I'm afraid I'll have to decline. I'm...swamped with work at the moment." He eyed the mound of envelopes he hadn't had a chance to get started on, most of them no doubt bills. "Why don't you consult your Yellow Pages and find someone else? I'm certain you'll find any number of P.I.'s willing to take on the case. Especially now, if, as you say, you have new evidence to support your story of a kidnapping.

"Or why don't you go back to the police with this new evidence? It seems to me that would be the thing to do."

"Police?" She sounded skeptical. "They couldn't help me before because they were too busy and they didn't put any stock in my idea that Debra had been abducted. I can't see them suddenly changing their minds even after hearing what I've just learned.''

Of course, she could have gone to Ryan Dennison. He would have helped, but once again she put the notion aside. She wanted to find Debra without currying favors from her friends.

"Sorry."

He didn't want to become involved with her. The one time he'd unwittingly had contact with her it had cost him too much. He'd lost his best friend and partner, his job on the police force, his own self-respect and, for a while, even his sanity.

Eight years ago he and Hank had answered a late-night call involving a domestic disturbance near Central Park. He'd had no idea at the time what they would be walking into, no idea that they would find one of the city's largest pushers cold with the goods, or that they would become involved with one of New York's leading families.

At first it had looked like a plain case of an argument getting out of hand and resulting in someone getting roughed up. On further investigation they had discovered that the young female victim had marks on her neck indicating that someone had tried to strangle her and someone—either herself or another party—had pumped her veins full of drugs.

But it hadn't ended there. The man who had beaten the young woman was still in the apartment, hiding. He managed with the aid of a knife to overpower Jonas and Hank, then used the knife to threaten the young woman. Hank had found drugs in the bathroom just before that, and the man wanted them. He also wanted the woman dead. It was only through some quick thinking on Hank's part that the woman remained alive, but as a result, the man got away. Hank gave chase into the park, leaving Jonas to care for the woman.

And when it was all over, Hank lay dead in a pool of his own blood, his murderer gone. Jonas was stunned, unable to comprehend that Hank could be alive one minute and lying dead the next. For a while he existed in a state of stunned disbelief—and then came the guilt.

He felt that if he had followed Hank, as he should have done, then Hank would still be alive. He'd been so broken up, feeling so guilty at having to face Hank's wife with the news of Hank's death, that he hadn't noticed much around him for the first several days after it had all happened.

His first day back at work, Jonas went to file his report on that night's happenings and discovered that a report had already been filed. One that in no way resembled what had actually taken place.

The officer who had written it was one of the men who had answered Jonas's distress call after Hank had chased the young woman's attacker. His report had failed to even mention a young woman being involved at all.

Jonas had been outraged and insisted upon filing his own report. A few days later he'd been called into the captain's office, where he was told in no uncertain terms to "cool it."

He hadn't known what kind of a can of worms he was opening when he accused the daughter of one of the city's leading families of being involved in drugs and murder, but he had refused to shut up, and that was when the stuff had hit the fan. He was *ordered* to forget all about what had happened that night. A more experienced officer had taken over the case and made it clear that Officer Hank Wilson had been attacked and murdered by an assailant, or assailants, unknown. Apparently Officer Wilson had felt he had reason to suspect his killer of something illegal and had followed him into Central Park, where he was subsequently overpowered and killed.

Jonas had been furious. From mug shots, he'd identified the man Hank had chased as Derek Lassiter, and he had threatened to go to the newspapers with the truth if Lassiter wasn't arrested and convicted of Hank's murder. But subtle threats were made against his younger brother. At first they only concerned his future career as a lawyer, but when Jonas didn't knuckle under, they took on a more personal nature.

At one point, recognizing Lindsey from a newspaper article, he even attempted to find and question her. But he'd been outmaneuvered even in that. Miss Hamilton, he'd been informed, was under a doctor's care for a serious nervous condition associated with her mother's recent death.

Jonas was only a rookie; he had no proof of the truth of that night's happenings except what he *knew* in his own mind had actually happened. He had left the captain's office a broken man with nothing to believe in.

After that his life had bottomed out, and it was a while before he made it back to reality. When he was himself again, he'd made a vow to steer clear of the Hamiltons and everyone like them. He'd managed to keep that vow—until now.

He wasn't exactly blaming Lindsey for all of that—at least, not anymore. It was her father he'd placed most of the blame on at the time. But he was dead now, and time had helped to dull, if not heal, the pain. It was true that for a while he had clumped her and her father together in his mind, along with the man who had murdered Hank. He'd blamed everyone involved equally for what had taken place that night and afterward.

But later, when it was all over, when Derek Lassiter ended up getting his at the end of a .44 from his own people, and the horror of that night and what followed had dimmed, Jonas had begun to wonder about her part in it all.

Whatever had gone on between Lassiter and Lindsey before that night, she had nonetheless been his victim. There was no shame in being a victim. We're all victims in one way or another, Jonas knew. But Horace Hamilton hadn't seen things that way.

It wasn't until much later that Jonas got an inkling of why the man had been so worried about his daughter being involved in that night's occurrences. It seems Lindsey had been seeing Lassiter for a couple of months before that night. It was a well-known fact in her crowd that she was his "woman." And it was also well-known that Lassiter supplied them with the cocaine they were all so eager to get their hands on.

But by that time Jonas had already left the force.

Over and over in his mind, Jonas had replayed that night's events, and they always came out the same. There were always the ifs. If he hadn't urged Hank to answer the call to begin with; if he hadn't been so concerned about the woman; if he had followed Hank into the park... If only he'd shown more professionalism, maybe Hank would still be alive today. If, always if.

All that remained were the memories, the dreams....

He listened to her soft breath coming through the line and wondered at her having the nerve to call him after what her father had done to him in the past. But then, maybe she really didn't remember him.

Eight years was a long time, and the one time he had seen her, she'd been so out of it that she probably wouldn't have recognized her own mother. She hadn't appeared to recognize him yesterday when she'd visited him in his office.

Or maybe, he speculated, he simply wasn't an important enough piece of her past for her to remember. Even though her face had haunted his dreams for eight long years, that was no reason to assume his had haunted hers. And the past should be relegated to memory....

"Wait! Don't hang up. Please." Lindsey's desperate voice ringing in his ear brought him abruptly back from his own personal hell. "Just meet me for lunch—that's all—and listen to what I have to say."

"I don't think that would be a good idea."

"What is it with you?" she asked almost angrily. "Have you taken a personal dislike to me for some reason?"

From his glaring silence, she accepted the truth of her spur-of-the-moment accusation.

But why?

The only explanation she could find was the offer she had made him as a last-ditch effort, telling him to name his own price. Most people would have jumped at the chance. Still, it was the fact that he hadn't that had made her call him and not some other private detective today, especially considering the manner in which she and his brother had last parted.

Or did his refusal have something to do with his brother? Didn't the saying go, "Mess with my family, mess with me?" Was he angry on his brother's behalf because of their breakup?

"Please, I know you must have found my story incredible, but believe me, it happened."

"Look, my refusal has nothing to do with liking or disliking you personally," Jonas finally answered after a long silence.

And as he said the words, he knew them for a fact. His reasons for turning her down were quite simple, really. He didn't want to become involved with her. Her face haunted his dreams night after night, and a small part of him feared the hold she seemed to have kept on his subconscious mind all these years. No matter how you looked at it, she'd already cost him too much.

Whether she'd had anything to do with her father's buying her out of a possible prison sentence as well as the notoriety she'd earned as Lassiter's girlfriend, whether she'd had any knowledge of her boyfriend's activities prior to the night he had beaten her and murdered Hank, Jonas still felt it prudent to steer clear of her.

He had never really known what she'd been involved in. The files, the case, had been closed to him. And as a rookie, he'd been unable to do anything but buckle under to the system and let it take its course. What he'd learned he'd learned through friends in the department after he'd left.

Now he feared that she would spell trouble if he let her back in his life. And even if things hadn't gone the exciting route he'd originally planned, he had enough excitement to suit him.

Unlike fictional private detectives, he didn't chase criminals with guns blazing, nor did he rescue beautiful women who were all longing to throw themselves into his arms at a moment's notice. He worked long, hard hours in all kinds of weather, and the most dangerous thing he normally faced was boredom.

When he was being honest with himself and not feeling depressed, as he had been the day Lindsey had visited his office, he actually liked what he did for a living. It suited him. He was his own boss, and occasionally, as with the older couple getting ready to celebrate their fortieth anniversary, what he did made him feel good.

"Look, why don't you try one of the other men listed in the phone book, like I suggested? I can even give you a couple of names you might try."

"I have," she concurred. "I've called several other investigators. And I've done some checking on you, as well."

Jonas felt his chest become tight. "You had me investigated?"

Lindsey knew from his tone of voice and glaring silence that the idea of having his own habits scrutinized by others didn't sit well with him.

"Not that exactly," she clarified hurriedly. "All I did was ask a few questions—like who was the best in the business when it came to finding missing people. And strangely enough, your name kept cropping up. It seems you have quite a reputation among your colleagues.

"However, you also appear to be thought of as something of a . . . *prima donna*. I believe that was the term used most frequently."

Lindsey paused briefly before adding, "You're the best, and that's what I want, the very best to find Debra. She's been my best friend all my life, and I know she's counting on me to find her.

"And make no mistake." Her tone hardened slightly. "I *will* find her, one way or another, with or without *anyone's* help."

Her words dropped like stones down a deep-well, striking at the very heart of him. That was the kind of attitude he would have had if the situation were reversed and he'd been trying to find Hank. And despite himself, he couldn't still the spark of admiration for her that ignited somewhere inside him.

What should he do? It was beyond his power to help Hank, but could he help Debra? Was he really afraid of the woman on the other end of the line? And just what was it about her that he feared? A memory he'd carried around with him for years? The poor, battered face of a helpless woman from his nightmares.

He'd been wrong to listen to his brother in the first place and turn her away. And now there was new evidence for him to consider.

"Mr. Kingston, please..." She was still waiting for his answer.

"All right," he agreed. "I'll meet you to discuss this new evidence. But understand this—I'm making no promises."

"That's good enough." Lindsey managed to cover the excitement in her voice with a small cough.

"Lunch," he reminded her. "Where? When?"

"The Oriental Palace at one."

"Right," he answered slowly.

"Do you know the restaurant, or shall I give you directions?" she asked.

"I'll find it," he answered softly. "Finding things is what I do for a living. Isn't that why we're having this conversation?"

He rang off, leaving Lindsey to stare silently at the phone in her hand. He was a strange man, but she wanted him on this case. She couldn't decide if that was because of all the good things she'd heard from his peers or the strange coincidence of the color of his eyes.

Her nightmare always ended with a vision of turquoise eyes. And somehow, even when she awakened in a cold sweat, the sheets binding her to the bed a silent testimony to her restless thrashing in her sleep, those eyes comforted her. The last thing she remembered was not the horror. That came later. It was the eyes. Those beautiful blue-green eyes.

"I wasn't certain you'd come."

The throaty tones slid over his nerve endings like warm, flowing honey. He couldn't decide whether she knew the effect her husky voice had on people, or if she was totally unaware of it.

"Neither was I," he admitted honestly, having had a moment of doubt as he was leaving his office.

He took the seat directly across from her, accepted the menu from the hovering waiter and opened it at once. He scanned it closely, not because he was hungry but because it gave him something to do instead of looking at her. She was every bit as beautiful as he remembered from her visit to his office. She almost took his breath away.

For several moments the air around their table shimmered with a fragile, unbroken silence, a small pocket of quiet in the universal hubbub of a popular restaurant filled to overflowing with the lunchtime crowd.

Lindsey stared at the back of his menu with perplexed eyes. He wasn't exactly rude, but rather abrupt almost to the point of rudeness. She wondered if that accounted for the nearly palpable tension she felt in the air.

At last, unable to contain her curiosity, she cleared her throat and prepared to speak. "I'm going to come right out and ask you something that I've wondered about since leaving your office yesterday."

Jonas tensed, but when he lowered his menu, nothing showed in his eyes. "And what is that?" he asked carefully, meeting her glance.

Lindsey found his eyes, ringed with inky black lashes, every bit as beautiful and disconcerting as the first time she'd looked into them, but she refused to look away.

What was it about this man that appealed to her? Because something about him did.

Perhaps it was that he was what you would call a man's man, very attractive in a hard, ruthless kind of way. He was nothing at all like the men she came into contact with daily. He didn't ooze charm, and he wasn't trying to impress her with either himself or any idea he wanted to sell her on.

He was, in fact, very different from every other man she'd ever met, including his brother. It was hard for her to even think of him as being Brian Kingston's brother. She kept looking for the same self-interest she had learned to read into everything Brian said or did.

Jonas appeared to be quite another matter. He captured and held her profound attention in a way she found uncanny under the circumstances. She didn't even know the man, and perhaps she should be wary of him because of his brother. Maybe he harbored hidden traits that he shared with Brian, traits she hadn't had a chance to see just yet.

All at once she realized she was staring at him and thinking thoughts that she had no business thinking. And what was more, she suspected that if he knew, he wouldn't welcome her interest in the least.

Besides, she reminded herself sternly, she was here for Debra's benefit. First and foremost she had to consider Debra's welfare in her dealings with this man.

Her probing glance turned suddenly cool. She took a sip of hot, sweet tea and cleared her throat once again before continuing.

"Did your brother have anything to do with your decision to refuse me yesterday or your reluctance to meet with me today?"

Jonas carefully laid his menu down before answering, the damp palms of both hands sticking to the red plastic-covered vinyl.

"I prefer to keep personal relationships out of business. What's between you and my brother has nothing to do with me or this meeting."

He sipped his water, noting how good its coolness felt sliding down his dry throat. "And now," he murmured in an attempt to put things once more on a business footing, "I thought you had something important to add, some new bit of evidence guaranteed to make me change my mind."

"I have," she said slowly. But she wasn't quite finished with the subject of Brian. "But first, I think you should know, if you don't already, that Brian and I had a disagree-

ment last night. He won't—we won't—'' She floundered
momentarily beneath his steady gaze before continuing in a
crisp voice. "Brian won't be pleased if you decide to help
me.'' She held his eyes with her own, refusing to allow him
to glance away. She wanted to see exactly how the news of
their breakup affected him. "I hope you won't let that influence you this time," she added deliberately.

She had the clearest green eyes, like finely made glass,
Jonas noted abruptly, and realized that he'd remembered
that about her. Hadn't green eyes once sometime way back
in history, denoted a person as being a witch?

Green eyes and mahogany hair... His eyes traveled up
over the elegant knot of hair fastened to the crown of her
head. In the light it had a deep, rich, red gleam to it, but it
was darker than it had been eight years ago.

As though pulled by a string, his glance slid back to hers.
And though he tried to fight it, Jonas felt himself beginning to drown in twin pools of green fire.

Was this how Brian had felt whenever he was with her?
The thought slithered through his mind, abruptly breaking
the spell. He tore his glance from hers and looked across the
restaurant toward the small pagoda-shaped fountain spew-
ing water in the center of the room.

"Brian and I are brothers," he answered, his eyes never
meeting hers. "However, we pretty much go our own way
when it comes to business matters—and in most other areas,
too," he added softly.

Wondering what he meant by that, she said, "I just
wanted things out in the open. I didn't want you to agree to
help, and then change your mind later."

"I haven't agreed to anything," he reminded her shortly,
"except to listen. I'm not a man who is easily swayed," he
warned. "And as I've already told you, I never allow my
personal feelings to interfere in business dealings."

But that wasn't strictly true. He *had* allowed Brian to
persuade him before. And he wasn't certain that he wouldn't
refuse her again, and this time for reasons of an even more
personal nature.

Their waiter, noting Jonas's closed menu, approached the table. "Are you ready to order?"

Without looking at each other, they placed their orders. The young man departed swiftly, as though to serve them was his main priority in life. Jonas glanced after him before turning his attention once more toward the woman seated across from him.

"Are you a regular here?" he asked abruptly.

"W-what?"

"I asked if you come here often."

"Oh . . . yes, it's one of our—Debra's and mine—favorite places to eat."

"I see."

What did he see with those fantastic eyes as his glance swept the room? She studied him without appearing to. The set of his chin suggested a stubborn streak, and it was echoed in the no-nonsense set of his firm mouth. But the thin crinkly lines at the corners of his eyes told another, quite different story. Was there someone—a woman, perhaps—who had helped him to develop those deep laugh lines?

Her glance traveled up over the curve of the close-set ear nearest to her, its tip hidden by wisps of soft-looking dark blond hair. Either his hair was in dire need of a cutting or else he liked it lying against the collar of his sweater, the color of which was a perfect match for his eyes.

Men such as he appeared to be didn't usually take much note of such things as matching their clothes to their eyes. But women did. Had a woman picked out the sweater? The same woman, perhaps, with whom he shared laughter—and what else?

He was a man who owed his attraction not to the perfect symmetry of his features, as Brian did, but rather to an aura of strength and virility that he wore with ease and charm. The kind of animal magnetism that she'd heard so much about but never actually encountered. The kind that attracted women of all ages, in all shapes and sizes.

She noted the heavy shadow of his beard, then her eyes moved along the taut, forward thrust of his jaw—and darted upward to find his eyes fastened questioningly on her face.

She had been so immersed in taking stock of him, busily denying that she herself found him in any way attractive, that she was totally unprepared for the shock of those eyes looking directly into hers.

She who could hold her own in a boardroom full of men, all bent on annihilating any idea she put forth on whatever topic, felt the skin of face and neck grow hot with embarrassment.

Her first thought was to make a stammered apology, and then her usual self-control came into play. "You and your brother aren't very much alike."

"Bri got all the looks." He grinned without humor, and all at once an air of stillness—isolation—seemed to surround him.

Lindsey blinked, and the aura was gone. Had she only imagined it? She was beginning to realize that there was much more to this man than she had seen at first glance. Unlike his brother, she suspected that his emotions ran deep.

"Are you ready to tell me why you've brought me here? I assume this is the restaurant where your friend had her last meal."

It was a poor choice of words, he realized as she raised stricken eyes to his. "Sorry. But I assume this *is* the place where you overheard the conversation?"

"Yes." Lindsey was still recovering from the shock of what his words implied. Had he uttered the painfully suggestive phrase deliberately?

"And you're still of the opinion that your friend was kidnapped?"

"Yes."

Jonas eyed her keenly. "So tell me what happened to reaffirm that idea."

"I received a phone call this morning from the pharmacist who fills all Debra's prescriptions. We're old school friends. He's my pharmacist, too."

"Prescriptions?" he asked with narrowed eyes. "Has your friend been sick?"

"Yes and no. Not like you're thinking, nothing terminal, like cancer. Debra is an epileptic," Lindsey explained. "She takes medication to prevent her from having seizures." She paused in her explanation to ask, "Do you know anything about epilepsy?"

"Very little."

"Then let me explain briefly. If Debra doesn't take the medication regularly, she could have a seizure. And with the type she has, that could prove to be fatal."

"I'm sorry," he sympathized, "but I fail to see—"

"I'm getting to it," she said, forestalling him. "The day we had lunch together, I saw Debra take the last capsule in her bottle. I asked her if she was out, and she said yes, but not to worry, she was picking up a refill on her way home from work that evening.

"But this morning Wayne told me that Debra never arrived to pick up her medicine. He called me because he knew what might happen, and he thought I might know where she was.

"Now do you understand my concern? Debra hasn't taken her medication for over a week. I saw her have a seizure once when we were teens. It was horrible. I didn't know what to do to help her."

Lindsey urgently bent forward over the table, her eyes locked with his. "Please, Mr. Kingston, we have to find Debra before she has a seizure—if it isn't already too late."

Jonas once more found himself caught up in the spell of those green eyes, shimmering now with unshed tears.

At that moment the waiter returned with their food. Relieved at the timely intervention, Jonas managed to get his thinking back on track.

She'd almost gotten him under her spell, agreeing to do anything she wanted him to without any further persuasion on her part.

An instinct for self-preservation lunged immediately to the surface of his conscious mind, warning him against further involvement with her. She was trouble, or a catalyst for it, as he well knew. Surely he wasn't foolish enough to set himself up a second time as a target for her to take down.

Lindsey felt shaken, her mind filled with memories of the past. She looked down at the steaming food with a jaundiced eye. At the moment she was quite certain that if she took a bite it would choke her. She glanced across the table at Jonas. Would he help her or not?

With his eyes on his own plate, Jonas picked up his chopsticks and began to eat. After a time she followed suit. Maybe he had the right idea; maybe they needed time to digest the situation, as well as the food.

"Your friend," Jonas said, breaking the silence abruptly, "would she deliberately go without her medication?"

"Of course she wouldn't," Lindsey answered indignantly. "She isn't stupid. She's had the results of what could happen if she did that drummed into her head all her life."

"You've talked with this pharmacist friend of yours. Did he say whether Debra has ever forgotten a prescription before?"

"I didn't ask, but I think he'd have mentioned it if she had. He's very worried about her. I didn't want to alarm him by saying that she was missing, so I told him she had probably found another bottle in her medicine cabinet and forgotten all about the refill order she'd placed."

"Look," Lindsey whispered urgently, "Debra may have an adventurous spirit, but she isn't foolish. And that's why I called you."

She had laid all the facts on the table. It was time to get an answer from him. "So, what do you say? Will you change your mind and take the case?"

"I think you definitely have reason to be concerned." Lindsey heard the words with a sense of satisfaction. At last someone was going to help. "But I can't help you," he finished, plunging her into instantaneous despair.

"Can't?" She targeted his face with sharp green eyes. "Or won't?"

"I—"

"Are you tied up with another case?" she asked quickly.

He eyed her for a moment in silence, noting a new, stubborn glint in her eyes. "If you're about to tell me—again—to name my own price, forget it," he answered uncompromisingly.

"Then you *are* working on something else?" she persisted.

"Not exactly." He saw no reason to lie.

She frowned. "Then what?"

Jonas studied her for a time without speaking. There were lots of reasons he could have given her, but only one that would have truly satisfied her. And that was the one he wouldn't mention. Not yet.

"It really doesn't matter. What matters is your friend. I'm certain it will be easy to find another private detective. Money talks." A hardness that hadn't been there before entered his turquoise eyes. "As I'm sure you well know. At any rate," he amended, "it talks to most people, most of the time."

"But don't you see—" she leaned closer in agitation, gripping the table edge "—that's exactly why I want *you*. You don't give a damn about my money. You told me so, and I believe you. And that's why I know you'll do a good job. Please, not for my sake—for Debra."

She held her breath, waiting, hoping, watching the changes taking place in his face. And suddenly, looking into those fantastic eyes, she knew what his answer was going to be.

This man might be a puzzle to her, but she was confident of figuring him out, given enough time. And she wanted him on her side. He could find Debra. She would bet her life on it. She was already betting Debra's.

"All right," he agreed reluctantly, tearing his eyes from hers while a small voice inside called him every kind of a fool. "I'll do it."

He was going against everything he knew about her and everything he felt deep inside by agreeing, but his conscience wouldn't allow him to give any other answer.

"Thank you," she whispered, lowering her eyes to the table.

Tears of relief were very near the surface, but she couldn't afford to have him see them—to see such vulnerability. The very idea of displaying such emotion in front of him unnerved her. It was strength she needed to help her find Debra. Besides, she wasn't the kind to indulge in emotional outbursts, not even in private. In public it was unthinkable.

Her display of anger when she'd practically thrown Brian out of her apartment had also been out of character. This thing with Debra was turning her life upside down. It was turning her into someone she no longer recognized.

Chapter 4

The meal was finished and her purpose in coming here accomplished. Lindsey signaled for the waiter. Jonas watched as she paid the tab. She was easy to watch but hard to figure out.

He'd reached for the check a few minutes earlier and been informed coolly, as she took it from his fingers, that this was a business lunch and she would take care of it.

He let her. She probably could have bought the whole restaurant if she had wanted to. She certainly had the money. She had enough money to hire the best of private detectives. And he certainly didn't kid himself that he was that. As a matter of fact, if she had wanted, she could probably have hired a hundred private detectives exactly like himself. So why was she so set on having him?

And why was *she* doing the hiring? She must employ a dozen different people who could handle such a task. There had to be a lot of her father in her. And Horace Hamilton had been a man who expected a handsome dividend on every expenditure. True, she had offered to allow him to write his own ticket, but he felt intuitively that that had not been her usual style of doing business.

And unless, for some reason known only to herself, she was putting on an act, she had no memory of him from the past. Maybe she had heard about his tenacity in sticking with a case to its oftentimes bitter end and that had made him her number-one choice for the job. Of course, he remembered sourly, his tenacity eight years ago hadn't counted for much. He'd knuckled under to her father just like all the others. And that memory was a bitter pill to swallow, even today.

Brian, he recalled, had intimated that she was being taken advantage of by Debra. That didn't sound like a Hamilton to him. If he was to suspect anyone of taking advantage of a situation, it would be the reverse.

Maybe this Debra had run away because *she* was the one being bought and she didn't want to feel dominated by Lindsey Hamilton any longer. It was obvious to him that Lindsey had at least some of her father's traits. She was a successful businesswoman, if appearances were anything to go by. And though he'd taken note of her obvious anxiety on her friend's behalf, she still appeared very much in control.

And then there was always the possibility that this Debra was running some kind of a scam. Maybe she was the key to this whole thing. Could she have staged the conversation between the two characters so she and Lindsey could "accidentally" overhear it, then engineered her own kidnapping in order to collect a generous ransom with which to blow this town? It wouldn't be the first time such a scenario had been tried.

There was also the possibility, unpalatable as it was, that his own brother was involved. Brian had admitted to the fact that he didn't like Debra and her influence on Lindsey. And he'd asked Jonas to turn down the case. But would he go so far as to get rid of someone he felt was in his way?

Jonas knew his brother was a man who wanted a lot from life and wasn't above using unorthodox means to get it, but surely he drew the line at kidnapping and extortion?

He wasn't sorry that he'd decided to help Lindsey find her friend, but just for a moment he couldn't help feeling almost trapped—and bought, if not with her money then with emotional blackmail. Here he was again, involved with the Hamiltons, albeit willingly this time.

The last time, he'd sacrificed his friend Hank and his own pride to keep his brother from becoming a victim of one Hamilton.

Maybe this time, if Debra was indeed a victim, by helping her he could in some small way make up for being too late to save Hank. And maybe then the guilt, the nightmares, the dreams of the woman sitting across from him, would go away and leave him in peace.

And this time, a small voice whispered inside his head, *you'll be using a Hamilton, instead of the other way around. Take a look at her. This time she'll be your pawn, and she won't even know it.*

Jonas pushed himself away from the table abruptly and stood, drawing Lindsey's eyes. All at once he couldn't get out of her presence fast enough. If he was going to do this thing he wanted to get started, find the missing woman, prove his brother wasn't involved in her disappearance and be done with Lindsey Hamilton once and for all.

He thought he'd left all the bitterness in the past, yet suddenly he could taste it on his tongue.

Lindsey picked up her credit card and hurriedly tucked it away inside her wallet. "What now?" she asked, gaining her feet and hurrying after him. Lifting her voice, she asked, "What do we do now?"

"Now *I* go to work. You point out the waiter who served you on Monday, and then *I*—" he stressed the pronoun again "—take it from there."

"Your retainer?" she questioned. "What—"

"We'll discuss that later," he told her shortly, his eyes searching the room for the young man who'd waited on them. He expected her to point him out in answer to his question and was surprised when she didn't.

"He isn't here." She glanced reluctantly around the room. The businesswoman in her didn't like leaving a discussion involving money for a later date. But what could she do about it standing here in a crowded restaurant?

"I've been watching for him since I arrived. I expected him to serve us, but I haven't caught sight of him once, and the table where we sat is in his station. Perhaps today is his day off."

She gave him a tentative smile, but found it dying a quick death when he turned abruptly without a change in expression and started to walk away.

"But I can show you where the two men we overheard were seated," she said, stopping him with her words.

Jonas took note of the aura of privacy surrounding the tiny alcove, but it was a false one. He could see how it might indeed have been possible to eavesdrop on another's conversation without meaning to. Especially if the exchange had been an angry one.

"I think I should speak with the manager. If your waiter isn't here, then perhaps he can be persuaded to give us his address."

Jonas marched off, leaving her standing where she was.

Lee Wong, the restaurant's owner and manager, wasn't hard to find. He was quite happy, after Lindsey's brief explanation, to assist the lovely Miss Hamilton in whatever way he could. He told them that Rob Slater hadn't been in to work or answered his phone since last Monday, and if they found him, to please convey the message that he was fired.

Lindsey could barely keep the excitement out of her eyes as she thanked the man and followed Jonas's broad back out to the street.

"Are you going there now? To his apartment?" she asked, standing close to his left shoulder because of the throngs of people on the sidewalk. A sharp wind whirled down around them, blowing her against him.

Jonas caught a whiff of tantalizing perfume and drew back. "Yes," he answered shortly, thrown off balance by her close proximity, the sudden and unexpected feel of her beneath his hands as he steadied her.

"Do you think his not showing up for work the last few days has anything to do with Debra's disappearance?" she asked a bit breathlessly. She could feel the contact with him all through her body, despite her heavy coat.

Jonas hunched down into his jacket, eyes beginning to tear from the bitterly cold, stinging wind, and shook his head. "I doubt it. But he might have seen or heard something that can help us. It might be something he doesn't even realize he knows."

Lindsey's heart leaped. He'd said "us," and that gave her the opening she'd been looking for.

"I'm going with you when you go to his apartment. We can take my car." She nodded toward a long black limousine that Jonas recognized as it slowly made its way through the thick traffic to where they stood. "I told Mac to pick me up here."

Jonas darted a glance from the limousine to the woman and back again, his ire aroused. He'd been amused and then irritated by turns when she had stepped up and taken over the questioning of Mr. Wong, but he'd held his tongue, because the man appeared to be more susceptible to her feminine charms than to Jonas's straight way of talking. But he'd be damned if he'd let her run the whole show.

It appeared to him that, just as her father had in the past, she thought she could step in and high-handedly take over, make people—make him—do as she wanted. Well, she couldn't have been more wrong.

"No way." He shook his head and began to walk down East Fifty-fifth Street, both to get away from her and because his feet were becoming numb from the cold.

"What do you mean, 'no way'?" She planted herself directly in his path, making it impossible for him to move because of the crowds.

"I mean I'm not going anyplace in that." He nodded back toward the limo, which had drawn up to the curb. "Would you take an ad out in the *New York Times* if you were planning to murder someone? Lady, that limo would stick out like a sore thumb on any street, especially the ones we would be traveling down. And in any case, you're not going with me. I don't take my clients along when I work. That's what you're paying *me* for. If you could do the job yourself, you wouldn't need me. Those are the rules."

Lindsey heard him out, her face an expressionless mask. And when he was finished, she locked eyes with him and said, "I hired you, that makes you my *employee,* and as far as I'm concerned that means I call the shots. My employees do what *I* tell them to." She stood her ground, stubbornly refusing to be outstared, or outsmarted.

Anger gathered in his blue-green eyes, turning them the color of stormy seas. "Maybe I made a mistake in taking this job, after all," he told her with a set jaw, turning away.

Lindsey backed down a fraction, realizing that a show of force was definitely the wrong tack to take with this man. "Look, maybe this isn't your usual manner of doing business, but you have to realize that this is an unusual situation for me, too. And if—when—you find Debra, I want to be there."

"No." He refused to give in. "You heard the rules. They're really very simple. All you have to do is let me do my job."

She was tempted to tell him what he could do with his rules, but she wanted to go along and was pretty certain that after hearing her views on his rules there wouldn't be a snowball's chance in hell of her doing so.

"Please..." Somehow she had moved around to stand in front of him again, and one small, gloved hand found its way to the solid wall of his chest, resting there in silent entreaty. "Not for me—for Debra. When she's found, she'll need the comfort of someone close to her. And I'm all the family she has in the world. She'll need me. *You'll* need me."

Jonas moved uncomfortably beneath her delicate hand, feeling its weight like a heavy stone against his chest. Was this another attempt at manipulating him against his will to do her bidding? Or was she sincerely concerned for her friend's welfare?

He forced sarcastic words to the back of his mind and tried reason. "Look, you have no idea what surveillance is like. This Slater kid might not be home. As a matter of fact, there's a good chance that he won't be, since he hasn't been answering his phone. And that means long hours of waiting inside a cold automobile for his return. You have no idea how cold and boring it can get just sitting and staring at one point for hours on end. It might take days, weeks, for this guy to turn up."

"But we don't have days," Lindsey interjected swiftly.

"Wong said he hadn't been in to work since Monday. He could have moved to Timbuktu by now," Jonas warned.

She refused to give credence to such a thing. Debra *had* to be found, and not in days, or weeks, but now, as quickly as possible. And she was going along to see that it happened.

Jonas stared into her stubborn face, searching for a sign that she was weakening, but nothing had changed in the green eyes locked onto his. And as long as they simply stood there locked in disagreement, the only thing they were accomplishing was to freeze.

"Look, the longer we stand here, the greater the chance that your friend the waiter and anything he has to tell us might slip through our fingers," he insisted in a last-ditch effort to make her see reason.

She bunched his jacket in her anxiety. "Please." The word came hard. She wasn't used to saying it to get what she wanted, and she'd used it with this man too often already. But all she could think of was Debra, her best friend in all the world, and how she might need her right at this very moment. "We don't know what...state we might find Debra in. She may have been...abused.... She'll need me. She'll need the comfort of a woman. Her eyes pleaded with him far more eloquently than any words.

"All right." He gave in all at once, knowing it wasn't worth the battle and wanting to get in out of the icy wind slicing through his clothing to the vulnerable skin below. And, too, she was right. He didn't know what they might find when they found the missing woman. If she was an innocent victim, as Lindsey believed, she had probably been through a rough time. And if she wasn't, perhaps the sight of her "best friend" would loosen her tongue.

In either case, the woman standing before him would get tired of tagging along soon enough. This was probably no more than a lark for her. Not that she didn't truly want to find her friend, but being this close to someone like him, someone out of her usual sphere, might be the real attraction. So with a mental shrug he decided to let fate take its course and to give the woman her money's worth, let her experience the thrill of the chase with a real live detective.

And maybe, in the meantime, he would get an insight into what made people like her and her father tick, and whether she *really* had no memory of her part in the night of Hank's death.

"We go in my car," he said, qualifying his permission.

Lindsey wasn't about to push her luck. Telling him that she needed a moment to let Mac know about the change in plans, she turned reluctantly away, worrying all the time that when she turned back he would have gone on without her.

It took only a few minutes to speak to her driver, phone the office to let her secretary know she would be out for the rest of the day and then she was searching through the crowd for Jonas's tall figure and distinctive eyes. She spied him at last. His attention was focused in a direction she found somehow disturbing.

His magnificent eyes appeared to be glued to the gentle sway of a pair of well-rounded hips encased in tight black leather that displayed an alarming length of thigh. The young woman in question wore matching leather boots with heels at least six inches high and had long, improbably blond hair hanging nearly to her waist and swinging with each step as she disappeared among the other pedestrians.

So, his taste ran to black leather and blondes. Her glance met his and held for several heartbeats. He gave a slight shrug and glanced away. A moment later he was at her side, observing the slight color in her cheeks and wondering if it was caused by the bite of the wind or something altogether different.

In silence he led her to a side street where his car was parked. Lindsey made no verbal comparison between the comfort afforded by the ten-year-old green Ford sedan and the luxurious interior of the Cadillac he had forsaken.

Without bothering to tell her where they were headed, Jonas made a brief stop at his apartment. Lindsey sat in the car, watching the light fade as the sun, hidden behind dark gray clouds, dropped lower in the late afternoon sky.

Jonas returned in about fifteen minutes with his arms full. He placed everything on the back seat and climbed in beside her.

Lindsey noticed that he'd changed clothes. He was wearing what appeared to be some kind of thermal coveralls, and unless her eyes deceived her, it looked as though he'd put on about ten pounds since leaving her.

It was four o'clock when they found the two-story building in a lower middle-class neighborhood in Queens where Rob Slater had an apartment. Jonas parked his car strategically across from the alley that ran beside the building and turned off the engine.

They had ridden in silence since leaving the restaurant. While the car had been moving it hadn't seemed to matter, but now all at once the inside seemed to have shrunk. Lindsey sneaked a peek at the man by her side. He had reached behind him and brought forth what looked like a short, fat telescope. He placed it to his face and looked across the street toward the building.

"What do you see?" she asked curiously, breaking the silence.

It was getting dark, and though the building was situated fairly close, there wasn't much to see from her standpoint.

"A building," he answered shortly, still not comfortable with her sitting so close beside him in the car, his nightmare come suddenly to life.

Lindsey glanced at him reproachfully, unaccountably hurt by his unwillingness to talk to her.

After a moment of tense silence he spoke again. "There's a little girl about three standing at one of the upstairs windows in a diaper, eating a cookie."

"That's all she's wearing? A diaper?" Lindsey asked, aghast, with a shiver. The car was beginning to cool down in the frigid temperatures outside, and she couldn't imagine anyone allowing a baby to run practically naked in this weather, even indoors.

"That's all," Jonas answered. "This isn't exactly a wealthy neighborhood. Maybe a diaper is all she's got to wear. At least the kid's got a cookie."

Jonas reached behind him with one hand and locked the back door, then turned in the seat and, being particularly careful that his hand didn't come into contact with her shoulder, stretched his arm along the seat behind Lindsey, snicking that lock into place, as well.

"Lock your door and mine after I get out."

"Where are you going?" Lindsey asked quickly. He wasn't leaving her here, was he?

"I'm going to take a look around while there's still some light. I don't think our boy is home, and since we don't know what part he's playing in all this—if any—I want to get the lay of the land while I can."

Lindsey scooted hurriedly over in the seat, rolled the window down and called somewhat anxiously to his retreating back, "Will you be gone long?"

"As long as it takes," he answered sharply, thinking it served her right if she didn't like sitting alone on a street in this part of town. She should have stayed in Manhattan, where she belonged.

Not that he liked leaving her, because now her safety was his responsibility, too, but he couldn't very well take her with him. He didn't know what awaited him in the building, and he needed all his concentration on the task at hand for his own safety. Already it would be distracted by his concern for the woman sitting alone in the car.

He knew he should have left her at the restaurant, because one way or another she was going to do nothing but get in his way.

He stopped abruptly and pivoted toward the car. "Don't get out while I'm gone," he snapped. "You got that?"

Lindsey nodded, unable to speak over the sudden uneven beating of her heart. He really was going to leave her on this street, in this section of town, alone. . . .

"I don't suppose it's . . . unsafe . . . to sit here?" she managed to get out before he turned away. What she really wanted to say was, *Don't go. Don't leave me here alone. Please, take me with you.*

"You'll be all right. Just keep the windows up and the doors locked, and don't flash that coat around."

Lindsey glanced down at the mink he was referring to, then watched his long strides take him across the street toward the cavelike alley. She shivered. It didn't look like a place she'd want to be, especially not after dark.

Time slipped by. She wasn't certain how long she'd been sitting there; it felt like hours, but in reality might only have been minutes. She could have turned on a light to look at her watch, but she didn't want to draw attention to the car—and herself, sitting alone in it.

As the sky began to grow darker, the alley became a place of shadows, and every time she glanced into its yawning black mouth she gave a tiny shudder.

Where was he? Where was Jonas? Surely it didn't take this long to look at an apartment. What could be keeping him?

And still she waited. As time passed she began to fret, her eyes drawn again and again to one spot until she hardly dared breathe. Her head began to ache with the strain of trying to peer through the darkness to the alley's interior.

All at once Jonas's tall figure moved into view. But he didn't turn toward the car, as she had expected; he moved instead toward the front steps of the building.

From where she sat, she could see him enter the building. Lindsey watched with a sinking feeling as his tall, loose-limbed figure disappeared through the doors.

What now? Her eyes were drawn toward the gaping black hole, waiting like a beast of prey for its next victim.

How long would he be gone? How long, she wondered, before she should start to worry?

Chapter 5

Lindsey could only guess at how long Jonas had been gone when she began to get the strange feeling that she was being watched. She attempted to put the notion down as nothing more than a case of paranoia brought on by the lateness of the hour and the unfamiliar surroundings, but she continued to feel uneasy. Her uneasiness grew so strong that she began to be afraid of glancing at what was outside for fear of what she might see.

She peered down nervously at the large, round face of the watch on her left wrist, but it was too dark to make out the numbers.

Where was Jonas? Why was he taking so long?

She shivered, telling herself that it was from the cold and not because the short hairs were standing up on the back of her neck. It had grown so cold that not even the warmth of the fur coat could stave off the chill.

She'd observed very few people on the street since they'd parked here, and rather than feeling reassured by the fact, it added fuel to her increasing disquiet. The few pedestrians she had spotted had passed quickly, keeping their eyes straight ahead.

The harsh winter wind had been brisk when they left the restaurant after lunch, but now it appeared to have reached gale force. Old papers, tin cans and a flat piece of cardboard skipped down the sidewalk and flew across the street.

The condensed moisture on the windows began to frost over, creating a feeling of isolation in Lindsey's susceptible mind. She snuggled down into her coat both for warmth and to make herself less visible to anyone watching from a window or hidden someplace along the street. She wriggled frozen toes inside the thin heels and wished longingly for a pair of boots, not unlike the ones worn by the blonde who'd attracted Jonas's eye on the sidewalk earlier.

The creepy feeling of being watched didn't go away, and her sixth sense told her that whoever was watching her was very close by. All at once, in a sudden show of bravery, she withdrew a gloved hand from her pocket and wiped it across the window at her side. There, now she had a better view of the building directly across the sidewalk from her.

Had a curtain moved at one of the ground floor windows?

She was concentrating so hard on watching it that when the door to the building was suddenly thrust open, she gave an involuntary squeal of surprise and jerked back against the seat. Loud music and raucous laughter issued from somewhere within.

Lindsey felt her heart stop beating and nearly choked on her own breath as two large figures filled the doorway. Her eyes widened in terror as the young men, dressed similarly in faded, ragged jeans, leather jackets and boots, paused at the top of the broken concrete steps and looked down, directly into her astonished face.

The hair of the taller of the two was a brilliant shade of purple and stood up in rigid spikes down the center of his head, the tip of each spike dyed a dark red. The second man was bald as an egg. His scalp had been painted in rainbow hues that extended down over his ears. But it was his eyes that struck terror into her heart. The outer rims and eyelids had been painted dead black, making it appear as though the eye sockets were empty. However, when she looked into his face, light was reflected off the orbs like the flickering flames of twin candles set inside an empty skull.

She couldn't seem to take her eyes off them. Her one coherent thought was *Thank God the doors are all locked.* Then she thought about the glass. There was an awful lot of glass in an automobile. It wouldn't take much for two strong young men to heft something with enough force to shatter it.

Lindsey scooted toward the center of the seat as, their eyes locked on hers, the two began slowly to descend the wide steps. Her heart, surely at a standstill until now, began slowly to beat once again, moving the sluggish ice in her veins. Her throat had closed up, and sweat began to break out in places that minutes ago had been in danger of frostbite. She shrank back against the seat as far as she could, wishing that, somehow, she could become invisible.

A sharp rap on the door glass to the left of her caused her to jump as though she'd been shot. Emitting a high-pitched scream, she whirled to face this new attack.

Jonas Kingston stood looking in at her from outside.

Lindsey scrambled for the lock, expecting that Jonas would hurry into the car.

"Hurry! Get inside! Quick!" She shoved the door open, nearly knocking him off his feet.

"What the—"

"Hey!"

Jonas wrenched his gaze from Lindsey's frightened eyes to peer over the top of the car at the taller of the two men.

"Yeah?" he answered in a dangerous tone.

"You or your lady see a little dog about this high?" He measured about six to eight inches with his hands. "He's out here somewhere, probably lost."

Jonas bent down to peer questioningly at Lindsey. She swallowed, unable to speak, and after a moment shook her head firmly.

"Sorry, no," he called over the roof of the car.

"Okay." The pair moved down the last step and started to turn away. "Listen," purple hair called back, "if you do see him, his name's Buster and he belongs to my kid sister. She's crying her eyes out inside." He gestured with a thumb back over his shoulder. "The first apartment on the right. If you do happen to see him, take him in to her, will ya?"

Jonas nodded, and purple hair grunted. "Thanks." Then the pair moved off down the street, calling as they went, "Buster! Here, Buster, come on, boy. Where the hell are you, you little rat?"

Jonas slipped inside the car, closed the door and locked it, before glancing over at the woman at his side.

"You all right?" he asked. She was leaning back against the seat, eyes closed, her face a pale shade of gray.

"Who, me?" She straightened, gave a shaky laugh and answered, "Of course. They were only boys looking for their dog." She sounded fine, but in the brief second her glance had met his, he'd seen the remnants of fear and vulnerability in her eyes.

"Their little sister's dog," Jonas corrected her without expression, drawing her gaze.

They stared at each other in silence for about ten seconds. All at once her green eyes narrowed, then brimmed with laughter. Lindsey put a gloved hand over her mouth but couldn't contain her giggles.

The serious expression faded from Jonas's face as the corners of his eyes began to crinkle with amusement. There, she thought with satisfaction, she'd known those were laugh lines.

"You should have seen your face when I tapped on the window." He tried, but he couldn't hold the laughter inside.

Lindsey let her hand fall back to her lap, allowing the merriment—partly a release of nervous tension—to burst forth, chuckling so hard that tears started to her eyes.

"Me!" she cried. "What about you? You should have seen your face when I screamed."

After a few moments the laughter died down. Lindsey took a tissue from her purse and dabbed at the corners of both eyes. Her mascara was probably running down her cheeks in black irregular lines, and she was certain that after this her lips must be bare of any trace of lipstick.

But instead of reaching for her compact she snapped the purse shut and rested her head back against the seat, feeling very relaxed all at once. The silence stretched between them. It started out easy, comfortable, but after a while she sensed a brittleness to it.

Jonas had gone back to watching the building across the street, but Lindsey was watching him.

"It's getting colder in here," she observed with double meaning.

Jonas grunted, concentrating on the work at hand.

She shivered. "I wouldn't be surprised if we get snow before morning."

He grunted again. He didn't want to talk just now. It was taking some getting used to, realizing how easy it had been to share a moment of laughter with this woman. And he kept asking himself how he could so easily forget the past.

"I could certainly use a cup of hot coffee about now." She shivered again and drew her coat closer about her.

Without comment, Jonas reached over the back of the seat in one swift motion and rummaged around in the bag he'd brought from his apartment. He drew forth something that glistened even in the feeble light.

Lindsey stared at the silver bottle topped with a red cup and asked, "Are you kidding me? A thermos?"

"I always bring something along, just in case." He removed the cup, unscrewed the cap and half filled the cup.

"Just in case of what?" she asked, sniffing the tantalizing aroma of hot coffee filling the air.

"Just in case—" he couldn't help himself "—I run across a lady in distress—" his eyes glinted with humor "—who needs some.

"Here." His eyes met hers over the rim of the cup. Lindsey felt her heart flutter and begin to thaw. "I didn't bring a second cup." His voice sounded suddenly deeper. "We'll have to share."

"I don't mind." She lifted the coffee to her lips.

"Wait!"

Startled, she stopped with the cup just short of her mouth. "What is it?"

"There's a good chance we'll be here a while." His eyes slipped away from hers. "I could manage the coffee, but if you need a ladies' room later..." he murmured, suddenly feeling awkward.

Lindsey smiled against the lip of the cup. "Don't worry. I can always go inside here—" she nodded back toward the building beside her "—and beg Buster's owner for the use of her...powder room."

When she had drunk her fill of the steamy liquid, warmth stole through her body, catching up with the thaw that had already begun in her heart, and she handed the cup to Jonas.

He accepted it carefully, keeping his hands away from contact with hers. Things were happening too fast for him. He'd been used to thinking of her in the context of the past, lumping her in with the way he felt about her father. She'd never been a real person to him, only a vision from his nightmares. He couldn't switch to sharing laughter, or admitting attraction, all at once.

Concentrating, to keep his thoughts off her, he refilled the hard plastic cup. With his eyes on the building across the street, he held the cup in both hands, rolling it back and forth, enjoying its warmth, wishing he was anywhere except sitting beside this woman in the dark.

This was only a job, he kept telling himself, a job just like all the others he'd done over the past few years. The intimacy that had built between them was simply an outcome of their present situation, produced by being forced into such close quarters and the sense of isolation created by the night.

The heat from their breath and the coffee had steamed up the windows, adding to their anonymity, but making it hard to keep watch on their target. Jonas focused all his energy on keeping a spot wiped clean so he could see the building across the street and the alley running along beside it.

The woman beside him, suffering once more from the intense cold, gave a sudden convulsive shiver and accidentally bumped against his arm. As a result Jonas only just managed to keep the hot coffee from sloshing over the side of the cup and onto his lap.

"S-sorry," Lindsey murmured between chattering teeth as she hugged her arms around her for warmth. "B-but it's s-so c-cold." She pressed her knees together, shivered again and asked, "I s-suppose turning on the h-heater is out of the question?"

Jonas offered her the coffee and, when she was finished, placed the empty cup on the dash.

"Afraid so," he answered, feeling a bit guilty for her discomfort. He had known what they would be facing sitting in a car without a heater for hours in this cold. When he'd stopped at his apartment, he'd taken the time to layer his own clothing to prevent feeling the cold as intensely as she was. He'd tried to warn her. . . .

"Wait a minute." Without warning he twisted around in the seat.

Lindsey turned toward him at that exact instant and looked up directly into his glittering eyes. All at once she couldn't breathe as she became instantly aware of the rigid lines of his body, the heat that seemed to be emanating from him in waves—so close, so warm, so inviting. . . .

Jonas could barely make out the lines of her pale face as she gazed up at him. He felt his senses stir. There was something about his being stationed above her . . . A feeling of power moved through him, as though, after all these years, it was *his* turn to bend *her* to his will.

Tension, like a fine, silver thread, stretched out between them, seeming to shorten with each passing second, drawing them closer. Jonas was tempted—Lord, how he was tempted. . . .

"If you could move..." His voice came out in a whisper, sounding more intimate than he cared to admit. He cleared his throat. "I think I have something you'll want."

Lindsey could feel his restraint, his uneasiness with the situation. She knew, without knowing how she knew, that unlike most men who might find themselves in similar circumstances, he wasn't about to take advantage of her. He was resisting his normal, healthy, male inclinations, and she admired him for his restraint, but on a purely feminine level she wished he would give in to them....

Without moving as he'd requested, she murmured in whiskey-soft tones, "And what is that?"

"A blanket," he answered shortly. "Keep an eye on the building." And, almost pushing her aside, he reached over the back of the seat to get it.

This new position put him in even closer, more dangerous proximity to her, and he couldn't help but get a deep whiff of the perfume that had been teasing his senses all afternoon and evening. It was something light and airy, but there was a haunting quality about it. It made him think of spring flowers and clouds and long, cat-green eyes smiling up at him with an invitation he found nearly impossible to resist.

Maybe she really was a witch.

Cutting off such frivolous thoughts, he settled back in his seat, handing Lindsey a soft bundle that smelled a whole lot like the dirty trunk of someone's car.

"A blanket." Her voice reflected her letdown. "How wonderful. Thank you." Unfolding the large blue square without even considering its origins, she spread it from toes to chin, feeling an immediate relief from the cold—and a deep sense of disappointment.

"I feel as though I've hitched a ride on a magic carpet." She tried to recapture the brief moment of camaraderie they'd shared earlier to lighten the atmosphere. "What other surprises can you pull from your bag of tricks, Mr. Magician?" she asked humorously.

"No tricks," he answered flatly. "Just practicalities." With his eyes glued once more to the street, her perfume making him feel light-headed, he refused to play along with her fanciful mood.

Deflated, Lindsey apologized. "I know this is serious business. I haven't forgotten about why we're here."

Just why her statement should make him feel like a crass heel escaped him, but he made an effort to explain.

"I keep certain items packed in a bag in my apartment, ready for use. Experience has taught me what I might need on surveillance, when I can't just get up and walk or drive away to get things."

Lindsey stared at his profile in the dim light. "You take your work seriously. In that respect you are very like your brother."

He felt as though she was constantly comparing him to Brian, and for some reason the idea irritated him in the extreme. Did she compare every man she knew to his brother, or only him?

"Would you like to share the blanket with me?"

Jonas jumped at the sound of her voice coming from so close beside his ear. He'd thought she'd fallen asleep. "No, thank you." He'd been concealing his shivers under the guise of shifting position, and he thought that was a much safer prospect than climbing beneath the blanket with this woman.

"How long do you suppose we'll have to wait?" she asked, no longer able to completely hide the weariness in her voice.

"As long as it takes," he almost snapped, pouring another cup of coffee.

Obviously, as he'd figured in the beginning, she was getting tired of the monotony and discomfort. It came as no great surprise to him. Hadn't he warned her? Hadn't he predicted that was what would happen?

No doubt she was used to being pampered by everyone around her. What a shock this must be for her, having to suffer right alongside him.

He didn't know who he was angrier with—her for insisting on coming along, or himself for allowing it. He should have known better. Next time he would.

He had a feeling it might be a good idea to keep an eye on her. These days, everyone was suing everyone else for whatever wrongs or imagined wrongs they could find. He couldn't afford something like that happening to him, so he'd better take extra care and see that Miss Hamilton suffered as little as possible at his hands.

A small voice whispered far back in his brain, telling him how easy it was going to be watching her and wouldn't he like being in a position to have her care all to himself? But he wouldn't pay attention to it, or to the forbidden thoughts that sprang to mind whenever it spoke.

Lindsey sneaked a look at the man beside her and saw his jaw harden. What had she done now?

"How long have you and your friend known each other?" Jonas asked abruptly, feeling her eyes on him, needing to dispel that invisible bond he felt drawing them together once more.

Surprised by the personal nature of the question after his obvious withdrawal, she answered, "Years and years. We met in grade school and have been friends ever since."

"Is she wealthy?" he asked. Maybe talking would prevent Lindsey from offering to share the blanket with him again. And this was a good time to get a little background information on Debra to better help him determine whether she was in need of money and likely to engineer her own kidnapping to get it.

Disappointed because she had thought money meant nothing to him, she answered in a haughty tone, "No, Debra is just Debra. And don't assume that she's my own personal charity case, either. Debra is an independent woman with a mind of her own. She's a warm, caring individual with an exuberant personality, and everyone who meets her grows to love her."

Everyone, that is, except Brian Kingston, she was thinking, wondering if that man's brother, presently sitting beside her, could read her thoughts.

"I don't know what you've heard about her, but don't make the same mistake my father made. Debra doesn't want, or need, charity from anyone."

At the mention of her father, Jonas tensed. "He—your father—didn't approve of your friendship?"

"Approve?" Lindsey gave a forced laugh. "He encouraged it—after my mother insisted I needed a friend, and after he had had her and her family thoroughly investigated." There was a wealth of bitterness in the words.

"I guess he wanted to make sure you didn't associate with someone beneath your social level."

"Not *my* level—his! But the joke was on him," she continued in a low voice, more to herself than to him. "He thought that because Debra was 'infirm'—his word, not mine—she wouldn't be a destabilizing influence on me. Obviously, he didn't know either one of us," she added sadly. "I consider myself lucky to call Debra my friend."

"I think maybe your friend is the lucky one," he said gruffly, unable to hold the words back. What was happening to him?

Their eyes met, and now the frigid air sparked with static electricity, shimmered with heat. Lindsey held her breath. There was no use denying it; from the very first moment they'd met, each time his eyes touched hers she felt her heart turn over in response. What was happening to her?

A warm, liquid feeling began to steal softly through her whole body, making her feel trembly inside. She could almost feel his hard arms wrapped around her, taste his lips on hers. Her body swayed toward him, drawn by a sexual magnetism she knew she was powerless to resist.

From the corner of her eye she caught movement in the street. She could already feel his warm, coffee-scented breath blowing warm against her cold skin when a shadowy figure darted from behind a wrecked car and dashed across the street. Jonas's fingers touched her cheek, burning her skin, as the figure, bent low, moved stealthily up the steps of the building.

"There!" she whispered, fumbling to get a hand outside the blanket and point toward the building, wishing she didn't have to.

Jonas gave a start, shook his head to clear it and turned toward the silent, looming building. The place was in darkness, the street empty.

"What?" he asked. "What did you see?"

"Something—someone—ran across the street and up the steps."

"Are you sure it wasn't an animal? Maybe Buster has come home—" he began wryly.

"No," she snapped. "It was too big for that."

"All right, you lock the door and I'll go see. Stay put, you hear?"

She didn't answer.

"Did you hear me?" he asked impatiently.

She didn't like the idea of being left alone in the car again, but she answered, "Y-yes, all right. But what about you?"

"Hey, this is my job, remember? It's what I do for a living, what you're paying me for." The reminder was for his benefit as well as hers.

He was attempting to put things back on their real footing. They'd gotten carried away and much too personal a little while ago, and that must not happen again. He had to remember who he was, and who she was. Like chalk and cheese, oil and water, he and this woman didn't mix.

After first making certain that when he opened the door the light wouldn't go on, he moved outside. Lindsey placed a restraining hand on his arm, felt the muscles bunch impatiently beneath his leather jacket and halted him with her words.

"What about a gun? Are you carrying one?"

"Gun?" he repeated in surprise. "No, I'm not. I'm only going to *talk* to the guy, not shoot him. This isn't the movies. I don't carry a gun. They have a tendency to make people nervous, and then the people do things you don't want them to, like pull guns of their own.''

Withdrawing his arm from beneath her detaining hand, he slid from the car and sprinted across the street. Lindsey moved over against the door, trying to find him in the darkness, but it was as though once he'd left her he'd become a part of the night.

Chapter 6

Jonas sprinted across the street, the added weight of the extra clothing he wore restricting his movements somewhat, slipped into the deeper shadows cast by the building and headed for the front door. He eased the door open, holding his breath as the hinges creaked and, keeping his body pressed tightly against the wall, peered through.

There wasn't much to see. A trickle of light from outside cast long shadows into the hall. Rob Slater had an apartment all the way at the back.

After a lengthy moment of silence when every nerve in his body was stretched to the breaking point, he pushed the door open an inch at a time until he could slip through and into the hallway.

Stepping lightly, peering cautiously into the shadows around him, he made his way toward the door at the end of the hall. The one behind which Slater would be waiting if it had been Slater that Lindsey had seen. He was almost there, not more than a yard away, when a door beneath the stairwell burst open.

He barely had time to turn his head, deflecting a blow that otherwise would have rendered him unconscious, before a figure of blackness was upon him.

Lindsey sat huddled beneath the blanket. With Jonas's departure her nerve had gone, and now every whisper of sound became magnified tenfold in her mind.

She couldn't remember ever being in this part of town, certainly not after dark. And now that darkness blanketed the area, no one at all ventured forth onto the street. The windows of all the buildings were hidden by curtains, a few with black iron bars shielding them.

Living and growing up as she had, virtually beneath her father's thumb, she hadn't been allowed a normal child-hood, despite her mother's intervention, except when she'd stayed with Debra's family. And now some of those forbid-den pleasures, remembered from her youth, pleasures that would have outraged her father, came back to haunt her. Literally.

She saw monstrous shapes in the outlines of cars parked along the street, and the sound of the wind became the mournful cry of lost souls from every horror picture she had ever watched, curled up on Debra's couch with a bowl of popcorn on her lap and a glass of cola in her hand.

She knew how ridiculous she was being and chided her-self for allowing her imagination to run wild. In any case, she assured herself forcefully, she was safe in the car. As long as she didn't leave its confines, no harm would come to her. But she couldn't prevent a part of her from wishing for the safety of Debra's home with its thick walls and doors, and a telephone close at hand.

There was so much glass all around her. It wouldn't take much force, she thought again, to break glass. She'd read about people who were snatched directly from their cars after someone had broken out the windshields. That kind of thing had played a large part in several of the horror mov-ies she remembered watching as an adolescent.

All at once she shivered, pulled the blanket up past her chin till only her eyes were uncovered and peered over its uneven edge out the window beside her. A small voice inside repeated the litany *I told you so*. She should have listened to Jonas when he'd told her that this was no place for her to be.

Where was Jonas? Surely by now he'd had time to find out if Rob had come home, and speak to him if he had. Why didn't he come back and tell her what he'd learned.

That devilish voice wouldn't leave her alone now that it had finally made itself known. *What if he can't come back?* it asked. *What if someone was waiting for him? What if he's been injured? What if he's dead?* As the frightening thoughts ran through her mind, her terror grew to boundless proportions.

A door slamming somewhere along the block startled her into jumping and sliding farther down into the seat. She peeked warily out the window, seeking the source of the disturbance. Could it have been Jonas? Was he this minute on his way back to the car?

She quickly scanned the dark, empty street, taking particular note of the dense shadows. No Jonas. Then who? The skin of her scalp pulled tight, making the hair stand up close to her head. Again she felt that unsettling sensation of unseen eyes watching her. Twisting in the seat, she glanced behind and to both sides of her.

The blood in her veins formed ice particles, clogging the passage to her brain. She could no longer think rationally. All she could do was to feel. And all she could feel was fear. The muscles in her stomach knotted, and those in her legs, straining against the cold, began to jump. Her one thought was to get out of the car, out of the dark and into the light, where she wouldn't have to fear the shadows.

She reached toward the door handle, her eyes on the street, and jerked down frantically. It wouldn't open! Trapped! She was trapped in the car—trapped in the darkness! She began to pant, to whimper, her breath forming a continuous cloud of vapor around her head. She jerked harder at the handle, hurting her fingers, until, finally, a thread of reason gave her the answer. It was locked. The door was locked.

Her fingers twitched, and all at once the lock popped up, the rubber guard coming away in her hand. She stared at it without comprehension, and then another gust of wind slapped against the side of the car, hurling a piece of newspaper across the front windshield and blocking her view of the street.

Lindsey dropped the piece of rubber from nerveless fingers and scooted across the seat. She was not staying here alone a moment longer! She got stuck behind the steering wheel, the blanket's folds binding her in place, until she ripped it free and threw it toward the other side of the car. The door opened wide, and she all but fell into the street.

Her feet had no more than touched the pavement when a crash, emanating from the alley beside the building, jerked her glance in that direction. A dog? A cat?

She should have run. Fear certainly had her in its grip, but something turned her steps in that direction.

As she drew closer the sounds became more easily distinguishable. Heavy breathing, scraping feet, muffled thuds, a crash, and then soft curses.

Someone was fighting.

Hugging the bricks behind her, eyes screwed up against the blackness, she peeped around the edge of the building. It happened so fast she didn't see it, but the power of the blow slammed her back, and her head connected sharply with the brick wall behind her.

For a moment she hung there, suspended between blackness and time. Everything—thought, feeling, sound—slid slowly from her mind as blackness descended.

Jonas, from his position on the ground among the garbage and trash, heard the sound of two bodies colliding, then saw the one he'd been grappling with fall backward, and climbed somewhat groggily to his feet. He stepped over his assailant and caught the other figure in unsteady arms as she began to slide down the bricks towards the ground at his feet.

"Lindsey!" He grasped her shoulders. "Are you all right? Answer me!"

He shook her, saw her head flop back and forth, and bent as though to pick her up in his arms.

"What happened?" she muttered dazedly. And then, in a stronger voice, "Did *you* hit me?"

"Are you all right?" Jonas asked urgently. "Can you stand up by yourself?"

That was when Lindsey became aware of how close she was to his body. Her whole scope of vision was taken up by the breadth of his shoulders and chest. She heard his voice, felt his chest rumbling beneath her cheek. She could feel his arms where they'd slipped protectively around her, his warm breath on her neck, and all she wanted to do was sink against him and let him hold her for a long, long time.

"I—yes—I'm fine." She raised an unsteady hand to the back of her head, feeling for the bump growing beneath the thick dark hair and, finding it, whispered, "Ouch!"

"What?" Jonas asked quickly.

"N-nothing. Nothing," she repeated in a louder, stronger voice. "I'm okay. What about you? What happened to Rob?"

Jonas released her reluctantly, liking yet also resenting the feel of her in his arms. Once before, he couldn't help but remember, he'd held her like this under similar, yet at the same time very different, circumstances, and look how that had turned out.

"Unless I miss my guess, he's right here, with the beginnings of one hell of a headache."

"Damn! Man, what did you hit me with?" Rob Slater sat up slowly, rubbing a goose egg forming above his left eyebrow.

Lindsey cleared her throat, slipped her cold hands into the pockets of her coat and said, "He didn't hit you. I did—sort of."

The young man looked up as Lindsey stepped out of the shadows and into the feeble light.

"You? What are you doing here?" he asked with a puzzled frown.

"She's with me." Jonas decided they had been out here in the alley, exposed to any neighborhood thugs who might be attracted by the commotion, long enough. "I'm a P.I. working for Miss Hamilton."

Lindsey gave him a sidelong glance. Hadn't she been Lindsey a few moments ago?

"I haven't the foggiest idea why you jumped me and ran, but I—we—only want to talk to you." Jonas was still speaking.

"Talk? Then Louie didn't send you?"

"Louie?" Lindsey inquired.

"Yeah, Louie, my bookie." He put out a grubby hand and hoisted himself to his feet. "I owe him some money, and I figured maybe you were here to collect it." He rubbed his forehead. "With interest."

"Do you really think Miss Hamilton would be involved with a small-time hustler like this . . . Louie?" Jonas asked sourly.

"No, of course not, but in the dark . . ." The younger man shook his head. "What do you want with me?"

"Let's get off the street before we go into that," Jonas suggested, a hand beneath Lindsey's elbow.

Slater edged around the corner of the building, peered down the street in both directions and then, with a slight shiver, said, "That's okay with me."

The trio hastily made their way across the street and into the car. Jonas gave Lindsey a look when he discovered it was unlocked, but didn't say anything. Lindsey climbed gratefully beneath the blanket's fold and turned in the seat so she could see both Jonas's profile and the face of the man in the back seat.

"Where to?" Jonas asked, looking into the rearview mirror at Slater. "You want to stay here? Or you want to go someplace else?"

"There's a hotel a couple miles from here, straight down this street and then to the left. It's called The Den. I'd be glad of a ride there." He sat hunched down in the seat, staring out the window, checking out the street.

When they were under way, Jonas glanced up in the mirror and asked, "Why haven't you been at work since Monday?"

The younger man darted a glance toward Lindsey, as though embarrassed at having to admit what he was about to, and then away. "The guy after me knows I work there."

"It doesn't have anything to do with Miss Hamilton, here, or her friend?"

"What?" Slater asked in amazement.

"You heard me." Jonas spoke in a deep, almost threatening growl. "Miss Hamilton and her friend had lunch at the restaurant on Monday. You waited on them. What can you tell me about that day?"

"Tell you? Nothing—nothing at all. Why?" His glance slid from Jonas's face to the silent woman and back. "What's this all about? What am I supposed to be able to tell you?"

"You remember where the two women sat?" Jonas ignored the other man's question. "Did you wait on the table in the alcove behind theirs?"

"Yeah, I remember where Miss Hamilton sat. She always sits at my table and she tips good—real good." He offered her a slight smile before his glance hardened as it switched to Jonas's profile. "And no, I didn't wait on the table behind theirs. That's Dave's section."

"Do you remember seeing who sat there?" Lindsey couldn't help asking.

Slater's eyes screwed up in thought, but after a moment he shook his dark head slowly. "No, no, I don't. It was a madhouse that day, Mondays always are. I was so busy I didn't have time for a break.

"Then, about fifteen minutes before my shift ended, I spotted these two guys. I knew who they were even before Dave told me they were asking for me by name.

"I got out of there but fast. I haven't been back since. Tonight is the first time I even dared to show up at my place."

"Dave, huh?" Jonas said. "You know his last name? Where he lives?"

Slater shook his head. "No, we're not friends or anything. I just know him at work. Hey, man, are you going to tell me what's up."

"It's Debra," Lindsey answered before Jonas could stop her. "She's—I can't find her."

"Your friend?" Slater asked. "You mean that cute little blonde you always have with you?"

Lindsey stiffened at his familiar tone of voice, but answered, "Yes."

"Well, maybe she's still with the guy with the limp."

A sudden tension turned the air in the car thick enough to cut with a knife.

"What guy?" Jonas asked in measured tones.

"The guy I saw her leave the restaurant with that day," Slater answered patiently.

"I thought you said you didn't see anything," Jonas said.

"I said I didn't see the people sitting behind them. I didn't say I didn't see Miss Hamilton or her friend leave."

"Describe him," Jonas ordered. "Describe the man you saw with Debra."

"Well, hell, there's nothing to describe." Rob shrugged. "He was just a man, tall, about six-four maybe, dark complexion, like he came from a foreign country or something. 'Course you never know these days, the guy could live just down the street from you, I guess."

"Hair?" Jonas barked.

"Black, thick, real curly—kind of kinky, you know? And he walked off balance, like one leg was shorter than the other or something."

"How was he dressed?"

"Black suit, dark shirt." He shrugged. "I don't remember if he had a tie."

"Did you see anyone with him? Someone he might have had lunch with."

"I don't know. I just saw them, the blonde and this guy. They seemed to be on friendly terms. It kind of surprised me, 'cause she always came in with Miss Hamilton and left with her. I never saw her there with a man, and he hadn't been at lunch with them."

"You didn't see how they left? Whether they took a taxi or who drove?" Jonas persisted.

"Nope," Slater answered, sitting back in the seat. "There, turn at the next corner. The hotel is in the middle of the next block."

Jonas pulled up between two No Parking signs and stopped at the curb. "Here." He reached into the pocket of his jacket and drew forth a card. "This is my number. If you remember anything else or see the guy again, call me. If I'm not there, leave a message."

Slater took the card without looking at it and shoved it into the pocket of his jacket. "I'm real sorry your friend is missing, Miss Hamilton. I hope you find her real soon."

"Thank you, so do I."

Slater climbed from the car and turned to face the flashing red neon sign.

Jonas fished in his pocket, withdrew a bill, folded it and called, "Slater!"

The young man hesitated before turning back. "Yeah?"

When Slater bent toward the open window, Jonas slid the folded twenty into the younger man's palm.

"Call me," Jonas told him.

"Will do." Slater backed away. "Thanks."

"Oh, yeah." Jonas's voice halted him again. "Your boss, Mr. Wong. He said to give you a message. You're fired."

Jonas started the engine and pulled smoothly away from the curb, leaving the younger man staring after them.

"Do you think he'll do it?" Lindsey asked. "Call you, or remember anything else."

"Hard to say. Right now he's got a mighty big problem of his own. I have a feeling this Louie isn't the kind of guy you can put off for very long. But the twenty might remind him for a little while, and if he needs money bad enough, he might remember something worthwhile.''

Lindsey folded the blanket as neatly as she could in the small space and settled it between them on the seat. The car might look like a relic from the past, but it had a good heater.

''What do we do now?'' she asked, watching the lights outside speed by faster and faster as Jonas left Queens behind and headed back toward Manhattan.

''I think it's time to take you home. I'm sure you must have a headache. And I have a couple of things to check out.''

''What things?''

He took his eyes off the road long enough to glance in her direction. ''Well, the Oriental Palace is still open. Maybe I can find this Dave and see if he can add anything to Slater's description of the man he saw with Debra.

''And I want to take a look at your friend's apartment too. You wouldn't happen to know if she kept a spare key hidden anywhere?'' he asked.

''I have a key, just as Debra has one to my apartment, but you're wasting your time. I was there yesterday after I left your office, and there's nothing to see. I mean, I couldn't find anything missing.

''If she left on her own, as the police and you first suggested, she didn't take anything with her.''

Jonas sighed heavily, his grip on the steering wheel tightening. When would she allow him to do his job without interference?

''Do I come into your office and try to run your business for you?''

Startled at the idea, Lindsey shook her head.

''No,'' he agreed in clipped tones, ''so please, do me the kindness of allowing me to be the judge of what will be a waste of my time.''

''Sorry,'' she murmured, taken aback by his vehemence. After a slight pause she added, ''I want to go, too.''

"Look—" he began in exasperation.

"Come on. I didn't do so badly on the stakeout—"

"Surveillance," he corrected.

"Surveillance, now, did I? I did what you said, and I didn't complain about the cold." She glanced down out of the corner of her eye at the blanket lying between them and added, "Much. And actually, I helped you catch Slater."

Jonas opened his mouth to tell her that if she had done what he'd told her, she wouldn't have a headache now. And that under different circumstances her disobedience could have cost her her life.

What was the use? She wouldn't listen, and in any case, in this instance they would be on turf more familiar to her than to him. She might actually be of some help.

"All right," he agreed, surprising her into a silence that lasted all the way to Debra's apartment.

Inside the apartment, Lindsey followed him from room to room, the slight furrowing of her brows growing steadily into a full-blown frown.

"I don't understand this," she whispered, looking at the empty bathroom shelves. "When I was here yesterday, Debra's makeup bag, her curling iron, her comb and brush were there." She pointed toward the glass shelves.

"You were upset when you left my office," Jonas offered. "Maybe you expected to see them—"

"I don't see things that aren't there," she snapped, then stomped down the hall to the bedroom. Jonas followed and watched as she threw open the closet doors and began to pull at the clothes hanging inside.

"Well," he asked after a moment, "anything else missing?"

"I don't know," she answered shortly. "There are a few items I don't see. But they could be at the cleaners."

"You know which one she uses?"

"Well, of course I do. It's the same one I use."

"Good, you can call them tonight."

Lindsey glanced at her watch. "Too late. I'll call first thing in the morning. But I fail to see what good it will do us to know what clothes she has at the cleaners. I know there are things missing. I told you—"

"Have you ever tucked your makeup bag in your purse or taken a curling iron to the office with you on a rainy day?"

"I keep extras at the office. I don't take my things from home."

"Right," Jonas said abruptly, then turned on his heel and strode from the room. "For a moment there I forgot you aren't an average working girl like your friend."

At the tone of his voice Lindsey's head snapped back as though she'd been slapped. Was there something wrong in being the head of a company rather than an employee of one?

"So." She followed him slowly, wishing she could figure him out. "What do we do now? Leave?"

Jonas was in the living room, going through the things on Debra's desk.

"What are you doing?" she asked, outraged. Those were her best friend's personal papers.

"I'm looking for clues." He had dumped the wastebasket on the floor and was unfolding crumpled pieces of paper, pausing to look at each one before throwing it back into the basket.

"Clues?" She hadn't thought of that. It was just that seeing a stranger riffle Debra's personal papers set her on edge. "Well, you won't find anything helpful in there. I looked through them when I was here before. I thought maybe she had gone on a sudden trip."

Jonas gave her a sharp glance. "No," she said, answering his unspoken question. "I really didn't think she'd do that without letting me know beforehand, but I looked anyway."

She followed him as he turned without making a comment and left the living room. In Debra's bedroom, she stood watching as he removed a small leather book from the table beside her friend's bed.

"What are you doing now?"

Jonas tried the small brass lock and it popped up, allowing the book to fall open in his hands.

"That's Debra's diary!" Lindsey had moved up beside
him and glanced down at her friend's familiar writing.

To Lindsey's outrage, Jonas began to leaf through the
pages. "What are you doing? That's private—you can't read
that!" She reached out to grab the book from his hand, then
moved quickly across the room, keeping it out of his reach.

"What the—"

"I won't let you pry into Debra's private life!"

"I thought you wanted me to find her?" he snapped.

"I do," she answered indignantly. "But I fail to see
how—"

"Learning all I can about her routines, her thoughts, her
friends, the places she's likely to go to get away, the place
where she might seek shelter if she were afraid, is the only
way I have of finding her." Jonas locked eyes with her and
gazed at her steadily.

Lindsey gripped the diary in taut fingers. This was too
much like invading her friend's privacy, too much like her
own remembered humiliation at the hands of her father
when he'd found *her* diary and broken the lock to read it.

She cringed inside, remembering how she had suffered as
he'd read aloud from it. How he'd scoffed at her heartfelt
feelings. She'd been twenty years old and had recently lost
her mother. Her fear that she would never find anyone to
love her, that she would end up with someone like her father, interested only in money and position, was all there for
him to see.

And that was what had precipitated her move from his
house to the apartment on Central Park West—where she'd
almost died.

"Very well." Jonas pivoted on his heel and started from
the room. "If you don't want me to find her, then do it
yourself."

"No! Wait!" Lindsey hurried after him. She caught up
with him at the open front door, where he'd paused to wait
for her. "Here!" She shoved the diary at him. "I know you

have to...delve into things...personal things...." She couldn't meet his eyes. "It's just that it can hurt sometimes if the wrong people know too much about your innermost thoughts and feelings."

Jonas gazed down at the top of her bent head. It sounded as though she had firsthand experience with that kind of hurt. Who knew too much about her? Brian? Himself? Was she trying to tell him that she knew who he was?

"Please." She turned the full force of her green glance onto his face. "Read it later, after you've dropped me at my apartment."

"I promise I won't reveal anything I read in here," he said, accepting the book. "To anyone. I'm not a voyeur, I don't get my kicks from reading someone else's private thoughts and dreams—"

Lindsey's fingers touched his lips. "Shh. I know you don't."

It had started as an automatic gesture to show him she didn't need his assurance that he was a man to be trusted, but now, all at once, she became aware of the intimacy of the gesture.

Her fingertips tingled against his lips. His mouth felt moist and a little rough, as though his lips might be chapped from the cold, and warm, so very warm.

After a breathless moment she became aware of other things, like the changes taking place in his eyes, the pupils expanding as if he were in the grip of some powerful emotion. The muscles in his lean jaw became rigid, stretching the skin taut. Deep ridges formed at either side of his nose, and the muscles of his neck bulged, as though straining against a need to give in to some hidden urge.

A tight, curling sensation developed in the pit of her stomach. Her legs became weak and, in an attempt to steady herself, she rested her other hand against his broad chest. Now she could feel its rhythmic up-and-down movement as he breathed, and that only added to her agitation when she felt the tempo suddenly increase.

Jonas took her slight weight against his chest without moving. He was afraid to, in case the iron control he held on his senses snapped and he swept her into his arms so he could taste the ripe mouth now only inches from his.

The clank of the elevator as it settled into place jerked them abruptly apart.

Lindsey turned automatically to see who had arrived. An older couple, the man walking with a cane, stepped into the hallway. She recognized them as neighbors of Debra's, and gave them a polite smile and a nod.

Recognizing her, they called out a friendly greeting as they passed. The elderly woman was helping the white-haired man, with a hand beneath his arm as he rounded the corner and limped from sight.

"My God," Lindsey whispered all at once, her eyes going round. "That's it! The man with the limp." She turned to face him, grabbing his arm in her excitement. "Yesterday I saw a tall, dark man get off the elevator—right here—as I was leaving.

"He was carrying a suitcase." She glanced down the hall in the wake of the older couple and added, "It bumped against his leg as he walked away from me, because he walked off balance, as though one leg was shorter than the other."

"Why didn't you mention this before?" Jonas asked sharply.

"I didn't even remember it till now." Her eyes widened. "Does that mean someone came and got clothes for Debra?" she asked with excitement.

"It could mean that," he answered cautiously. He'd never before heard of kidnappers so solicitous of their victim's welfare that they risked capture for a change of clothes, a curling iron and a makeup bag.

"Fingerprints!" Lindsey pounced on the idea. "Couldn't the police get his fingerprints from Debra's apartment?"

"Possibly, but I doubt it. Do you seriously think our man would be so careless as to leave fingerprints? He's already

Enjoy Four Silhouette Sensations plus a cuddly Teddy and extra Mystery Gift

▲ Absolutely Free! ▶

We're inviting you to discover why the Silhouette Sensation series has become so popular with our readers.

Here's a truly sensational FREE offer.

We'd love you to become a regular FREE reader of Sensations and discover just why these modern love stories with a twist in the 'tale' have become such a popular series. As a welcome we'd like you to have four Silhouette Sensations, a cuddly Teddy and a Mystery Gift ABSOLUTELY FREE.

Then, each month you can look forward to receiving four brand new Sensations, delivered to your door, postage and packing FREE! Plus our FREE Newsletter full of author news, competitions and special offers.

Turn the page for details of how to claim your free gifts!

FREE BOOKS COUPON

Yes Please rush me my four FREE SENSATIONS and two FREE GIFTS! Please also reserve me a Reader Service subscription. If I decide not to subscribe, I shall write to you within 10 days. If I decide to subscribe I can look forward to receiving four brand new Silhouette Sensations, each month, for just £7.40 (postage and packing free). I may cancel or suspend my subscription at any time. I can keep my free books and gifts whatever I decide. I am over 18 years of age.   5S3SS

Ms/Mrs/Miss/Mr _____

Address _____

_____ Postcode _____

Signature _____

FREE

FREE

No Stamp Needed

Reader Service
FREEPOST
P.O. Box 236
Croydon
Surrey CR9 9EL

SEND NO MONEY NOW

messed up once by allowing someone to overhear him in a restaurant. He isn't likely to be that stupid again.

"And besides, you haven't been able to convince the police that your friend is in any danger. Remember, her boss says she's visiting a sick relative."

The excitement died slowly from Lindsey's green eyes. "If only something would turn up about the theft. Then the police would be forced to believe me."

"Come on." He took the key from her slack fingers, slid the diary into his pocket and closed the door. "I think it's time I took you home. You've had enough detective work for one day."

In the car Lindsey asked, "What good have we done? We're no nearer to finding Debra than we were yesterday."

"Already worried about making a bad investment in hiring me, huh?" he joked wryly, surprising her.

"Never mind." He shook his head when she started to protest, then concentrated on his driving for a moment before correcting her. "You know, you're wrong about that. We know several things we didn't know before tonight."

He counted off the facts. "We know that a tall, dark-complexioned man who walks with a limp was seen with Debra at the restaurant, the last place we can pinpoint her whereabouts. We know that same man showed up at Debra's apartment with a suitcase. And after his visit, personal items belonging to Debra are missing from her apartment.

"We have a description of the man and an eyewitness who saw him in Debra's company. And we also know that your friend is alive, most likely in good health, and probably somewhere not too far away."

"I'm sorry," Lindsey muttered after a long moment of silence, "but that doesn't seem like very much."

"Maybe not," he agreed. "But it's a lot more than we knew yesterday."

They had arrived at Lindsey's building. Jonas drove into the underground parking lot, and they took her private elevator up to the penthouse suite. She unlocked the door and turned toward him.

"Would you like to come in for a sandwich or something?" There was nothing provocative in the question. She saw him hesitate and said, "It's been a long time since we had lunch, and I'm going to make myself something. You're welcome to stay."

Jonas studied her face. There was nothing but politeness reflected there, but in the depths of the green eyes he thought he detected something more. And he knew he was too weak in his present state of mind to handle it.

"Not tonight." He backed toward the elevator. "I have a few things to check out yet before I call it a day. I'll call you if I find out anything of value."

Lindsey watched him go. "Jonas!"

He looked up.

"Here. You'll need this." She extended one hand, something shiny on the palm. A key. "It unlocks this elevator. You won't have to be announced by Willy each time you want to see me."

"Thanks." He lifted the key, warm from her hand, and slipped it into his pocket.

His last sight was of her standing in the open doorway, one hand raised, a small smile on her lips, a lonely look in her green eyes.

She had called him Jonas—and he liked it.

Chapter 7

Jonas made his way down the street to the pharmacy at the end of the block. It was almost ten in the morning, and the streets were crowded.

As he reached the door it was opened from inside, and a slender young woman with close-cropped black hair moved past him, holding the door for him to enter.

He murmured, "Thanks," but she was gone without a backward glance.

He paused for a moment to look around, then spotted what he was looking for and made his way slowly past rows of cosmetics, jewelry and hair-care products to the elevated, glass-enclosed pharmacy at the back of the store.

A tall, bespectacled man with thinning blond hair was standing behind the enclosure counting pills.

Jonas waited patiently until he'd finished, then asked politely, "Are you Wayne Riddell?"

"Yes, I am. What can I do for you?"

Jonas showed him the card identifying him as a private investigator licensed by the state of New York. "I'm working on a missing person case involving a customer of yours, Debra Foley."

"Debra? Missing?"

"That's right. I've been hired by Miss Lindsey Hamilton, with whom I understand you are also acquainted, to find her. If you'd like to give her a call, I'm certain she'll confirm that she hired me to find Miss Foley."

"Lindsey sent you?"

"That's right."

"Excuse me for just a moment, please." Without waiting for Jonas's reply, the pharmacist moved to his computer, gave Jonas a quick glance and punched something up on the screen. Then he dialed the phone, identified himself and asked for Lindsey, then waited a moment for her to come on the line.

Jonas craned his neck so he could watch as the man spoke into the phone and saw Riddell dart a glance in his direction, then turn slightly away and address a remark into the receiver. After a few words, he gave a slight nod and his shoulders relaxed.

Okay, Jonas thought with disgruntled sarcasm, so he looked like hell this morning.

He should have let well enough alone, should have told Lindsey Hamilton to find someone else to play detective with. Last night he'd almost literally run from her—or was it himself he'd been running from?—and this morning he was ashamed.

His sleep had been restless, filled with dreams of her. But in his dreams he'd been trying to find her, and every time he came close to her, either Derek Lassiter or Hank would step suddenly in front of him, blocking his way, and for some reason he'd been afraid to try to move around them. So he'd spent the night in pursuit of an elusive Lindsey, knowing that there was some urgent reason he had to get to her, but never quite reaching her and never quite understanding what the urgency was all about.

Why, when he was with her, did he find her so fascinating, everything from the way her green eyes tilted slightly up at the outer edges to the deep, husky tone of her voice? Why, when he was with her, did he find it impossible to sever the fine, silver thread of attraction he could feel building between them?

At home he had tried to wipe her image from his mind, sought haven from the torture of his own guilt in the oblivion of sleep. But every time he had closed his eyes, he'd seen himself sitting beside Hank in the dark, the smell of blood in his nostrils, blood on his hands, on his clothes, soaking the ground, turning it to red mud.

He hadn't thought he blamed Lindsey for Hank's death or his own downfall at her father's hands, yet somehow the attraction she held for him had gotten all mixed up inside his head with his own guilt over what had happened to Hank and made him feel as though it was wrong to think about her in that way.

A flash of how her eyes had looked sparkling with laughter, the curve of her beautiful mouth, darted through his mind. Even now, in a public place, he felt his blood begin to heat at the memory. And later, at the door to her apartment, he'd wanted to haul her into his arms, taste that mouth, see those green eyes burning with passion for him.

Jonas shook his head to clear it. The pharmacist was still on the phone, his pleasant face wearing a look of concern rather than suspicion. Jonas focused his attention on the display of sunglasses to his left.

"Excuse me," Riddell called.

Jonas looked up.

"If you'll come around this way, there's a small room where we can talk privately."

Jonas waited patiently while the other man unlocked the door, then stood back and allowed Riddell to precede him inside.

The pharmacist flipped a light switch, and the room came into focus. Jonas glanced around at the sparse furnishings. The place reminded him of his own office, he thought wryly.

"Have a seat." Riddell gestured to one of the two straight-backed chairs sitting on either side of a scarred, round wooden table and took the other one for himself.

"Smoke?" he asked, taking a crumpled package of cigarettes from the pocket of his white smock and holding it up for Jonas to see.

Jonas shook his head politely.

After a long drag and a heavy sigh, Riddell sat back in the chair and met Jonas's eyes. "Now, what can I do to help?"

"Have you heard anything at all from Debra in the last week?"

"No." Riddell knocked ash off into a white plastic ashtray. "It makes me angry to think something might have happened to Debra. You know, you read about things like this happening to strangers—but Debra?" He shook his head.

"Does Debra always pick up her own medicine?" Jonas asked.

"Yes," Wayne answered readily, then hesitated. "Well, Lindsey has picked it up for her a couple of times when she was sick. But Debra makes a practice of picking it up herself."

Jonas folded his arms on the table and asked, "Is there anything you can tell me about Debra that might be of help in locating her? For instance, do you know any of the men she dates, or has dated in the past?"

Riddell shook his head. "Not really. It's been a long while since she brought anyone over for Cheryl—that's my wife—and me to meet."

"What about family? Does she have any that you know of?" Jonas persisted. Lindsey had insisted Debra was an orphan, but he asked the question nevertheless. You never knew what could turn up in a case like this.

"The three of us, Lindsey, Debra and myself—" Riddell was speaking as if he hadn't heard the question "—knew each other in school. I don't know if you knew that." He looked up to see Jonas nod. "We weren't real close until our junior year, when the three of us got teamed up for a science

project. Debra and I were pretty average, but Lindsey..."
He shook his head. "I always kind of felt sorry for her."

"How's that?" Jonas asked.

"Her home life. Not that I'd say anything to her face about it, but her father..." He clicked his tongue and shook his head. "He treated her pretty badly, in my opinion. She wasn't allowed to date or associate with anyone except Debra. She wasn't allowed to attend any school functions.

"It's like she was a prisoner or something. I know some people envied her the clothes and the money." He shook his head. "But not me. It must have been hell growing up the way she did, money or not."

"Debra?" Jonas frowned, trying to get him back on the subject at hand.

Even though he wanted to know more about Lindsey and what she had been like growing up, what kind of an influence her father had been on her, now was not the time. He needed to learn all he could about Debra so he could get a more rounded idea of what she was like and what she was likely to be capable of—where she might go if she was hiding.

"Right. Debra." Riddell nodded, then shrugged. "I don't really know what to tell you. I don't keep up on women things, like who she dates and so forth.

"I do know that she doesn't have any family, though." He paused to glance down at the glowing tip of the cigarette. "She lost her parents her sophomore year in college. My wife might be able to tell you more than I can. I'll be happy to give you our address and let her know you might be coming by later to talk to her.

"Just one thing. She's pregnant and it's been a difficult pregnancy, so go easy with her, all right? Play down the missing thing about Debra. Maybe you could talk to her with someone else there, like Lindsey. She and Cheryl get along great."

Jonas agreed. "I'll be careful what I say, and I'll talk to Lin—Miss Hamilton about accompanying me." He watched as the other man ground out the cigarette butt in the ashtray, took a mint from his pocket and popped it into his mouth.

"I guess I haven't been much help, have I?" Wayne asked, sucking on the candy.

"On the contrary," Jonas assured him, "everything helps. And I could use your help with something else, too. I'd like to station myself somewhere inside the store for a while, just in case someone does come in to pick up Debra's prescription. If anyone does, I'd like you to give it to them and signal me immediately afterward. Give me a nod.

"After a while, just in case someone is casing the place—someone who wants Debra's prescription—I'll move outside and across the street, where I can keep an eye on the front door."

"You sound like you think there's something sinister involved in Debra's disappearance. Is there a chance something...bad has happened to her?"

"I'm just being cautious. You know the old saying, 'An ounce of prevention—'"

"'Is worth a pound of cure,'" Riddell finished with a small smile. "Okay, I get the point. What makes you think someone is going to come for the prescription?"

Jonas figured that no matter who was involved in Debra's disappearance, and whether she had engineered it herself or not, the fact of the missing personal items pointed to her being alive and healthy, and whoever had her would want to keep it that way.

"Let's just say I have to consider all the possibilities."

Riddell hesitated, as though he wanted to say something more, but he only shrugged before finally agreeing. "All right. If it will help Debra, I'll do it."

Jonas stood and stretched out a hand. "Thanks." They shook hands. "I'll stay inside for a while, and I'll let you know before I leave the building."

"And all I have to do is nod toward whoever it is?" Riddell asked quickly.

"That's all," Jonas answered, "Or point, if I've gone outside. I'll take it from there."

At eleven o'clock a young woman entered the store and made her way to the back, taking up a position beside Riddell. Jonas moved slowly from aisle to aisle, apparently looking for something he couldn't seem to find, but in reality keeping a close watch on the pharmacy and anyone who headed back in that general direction.

The morning dragged by, and eventually Jonas signaled Riddell that he was leaving the building. Outside, he crossed the street to take up his post in front of the bank.

Jonas knew he would be virtually invisible here. No one would take notice of him among the steady ebb and flow of people, unless someone was looking for him. And he was counting on the fact that no one was. The kidnappers thought everything was neat and tidy. No one would be looking for a young woman who had asked for time off from work to stay with a sick relative.

He'd been standing on the corner for almost two hours when all at once Riddell appeared in the door across the street, gesturing frantically. Jonas figured maybe he was about to get a lucky break and ran across the street against the light, earning the wrath of several drivers, who honked at him in protest. An angry cab driver stopped in the middle of the intersection to shake his fist and yell expletives in a tongue Jonas didn't recognize.

Riddell stood before the large plate-glass window filled with sale advertisements, literally wringing his hands. "Hurry, hurry, or you'll miss him."

"He's inside?" Jonas asked, trying to peer around the man's narrow figure.

"No, no, he's there—there—" He pointed into the crowd moving down the street away from them. "Damn! He's gone."

"You saw him? You could identify him?" Jonas asked quickly, trying but failing to see where the man beside him was still pointing.

"No, I didn't see him. I'm sorry. I left the prescription counter for a few minutes. My assistant took the call and she gave the medicine to the man."

"Whoa, wait a minute. What call?" Jonas took the other man's arm and directed him out of the way of several people trying to exit the store.

"Debra said to give the medicine to this man—"

"How do you know, if you didn't take the call yourself, that it was Debra?"

"No, you don't understand." Riddell felt around inside the pocket of his white lab coat. "Here, she sent a note."

Jonas took the note, read the sentence and glanced closely at the signature. "That's her handwriting?" He fixed a sharp eye on the other man's face. "You're positive?"

"Yes, or as positive as I can be, under the circumstances. That's the way she always writes her name. More like it was printed and just all tied together that way." He pointed to the signature at the bottom of the paper.

"She called *and* sent a note," Jonas muttered with a puzzled frown.

Riddell nodded.

"I'll need a description of the man." Jonas shook the paper in frustration. This was just great. Here he was waiting all damn day for someone to show up and when he did, this had to happen. Talk about a comedy of errors.

Face it, a small voice inside chided. You're sore because you don't like the idea of having to explain to Lindsey how the man literally slipped right past you without your seeing him.

"I'm sorry," Riddell apologized. "I should have been there. I just stepped out for a minute." Jonas smelled mint on his breath and guessed what he'd stepped out for.

"You didn't tell your assistant to call you in case something like this happened?" Jonas asked tautly.

"No, I guess I had the mistaken notion you wanted this kept just between the two of us."

"The description," Jonas reminded him shortly. Damn, he'd been so close. He'd undoubtedly seen the man enter and exit the place, without knowing it was him. He followed the other man back inside in frustrated silence.

Inside, the assistant pharmacist, the young woman Jonas had watched arrive earlier, kept darting worried little glances in Riddell's direction, as though she expected him to request her resignation on the spot.

Jonas did his best to clamp down on his anger and put the woman at her ease, realizing she wouldn't be as apt to remember the details as clearly if she was under too much stress.

After taking a small spiral notebook from his pocket, he wrote down the woman's words as she gave him the description of the man who had handed her the note and accepted the bottle of medication.

"You're certain about this?" he asked, looking over what he'd written down.

"Yes, I'm positive." She looked from him to her boss and back again. "Is s-something wrong?"

"No, everything is fine, just fine. Thanks," Jonas assured her. He started to turn away, then quickly turned back. "Has either of you ever seen this man in here before today?"

The woman shook her short, dark curls. Riddell shrugged and shook his head, too. Jonas nodded and walked away, with Riddell following close on his heels.

"Something is wrong, isn't it? You looked very strange back there. What is it?" Riddell asked, watching Jonas's face closely.

"Nothing," he denied. "Look, I gotta go, but I'll be in touch. Thanks again." He turned away, then spun abruptly to face the man again. "You won't forget to mention to your wife that I'll be dropping by to talk to her some time soon, will you?"

"No, I won't forget," the other man answered.

Jonas moved off down the street toward his car. Something was wrong, very wrong, or else very right—depending on how you looked at it. The description of the man who'd picked up the prescription didn't in any way match up with the dark, limping man.

So what did that mean? Had he paid someone to pick up the medicine? A stranger, perhaps? Or a friend? Or was this the *second man* from the restaurant—the accomplice? It made sense, and if it was true, then now they had descriptions of *both* kidnappers.

Chapter 8

It was six o'clock by the time Jonas finally reached his office. He'd almost given it a miss, but decided to check on his messages, since he didn't employ an answering service. He unlocked the door, threw his jacket on the coat tree and heaved a tired, dispirited sigh.

He'd just spent a fruitless half hour interviewing Dave, the waiter from the Oriental Palace. He'd been hoping to confirm his suspicions that the second man, the one who had picked up the prescription earlier that day, was also the man who had lunched with the dark, limping man the day Lindsey and Debra had overheard the conversation about the theft.

But it had been a waste of time. Dave couldn't, or wouldn't, give him a good description of either man. He said he couldn't recall the two clearly, but did add that they weren't regulars.

Jonas had been very careful during the interview not to plant any information in Dave's head. What he needed were real, honest-to-goodness facts, not something someone suddenly "remembered" because he wanted to help.

He needn't have worried about Dave doing that, though; the man was a veritable sphinx when it came to divulging information. Jonas had been wondering if perhaps he should have jogged the man's memory a bit more when, as he was leaving, Dave had called out to him. He did remember one thing about the pair. One of them appeared to have something wrong with his leg. He limped.

After that Jonas had stayed to talk with a few other employees, but no one had anything to add to what he already knew. He left several of his cards, asking anyone who remembered anything, anything at all, to give him a call.

It had been a bad day from beginning to end. His feet hurt, it was starting to snow and he was sure he had frostbite on his nose. At the moment he wished he'd followed his aunt's advice and become a lawyer. Then he could have hired someone else to do all this legwork while he sat back and drew a nice fat retainer from his client while staying warm inside.

Just as he sat down heavily in the chair behind his desk, the phone began to ring. Maybe this was it. Someone had remembered something about the two men. He grabbed for the receiver.

"Hello?"

"Jonas? Brian here. Where the hell have you been for the last eight hours? I've called your office at least a dozen times today, and I called your apartment, too."

Jonas allowed his shoulders to droop as he loosened the top button of his shirt and rested back against the cushion of the chair. "I was out. I'm working a case."

"Yeah, well, drop everything else, 'cause I've got a big one for you. Wait until you hear this. You won't believe it."

Jonas hadn't heard so much excitement in his brother's voice since they were kids.

"You know that conversation Lindsey Hamilton told you about when she visited your office—the one she and her friend supposedly overheard? Well, hold on to your britches, brother, 'cause you won't believe what I'm about to say.

"Mayor Dennison paid me a visit this morning. It seems this friend of his returned last night from a trip to Europe and discovered his house had been burgled. Get this." He paused dramatically, and Jonas felt the hair stand up on the back of his neck. "The only thing missing was a set of hand-carved, jewel-encrusted, ivory snuffboxes dating back to the early eighteenth century."

Jonas pushed himself up in the chair. "I'll be damned! So it was all true," he muttered beneath his breath. This wasn't a hoax thought up by Debra to extract money from her best friend. It seemed he owed the woman an apology—if he ever found her.

"Do they have any suspects?" Jonas asked.

"Several," Brian responded dryly. "They think it was an inside job, one of the servants. It seems the alarm system was turned off, and that has to be done with a key. The strange thing is, there was a fortune in stocks, bonds, CDs and jewelry in the safe, but nothing else was touched.

"The Morgans, the victims, returned two weeks early from their trip because the wife became ill quite suddenly. The house was all closed up, and the servants had all gone on vacation, too.

"Mayor Dennison told the Morgans to move into a hotel, leaving the house closed up as though no one has returned. He figures that if the thieves think no one has tumbled to what they've done, it will give the authorities time to find the missing items—and the thieves—before they get nervous and decide to fence the stuff out of the country. He told the D.A. he has two weeks to find the stuff, or else."

"And how do you figure in all of this?" Jonas asked. His brother was an assistant district attorney, not the one who would usually be approached by the mayor in such a case.

"That's the best part." Brian almost laughed aloud with glee. "I was informed by Dennison that if I could solve this caper, he would be very pleased, very pleased indeed. Do you have any idea what that means? It means once the present D.A. is out, I can write my own ticket as far as the D.A.'s office is concerned."

"Do they have a particular suspect in mind?" Jonas asked softly.

"Not really. They're looking for all the servants, tracking them down one at a time. But they've all scattered to the four winds." He paused, then continued, "And that's where you come in. I want you to help me find them. Find the servants and we'll find the stuff one of them stole."

"What about Debra?" Jonas asked into the silence.

"What about her?" Brian asked stiffly.

"Look, I told you I was on a case. I'm helping your—I'm helping Lindsey Hamilton find her friend."

The wire crackled with a heavy silence. "I really *need* you on this one, Jonas."

"I'm sorry, I can't do it, Bri. I've already taken on the case for Miss Hamilton. It wouldn't be ethical for me to work it from your angle, too. You understand that, don't you?"

The air was pregnant with unspoken words. "Sure," Brian finally said. "Sure, I understand. Just forget it."

"Bri, I'm sorry."

"I said forget it. I'll talk to you later." Brian slammed the receiver down angrily.

Lindsey stepped off the elevator into the underground parking garage, her mind on Jonas and whether he'd learned anything new, not on the office, where she was going to put in a few late hours. She caught an unexpected movement from the corner of her eye and clutched her briefcase and handbag to her in a protective manner.

"Oh, it's you," she said a moment later. There was no welcome in her voice, but she relaxed, still feeling a bit heady from the surge of adrenaline flowing in her bloodstream. "Brian, what are you doing here?"

"Waiting for you. He smiled a bit sheepishly and moved closer.

"Me? What for?" she asked sharply, past being unable to resist his brand of charm.

"I wanted to ask you to have a drink with me before I went home this evening."

It wasn't hard for him to read the look that sprang immediately into her eyes. He took a step closer, drawing his hands from the pockets of his dark wool coat.

"Come on, Lin, don't refuse me. We've been friends for a long time. Just a drink. That's all, I swear. I don't want you mad at me."

He took her forearms in a light grip and drew her closer. "I'm sorry, truly I am, that we parted the way we did." He searched her stiff expression for a sign of softening. "Please, can't you forgive me for the other night?

"I admit I was being insensitive—I think that was the word you used." His look grew intimate, his voice coaxing. "Please? Allow me to make amends in some small way. Just a drink...." He could see the uncertainty in her face. "Come on...." He shook her arms slightly in a cajoling manner.

Lindsey looked deeply into his eyes. She wasn't fooled for a second by his act of false humility. He was up to something, and she wanted to know what it was.

"What is it you want from me, Brian? It's late, and I'm tired—very tired—and besides that, it's freezing here."

He drew back slightly, his dark eyes hardening imperceptibly. "I came to apologize, which I've done, and to ask you to have a drink with me to show there are no hard feelings." He raised his hands palms up. "That's all. I swear."

She didn't believe him, and she didn't really want to go anywhere with him, but . . .

"All right, I accept, on the condition that we have one drink, and you don't try and persuade your way back into my life. Agreed?"

"Your wish is my command." With a hand beneath her arm, he led her to his sleek, candy-apple-red Corvette and assisted her inside.

Lindsey looked around her at the car's luxurious interior, sniffed the new car smell and thought about the hours she had spent recently in his brother's automobile. There was no comparison, yet she would much rather be in Jonas's car right now, even parked in the dark on a street in Queens.

The thought in no way pleased her. She and this man's brother were like the opposite ends of a stick, a whole pole apart, and in any case, the attraction appeared to be all on her side.

It took only a few minutes to reach one of the bars near where her offices were located in Manhattan. They were seated at a corner table in the dim recesses before either spoke again. Lindsey was drinking a fruity wine cooler, and Brian a Scotch on the rocks.

"So, has little Debra showed up yet?"

Lindsey held her glass a little tighter and gritted her teeth before answering. "No, she hasn't." She resented the disparaging note that was always evident in his voice whenever he spoke about the other woman and wished she'd made more of an objection to it during their relationship.

"I hired someone to find her."

Now why hadn't she simply come out and said she'd hired his brother to do the job?

"And has he come up with any leads?" Brian ran a finger around the rim of his glass.

"No...." She faltered, feeling silly for the subterfuge. She took a drink, met Brian's glance head-on, and said, "It's Jonas. I hired your brother to find her.

"Look." She leaned forward. "I don't know why you tried to keep Jonas from helping me—no!" She held up a hand as he opened his mouth to protest. "I know you didn't want him to. Let's not pretend otherwise.

"The thing is, Jonas now believes, as I do, that Debra was abducted. And what's more, I believe he'll find her."

"You seem to have developed a lot of confidence in my brother's capabilities rather quickly," Brian reflected softly, his eyes on the table's shiny surface.

"Yes, I suppose I have," she answered, watching his face. What was there about his expression that caused the uneasy feeling she felt creeping over her? She didn't realize she was going to ask the next question until she heard her own voice speaking. "Is there some reason I shouldn't?"

"No," he answered quickly.

Too quickly?

He hesitated before going on. "It isn't anything to me what you—or Jonas, for that matter—decide to do."

His gaze slowly touched hers, slid sideways and came slowly back again. "I care about you, Lin, even if you don't believe me," he added softly, seeing her green eyes begin to ice up.

He stretched out a hand and covered hers. "And I have to be honest with you. Jonas is every bit as good a detective as I told you he is. He's a good man. And he was a good cop."

"I didn't know your brother was on the police force," she said sharply.

Brian gazed at her in silence. She got the impression that he was waiting for something. For her to add something to what she'd already said?

When she didn't, he answered, "Yes." His glance shifted from her face to the wall. "He left the force suddenly, without telling me."

"Because he wanted to become a private detective?"

Again he gave her that strange look, then shrugged. "I...suppose that had something to do with it. The other thing isn't important, anyway, and besides, I believe his side of the story."

"Story?" A tiny knot of apprehension began to grow in the pit of Lindsey's stomach. "What story is that?"

"It doesn't matter. It was all over a long time ago, and it's best forgotten. Cops die every day in the line of duty. And Jonas wouldn't thank me for bringing it up now. Please..." He paused, as though searching for the right words.

"Don't say anything to him about my mentioning this, will you? He has a low boiling point. Always has had, even when we were kids. It's put him in a few bad spots over the years, and I don't want him mad at me."

"I don't understand," she whispered softly. Obviously he had brought her here specifically to talk about this, so why didn't he clarify the whole thing?

She withdrew her hand from beneath his. "What did he do? Does his . . . temper have anything to do with the trouble you mentioned, with why he left the police force? With someone's death?"

Brian shifted uncomfortably and wouldn't quite meet her eyes. "I told you—it isn't important now. And of course he didn't have anything directly to do with his partner's death." He made an attempt at a laugh. "This is all getting out of hand. And if it makes you feel any better, the charges were dropped when he left the force. In any case, everything was hushed up. I don't need to tell you how that works."

"What do you mean by that?" she asked curtly.

He looked surprised by her sharpness. "I only meant that you must be familiar with how justice sometimes works outside the law."

Before she could comment or ask another question, he glanced down at his watch. "Blast, look at the time. I have an appointment at seven-thirty."

Taking a last sip from his glass, he fished out a couple of bills and laid them on the table.

"I'm sorry, Lindsey, but I lost track of the time. I need to go." He stood, assisted her to her feet and into her coat. "Do you mind if I get you a cab?"

"No," she said, more suspicious than ever. "It's not a problem."

Out on the street, she stopped him with a hand on his sleeve. "Brian, you know you can't simply start something like this thing about your brother and then drop it without any further explanation. If you don't explain what this is all about . . ." She hesitated, then continued in a firm voice, "I'm going to have to ask Jonas about it myself."

Brian grabbed her by the shoulders urgently. "Don't do that, please, for your own sake. It's best not to dredge up the past. Leave well enough alone. I thought you knew. . . .

"It doesn't make any difference to his helping you find Debra. He's a damn fine detective—that's all you're interested in." He paused to eye her closely. "Isn't it?" Without giving her a chance to answer, he released her abruptly and turned back to the street.

Snow began to fall in large, fluffy white flakes. Lindsey shivered, but she couldn't be certain if it was a result of the cold or because of the unanswered questions whirling around inside her head.

What had caused Jonas to leave the police force? What were the charges that had been dropped against him? What had happened to his partner? And what did his *temper* have to do with it all?

She didn't recall seeing any signs of excessive temper in her dealings with the man, though there had been a time or two, she recalled, when he'd looked angry about something. And in the car, he hadn't wanted to talk to her at first. But she'd put that down to his being upset at her wanting to go along with him.

This was ridiculous! Jonas was—Jonas, the man with the eyes from her dream....

Brian waved, and a yellow taxi with a dented right front fender pulled over to the curb. The driver rolled down the passenger window and called, "You need a lift, buddy?"

Brian glanced back over his shoulder at Lindsey, his hand reaching blindly for the taxi door. "Just forget all about what I said tonight, okay?" He pulled the door open, almost thrust her inside and bent to hand the driver a folded bill. "Take her wherever she wants to go."

Lindsey gave her home address to the man, all thoughts of the office gone, before turning her total concentration to Brian's innuendos.

She could feel the blast of warm air from the taxi's heater against her skin, but it couldn't penetrate any farther. From somewhere deep inside a coldness was spreading through bone and tissue alike, turning her blood to ice in her veins.

Brian stood with his hands thrust into the pockets of his coat, staring at the vehicle disappearing in the distance. A slight smile began to creep over his self-indulgent lips, to crinkle the corners of his jubilant brown eyes.

"Sorry, bro, I know that was a rotten thing to do," he whispered under his breath. "But I need your help a hell of a lot worse than she does. And besides, if you help me you'll be helping her, too—if that's what you're *really* after."

Once Lindsey had time to stew about things, he knew she would confront Jonas with her unanswered questions. And that would be the end of the Jonas-Lindsey pact.

Shoulders thrust back, whistling a tune, he almost danced down the snow-covered street. The appointment he'd mentioned to Lindsey was pure fabrication. He was going to go home, build a fire, make himself a drink and sit back and wait for the seeds of doubt he'd planted to take root.

It shouldn't be long. He would spend the time putting together all the data on the theft that the police had gathered so far and have it ready for Jonas when he called.

And he *would* call, of that Brian was certain.

Chapter 9

Jonas drove into the underground parking garage, pulled into a slot and climbed from the car. He used the elevator key Lindsey had given him the night before and punched the button that would take him to the penthouse suite. He should have called, he supposed, but it wasn't until the last minute that he'd decided to fill her in on the fiasco at the pharmacy.

After he'd rung off from talking with his brother, he'd listened to the messages on his answering machine. There had been three calls from her asking him to call her back. But feeling as he did, confused and vulnerable where she was concerned, he'd delayed that call while he read Debra's diary.

He hadn't found what he'd been looking for in the pages of that book, but what he *had* found was very disquieting.

He'd hoped to find reference to people and places that might help him to locate the young woman. What he'd found instead were the dreams and frustrations of a romantic young woman living with the restrictions created by a brain dysfunction she couldn't control. His heart had gone out to her as she had poured out her longings for a normal life, not one controlled by a dependence on medication, and the fears that she would never find someone to love her.

She'd had a particularly bad experience during a trip to Europe when she was still in college, and she hadn't quite gotten over it even after all these years. The man she'd been seeing had been horrified to learn she wasn't "normal" and had left as fast as his legs would take him.

And though he'd begun to feel like the snoop Lindsey had accused him of being when he'd first taken the diary, he'd continued doggedly to the end.

The thing that unsettled him the most were the references to Lindsey and what a good friend she had always been. It appeared that though Debra sometimes found her overprotective, and at times quailed beneath the feeling of being smothered by her friend's attitude, she understood that Lindsey's behavior sprang from her own unhappy childhood. Debra suspected that Lindsey thought she would never be loved for herself alone, and Debra's heart ached for her friend, but she didn't know how to help her.

The diary had also shown that Debra was greatly concerned about Lindsey's relationship with Brian. She called him empty and shallow, a user who would take advantage of Lindsey until there was no more profit in it and then throw her away when the next woman came along who could push him farther up the ladder of success. In addition, there had been a mention of a pass Brian had made at Debra while Lindsey was out of town. And that explained Brian's unwillingness to help locate the young woman.

Debra felt that Lindsey was running away from something, maybe someone from her past.

Debra had also mentioned something about a recurring nightmare that Lindsey refused to discuss with her.

Did it have anything to do with Lassiter, Jonas had wondered as he'd read, and the night he and Hank had saved her from certain death at the man's hands?

All in all, the diary had offered few clues to help him in finding the missing woman. However, it had raised several questions about Lindsey in his mind. He was curious about why she had done the things she had in the past—like become involved with Lassiter in the first place.

Was she not the hardheaded businesswoman she appeared to be on the surface? Was she as emotionally insecure and defenseless as Debra seemed to think she was?

Or was that wishful thinking on his part because of the attraction he felt toward her?

The elevator slid to a stop and the doors slid automatically open, bringing him into the present. He hesitated before getting out. It really *was* too late to be making a call of this nature. Normally he would have waited until the next morning, then phoned his news to the client. Perhaps that was what he should do now.

But then, he reflected, there hadn't been anything normal about this case, or the people implicated in it, from the very beginning.

He should have known better than to become involved in any plot his brother had a hand in. However, like a fool, wishing he and his brother were closer, feeling guilty because they weren't, when Brian had called asking him to see a friend—one who was probably being set up to lose a chunk of money—Jonas had agreed to listen and then turn down the case.

Brian hadn't told him her name, or when to expect her. He'd said she was wealthy and very beautiful, and warned Jonas not to fall for her.

Jonas had been stunned when she had turned out to be a specter from his own unhappy past. But it had made complying with his brother's request that he turn down her case very easy, almost enjoyable.

As a matter of fact, the longer she'd remained in his office, stirring up unpleasant memories, angering him by not acknowledging their previous acquaintance, the more he had relished the idea of thwarting her in some small way. Until he began to think about Debra—and Hank.

After she had left him, he'd been plagued by memories. He'd never really known her part in things. Her presence had been so swiftly, so completely deleted from the record, and she'd disappeared so quickly. He'd never seen or heard about her again—except in his dreams—until now.

He'd almost welcomed her call yesterday morning and had known, down deep inside, that he would probably end up taking the case. He had to—for Hank.

In a moment he was standing on plush gold carpet, his hand reaching toward the doorbell.

The door opened almost immediately, and Lindsey met his glance with a look he couldn't quite interpret. Was it wariness he saw in her eyes?

"I should have called first," he acknowledged abruptly, "But I wanted to talk to you face-to-face."

Why was she just standing there, her body blocking the entrance, as though he was the last person on earth she had expected to see and she wasn't about to allow him inside?

"Is something wrong?" he asked.

"No, nothing." Her hair shimmered like silk in the glow of the hall light, swaying against the shoulders of her cranberry red sweater as she shook her head in denial.

"I know it's late...." He almost stammered his reply as the magic she could so easily weave around him began to take hold. "I should have called," he repeated.

She felt caught off guard by his sudden appearance when she had been thinking about him so strongly. It was almost as though she had conjured him up.

Since leaving Brian on the street in front of the bar that evening, she hadn't been able to get what he'd said—or, rather, hinted at—about Jonas out of her head. And she didn't want to fear him, she wanted to trust him, trust the legacy of her dreams.

Her eyes focused on his face. Should she simply ask him about what had happened so long ago, why he'd left the police force? He was a proud man; she had learned that when she'd offered to "buy" his services. He wouldn't respond well to her questioning him about his past, she knew that instinctively.

She wanted to believe that whatever the reason for his leaving, there was nothing criminal about it. She wanted to tell him he shouldn't be ashamed, whatever the reason.

Lindsey knew all about shame. It could destroy you—if you let it. Stepping back, she said softly, "Come in."

But now it was Jonas who hesitated. "This can wait until morning."

"No, I'm glad you came by. I want to hear what happened today. I've been curious since Wayne Riddell called me at the office this morning."

Jonas couldn't take his eyes off the sway of her narrow hips beneath the white wool skirt as she moved from the hallway to the living room. She seated herself on a low russet upholstered chair, folded her hands in her lap and sat looking up at him.

Ill at ease, he took up a stance behind the couch across the room from her. He sensed that she wasn't as relaxed as she would have liked him to believe, and that kept *him* on edge, because he couldn't fathom the reason for her nervousness.

"Please." She gestured briefly, then clasped her hands in her lap. "Sit down."

Jonas ignored her invitation, watching her face keenly. Where was the confident, almost arrogant, woman who had finagled her way on to the surveillance with him? The woman bold enough to come looking for him at night in a part of town even strong men had sense enough to shy away from?

Lindsey swallowed. His stiff attitude was making her feel more nervous than ever.

"Someone picked up Debra's medicine this afternoon," Jonas said without preamble.

"What?" She gripped the arms of her chair. "Who?"

"I don't know. I thought you might be able to shed some light on that question. Debra called ahead and sent a note saying it was all right."

"B-but they must have forced her to make the call, to write the note."

"You think so? Maybe she wanted to write it. Maybe she isn't a kidnap victim after all," he taunted, surprising even himself.

Lindsey rose to her feet. "Surely you don't believe that? How can you even suggest it?" Her eyes flashed green fire, and the fingers of both hands curled like talons with her anger.

Still wearing his heavy wool jacket over a white, cable-knit sweater, his own hands shoved into the pockets of his gray trousers, Jonas relaxed and admitted, "You're right. I don't believe it."

"Then why did you say it?" she asked in confusion.

But his answer was a shrug as he moved around the room, crossing the Oriental carpet to stand before the tapestry hanging over the fireplace.

"Who picked up the prescription?" Lindsey asked, following him with her eyes. "Was it the man from the restaurant? The one with the limp?"

"No. I don't know who he was."

"You don't know!" she repeated accusingly. "Didn't you question him?"

"I couldn't. I was across the street from the drugstore when he arrived. He came and went without my even knowing."

"How could that happen?" She jumped up and rounded the ornately carved coffee table and moved closer to him. "Are you telling me you let him slip through your fingers?" She was almost beside herself with disbelief, uncertainty and fear for Debra. Blinding anger came a few seconds later.

"I'm paying you for results, not excuses. I thought you were the best money could buy—or was that simply another one of your brother's little exaggerations?" she said scathingly, resorting to contempt to hide her jumbled emotions. She'd hired him to find her missing friend, that was all she'd wanted from him at the time. But now...

"I *am* good at what I do." He faced her challengingly. "But I'm not for sale." His eyes traveled over her figure suggestively. "Not at any price," he added, meeting her shocked glance.

Lindsey felt her face flame. Was he suggesting . . . ?

"You have an elevated opinion of yourself, Mr. Kingston. That seems to be a family trait."

"And are arrogance and egomania Hamilton family traits?" he asked angrily, drawing his fists from his pockets.

"How dare you?" she whispered furiously, nearly choking on her anger.

"Oh, I dare lady, I dare plenty. But I've had it with you. You don't want a private detective. You want a puppet whose strings you can pull. Well, I don't dance to anyone's tune except my own. Get yourself another sucker you can lead around by the nose. I'm through!"

"Where are you going?" Lindsey asked quickly, following him to the door. She didn't want him to leave. She needed him. He was all that stood between Debra and danger.

"Home. I'll give whoever you hire to replace me access to what I've learned so far. Just send him over to my office in the morning." He didn't bother turning around.

His hand was on the elevator button when she asked in a contemptuous tone, "You're quitting, just like that? Walking away from the case?"

Jonas hesitated. "It's for the best."

"Best for whom? Certainly not for Debra—and not for me," she added honestly, desperately, knowing in that instant that it was truth.

He turned slowly to face her, knowing he should just leave. If ever there was a time when he should simply walk away without a backward glance, this was it.

"I don't want anyone else," she murmured in a voice that caused his nerves to quiver like the taut strings of a violin. "I chose you."

"What are you saying?"

She couldn't help herself. "Stay," she breathed, her glance locking with his, a deeper message flashing from her glowing eyes.

She could feel the surging power of his presence across the short distance separating them. She watched his eyes move over her face, her hair, her body. The sensation of his having touched her, though only with his glance, sent warmth flashing through to her soul.

What was this thing between them, this chemical combustion that took place whenever they inhabited the same space? From the first, she'd been drawn to him by the color of his eyes, because she'd seen them in her dreams.

But it was much more than that. Something inside him called to something inside her. And it was growing impossible not to answer to that call.

This anger between them was a part of it, but only one small facet of the whole. She was intrigued with the idea of letting go and finding out what would happen if she gave in to her emotions. But a deep-seated fear that with this man she could lose her identity held her back.

She closed her eyes in indecision for a moment, and felt the rough touch of his palm even before he reached out to cup her cheek. Without thinking, she leaned into his hand. With a little shiver, she felt his hand glide down her neck to her shoulder. Oh, please, she prayed silently, don't say anything more, just hold me—kiss me.

"Is this what you really want?" Jonas asked softly. "Are you looking for stud service, rather than a private detective?"

Lindsey's eyes shot open as she jerked away from his touch. He thought she...! He had it all wrong. Didn't he, too, feel this captivating enchantment that wound its way into her being whenever they were together? How humiliating. Her glance wavered; she couldn't look at him.

"Get out!" she whispered. "Get out! I don't want you on the case any longer. I'll get someone else to find Debra. I've had it up to here—" she gestured "—with the Kingston men."

She whirled and pressed the elevator button, keeping her back to him until she could regain her composure. She couldn't let him see how deeply his contempt affected her.

But Jonas had other ideas. He stood close behind her, almost touching her. "I came here to give you an update on what I've learned, and I'm not going until I've done that."

Lindsey twisted around, found him much too close and drew back against the wall.

Against his will, Jonas was affected by the glimpse of despair in her eyes, the slight trembling of her lower lip. His glance was drawn to her breasts straining against the soft material of her sweater and the increased tempo of her breathing. He felt his body stir. However, nothing showed in his face when his eyes moved back to hers.

"I have a description of the man who picked up the prescription," he continued. "And it isn't the same man you saw at Debra's apartment, or the man with whom Slater saw her leave the restaurant."

"Not the same? Then it must be the other one. It must be the second man we heard discussing the theft." She hesitated when he didn't immediately answer. "Or is it someone else altogether? Are we now looking for three men in a city of 7.2 million people? Men no one seems to know anything at all about, and who seem able to slip past even you? How many more? How many more before you do your job and find Debra?" She wanted to hit something in her frustration.

He'd expected her to be upset by his news, but not wavering on the brink of hysteria. He drew closer and placed soothing hands on her shoulders, a move that surprised him as much as it did her.

But Lindsey didn't want his sympathy, and she twisted unexpectedly away, leaving his hands dangling in space.

"What is this?" he asked in a tight voice, his eyes narrowed on her face. "There's something more to your anger than the fact I didn't get the man at the pharmacy."

Now was her chance to speak. She couldn't explain about her tangled emotions concerning him, but she *could* broach the subject of what Brian had said to her at the bar. "I—I'm worried," she said, delaying, keeping her face away from his, unable to put words to the multitude of questions that trembled on her lips.

"What's *really* bothering you?" he asked, crowding her up against the wall. "Is it that I still haven't taken the bait you've been dangling before me, like a red flag in front of a bull?"

"B-bait?" she stammered, taking shallow breaths to keep her chest from coming into contact with his.

"Don't play innocent with me. We both know that's a lie, don't we? Or have you simply decided to quit playing your little cat-and-mouse games?"

Lindsey had never seen eyes that looked so cold.

"I don't understand."

His eyes grew colder. "I think you do. You didn't ask for references when you came to my office, and you admitted to making inquiries about me. Surely you learned about my past—*all* about my past?"

"Your brother sent me to you. He said—"

"You know my brother well enough to know he tells people whatever story best suits his own purposes at the time."

"No." She shook her head clutching at the door behind her. His sudden attack was making her feel ill. "I didn't know what else to do. I believed him when he said you'd help."

"Don't lie!" He grabbed her and shook her.

He knew his anger was out of proportion to what was happening here. She was eyeing him with fear and all at once he couldn't take that. It wasn't fear he wanted to see in her green eyes, but desire....

And he couldn't handle *that* realization, either.

His jaw clenched while his eyes fastened on her trembling lips. Feeling something inside him grow taut in his anger, he gripped Lindsey tighter and jerked her against him. He wanted to throttle her for all the unhappiness he'd suffered in the past. Whether she'd been a part of it or not didn't matter; he simply needed to expunge the feelings he'd kept locked inside all these years.

Lindsey began to shake in his hold. Seeing the blazing anger in his eyes, she searched desperately for the meaning behind his words. What had made him so angry with her?

Once there had been another man who had made wild accusations against her, yelled at her, backed her into a corner—hurt her.

"You're hurting me." Her throat had closed so tightly that she had difficulty getting the words out. "Please..." She twisted in his hold.

Panic made her green eyes darken, stretched her pupils to their limits. She was breathing in short, soft gasps, her chest rising and falling rapidly, her stomach churning dangerously.

He was hurting *her?* She was killing him slowly in his dreams night after night. She had him so mixed up he didn't know if his head was up or down.

"P-please..." she hiccuped softly, her eyes pleading.

But the fire of anger burned within him, turning his blood to molten lava. The innocence of her pleading glance was lost on him, instead he felt only the fiery demand to make someone else pay for what he'd been put through.

His temper erupted in explosive action. He didn't know whether she was to blame for the past, and at that moment he didn't care. He hauled her unceremoniously against his chest and fastened his hard mouth to hers, grinding her lips against her teeth. Hearing her moan of pain, he knew a moment's satisfaction at having caused her a small measure of what her father had doled out to him.

Maybe what he really needed was to use her to get even with her father and then be done with her and the past once and for all.

And so the kiss Lindsey had looked forward to with breathless anticipation was not a kiss at all, but a violation.

She couldn't move. Stunned, her head forced back, she stood rigid beneath his marauding hands and mouth. He surrounded her, absorbed her, left her no room to maneuver, and for several seconds she couldn't even think.

All at once the past had her in its strong grip, and she was blindingly, sickeningly, terrified of him. She wrenched her lips from his with a moan of despair and in a desperate move wedged her arms between them and pushed against his chest with all her might.

The real panic in her cry snapped Jonas back to his senses. Thoroughly shocked by his own behavior, he had already begun to loosen his hold on her. It was an easy task for her to free herself and pull away.

Before he could find his voice to apologize for his actions, before he could offer an explanation, she was gone, running down the hallway, a shaky hand covering her trembling mouth.

Lindsey barely made it to the bathroom before she was thoroughly sick. Dropping to her knees beside the commode, shivering violently, she hung her head over the bowl and retched.

After a time she became aware that she was no longer alone. Strong fingers took her head in a gentle, if somewhat clumsy, grasp. She held on to the bowl with both hands and continued to be sick.

When at last she was feeling better, she sat back against the wall, legs folded beneath her chin and eyes closed. She was too ill at first to think about it, but when the churning in her stomach had begun to subside, she felt embarrassed for his having seen her in such a state.

Her eyes on the floor, she reached up and felt around on the shelf beside her. A bottle of mouthwash was handed to her. She accepted it without comment and rinsed her mouth. The plastic bottle was taken away, and hard rough fingers gently raised her face, while a cool, damp washcloth smoothed her forehead, cheeks and chin.

She sensed that he wanted to apologize, and when she couldn't resist his compelling personality any longer, she allowed their glances to meet. His eyes were filled with shame.

"I have never, to my knowledge, literally made a woman sick with my kisses—before tonight...." He tried a smile that didn't quite come off, sobered and whispered, "I'm sorry."

Lindsey swallowed and looked away. To be honest, he wasn't completely responsible for her extreme reaction. He'd been rough, but it hadn't been his face she saw, his hands she felt, his voice whispering vile threats in her ear. "It isn't your fault—at least, not totally."

She made a move as though to get to her feet, and he helped her. "I had a...bad experience once," she explained haltingly. "It was a long time ago." She turned toward the sink. "It's hard to forget. Sometimes I do for a while, but...some things have a way of bringing it all back."

Jonas caught her arm carefully, mindful of the soreness she might already be experiencing from his earlier treatment of her. "Tell me about it. Was it...rape?"

He'd never really known exactly how badly Derek Lassiter had hurt her. Those facts, along with everything else, had been repressed by her father.

"No." She used her other hand to push the hair back from her damp face and looked at him. "Not that—thank God."

"But he hurt you," he said with certainty. He could see the memories in her dark, turbulent eyes.

"Yes," Lindsey whispered. "He hurt me."

"I'd make him pay for that, if he were here right now," he muttered from between taut lips as he lifted a curl from her cheek with unsteady fingers.

She was so lovely, even now, with her face flushed from her recent bout of nausea and her eyes bright with remembered pain. And he ached inside with need for her even as he felt ashamed of his need at the same time.

"It's too late for that," she told him flatly, mildly shocked at his vehemence. "He's already paid. With his life."

Jonas's face hovered above hers; he could feel himself being drawn toward her. How was she able to do this to him even when he wanted to resist? His dreams were haunted by those green eyes of hers, eyes that at times seemed to look deep inside him, clear to his soul. And since meeting her again, she'd begun to haunt his days as well as his nights.

He'd been fooling himself this past week, ever since sending her away from his office that first day. Nothing, not even his brother's priŏr attachment to her, he now admitted to himself, would have prevented him from seeing her again. Her memory was too firmly ingrained in his mind for him ever to be able to forget her for long. Wasn't that what he'd been trying to do these past few years?

A muscle worked in his jaw, his throat closed up, and for a moment he couldn't speak. Could the dead see? Was Hank watching him right at this moment, condemning him for even thinking such thoughts about this woman?

Forgive me, buddy. If, wherever you are, you can still feel emotion, then you have to know and maybe understand better than I can what I'm feeling right now. Just once he had to feel her mouth beneath his, not in anger but in passion. Just one time....

His face began to drift toward hers. "I...need to brush my teeth," she breathed, knowing he was going to kiss her. Dreading it...wanting it....

"Later," he whispered against her mouth, knowing all at once that one kiss would not be enough. "Much later."

His lips closed over hers for a brief second. "Please..." she protested weakly, drawing back a little, then catching fire from his touch. "I'm—"

"Delicious," he murmured, recapturing her lips with his, tasting the minty flavor of the mouthwash. And then, at last, she was in his arms, willingly, crushed against his chest, his mouth taking hers in a kiss of shared desperation.

It was better than his dreams, the feel of her in his arms, her body molded tightly to his. She was warm and alive, responding as he'd hoped she would. Jonas felt his heart quicken; the muscles in his arms and legs first grew taut, then weakened and his stomach clenched. He was certain that if he let her go, he would topple over like a felled tree, unable to stand on his own two feet. She was doing this to him; she had that much power over his senses. For a moment the realization made him want to back away from her.

Lindsey felt him tremble and was awed that she could cause such a profound reaction in him. He was such a strong man, so independent, so sure of himself, yet he quivered at her touch and that excited her all the more.

Jonas drew back, releasing her a tiny bit, so that he could look at her. He lifted her face with unsteady fingers and watched the twin crescents of her eyelashes flutter against her cheeks, hiding her expression from him. In her sudden shyness, she was the most perfect thing he'd ever beheld.

He caressed her lower lip with his thumb, moving back and forth, testing its softness. He drew it down, dipped the pad of his thumb into the moistness of her mouth, heard her gasp of surprise, then rubbed his thumb against her teeth.

Lindsey opened her eyes and shivered, captivated by his gaze riveted on her mouth. Twin smoldering flames of desire flickered in the blue-green depths, startling her with their intensity. Until this moment she hadn't fully believed that he, too, could feel the tumultuous disturbances she always felt whenever they were together.

It had been so long—forever, it seemed—since she had allowed a man close enough to move her on this level. She sensed that Jonas had found the secret of her innermost self, found the key and unlocked her heart, captured her body and soul, without his even realizing it.

Jonas let his hands slip around either side of her head, his fingers smoothing the hair back from her face. Bending forward, he touched the tip of his tongue to an ear, moved it gently to the lobe. Taking the soft lip of skin into his mouth, he tugged on it gently.

Lindsey felt her knees go weak and sagged against him, her heart turning over in her chest, unable to withstand the sensations he provoked. She hesitated for a moment, then buried her face against his neck so he couldn't see the effect he was having on her.

But Jonas wasn't deterred; he lifted her hair once again and pressed a kiss against the back of her neck. Lindsey squirmed against him, her hands dropping from his chest to his waist, then lower. Jonas sucked in his breath as one hand came into intimate contact with the source of the heat spreading through him like wildfire.

"My God," Jonas moaned, pressing his hot face against her shoulder. "Do that again."

"W-what?" Lindsey asked in confusion.

"That," he whispered, pressing her warm palm flat against his groin.

"O-oh..."

Taking her by the shoulders, he drew her up onto her toes, his mouth devouring hers. Over and over, without letting her catch her breath, he pressed his lips to hers, drawing every ounce of response he could wring from her. His tongue touched, teased and taunted hers, flicking against her inner lips and teeth in slow gentle strokes, drawing back, then returning to provoke a response.

And Lindsey responded as eagerly as he could have wanted. She entwined her arms around his neck, flattening her breasts against his chest, and answered kiss for kiss. At the end of the onslaught they could not speak, could barely stand.

"I'm going to love you like you've never been loved," Jonas promised when he had his breath back, bending over her, one hand slipping slowly down her hip to the hem of her skirt.

Lindsey could only catch her breath in answer as his hand glided slowly up the outside of her thigh, then around to the inside of her leg, where his fingers encountered not the satin smoothness of skin, but silk.

"I'm going to kiss you till we're both exhausted." His fingers became entangled in silk and lace. "And then I'm going to strip the clothes from your body," his tongue outlined her mouth, and then he drew the soft swell of her lower lip into his mouth, "piece by piece." His lips traveled along her jaw to the delicate underside of her chin. "And then I'm going to kiss you again."

With his cheek he pressed the neckline of her sweater aside and, with his tongue, drew a moist line along the swell of her breast, above her lacy bra. "Every inch of your body is going to know the touch of my lips, the feel of my hands, before I'm through," he promised.

He drew back suddenly and locked glances with her, so close they breathed the same air. "And you'll never forget me." He gave her a little shake. "Never again—do you hear?"

His hands slipped down to her hips and drew her in against him, pressing their lower bodies together in a fevered frenzy of passionate need.

"Yes," Lindsey moaned, feeling his powerful body rippling with tension. "Yes." Her fingers crawled up his chest, slipped beneath his jacket and pushed the garment from his broad shoulders. She could feel the damp material of his sweater sticking to his back, and her senses swam.

Weakness stole over her, and she leaned into him more deeply for support. Jonas used the opportunity to place his leg between hers and with one hand pressed every inch of her sensuous, curvaceous body to his, while the other hand began to draw the sweater up over her waist to her head.

"Not here," she begged, knowing she wouldn't be able to stand on her trembling legs for much longer.

With quick understanding, Jonas lifted her in his arms and carried her, with her directing his steps in between the kisses she pressed on his cheek, neck and chin, to her bedroom. There he set her on her feet beside the large canopied bed.

Without waiting for an invitation, he pulled the sweater from her body and stopped abruptly, turned to stone, his breath strangled in his chest at the loveliness revealed to him. His eyes drank in the sight of smooth satin skin and high, supple breasts, sights that he'd only been able to dream about until now, bared for his leisurely examination.

With shaking fingers he found the front fastening of her lacy bra. It took only a second, and then he had released her breasts into his waiting hands. For a long moment, without moving, he gently cupped the warm, supple flesh before lowering his head and saluting each breast with a kiss of reverence.

The perfume of her skin filled his nostrils, causing him to become enervated with feelings he didn't quite understand. Their joining meant more to him than he was able to acknowledge, even to himself. But he thrust the unsettling thoughts aside, even as his hands, hard and callused, moved unerringly against her, bringing her pleasure she'd never known.

Lindsey gasped and closed her eyes as his thumbs flicked lightly against her throbbing, puckered nipples. She was discovering a new, passionate woman alive inside her. A gentle moan escaped her lips as a large masculine hand moved steadily downward to rest warm and hard against the front of her skirt. She could feel his heat, even through the material, against the tender skin of her belly.

She wound a leg around one of his, and her soft curves molded themselves to the contours of his lean body. With his control almost at an end, Jonas lifted her face to his. Taking her mouth hotly, exploring its tender insides, delving deeply with his insistent tongue, he brought them both to the brink of ecstasy.

Tentatively Lindsey slipped her hands beneath the bottom of his sweater and pushed it up, feeling the springy mat of dark hair covering his chest. Once she'd pulled the sweater from his head, her fingers returned to drift through the soft hair.

All at once she wanted to feel those soft curls against her skin, and she dropped her cheek to his chest. Her lips curled slightly at the tickling sensation, and then she pressed her face against his chest and offered him a shy salute.

She felt the soft springy hair and caressed the skin beneath with her moist tongue. Lindsey moved her face all over his chest, leaving tiny kisses behind, while her hands began a foray of their own along muscled ribs to his narrow waist and the rigid bones of his spine.

Her exploring fingers released primitive yearnings he couldn't control, and Jonas captured a roving hand and pressed it against him, centered over the heat of his arousal, causing the flames of desire to rage nearly out of control.

Drawing back a little, he found the fastener of her skirt and released it. He drew the fabric slowly down her hips, a little at a time, looking up into her eyes from his bent position as her skin was exposed to his hungry gaze. By the time the skirt lay in a pool around her ankles, he could feel his heart kicking against the wall of his chest.

With shaking fingers, still on bended knee before her, he reached up toward the elastic band of her briefs.

All at once Lindsey felt—naked. She stepped back out of reach, folded her arms over her pointed breasts, and looked away. What was she doing here, like this, with this man? Was she so eager for a man's caresses that this was what she had come to? Making love with a man she hardly knew, one she wasn't one hundred percent certain she could trust?

Jonas watched the expressions chase themselves across her pale face. For a moment he'd forgotten exactly who they both were. She was, after all, a *Hamilton*.

"Have you changed your mind? Or is it my brother?" he asked softly, his voice shaking, not really wanting to hear her response, dreading it.

Lindsey swallowed with difficulty and allowed her eyes to move slowly in his direction. Just for an instant she glimpsed a vulnerability in his face that she would never have equated with Jonas Kingston.

"I've never made love with your brother. I don't do this kind of thing." She gestured with one hand, while the other hand preserved her modesty. "I..."

He was so relieved to know her hesitation wasn't because she was having second thoughts about him, thinking of the difference between them and their backgrounds, that his thinking never traveled beyond that one point.

He straightened and moved eagerly toward her, his bare foot coming down on the skirt lying on the floor between them, then slipping out from under him, pitching him forward. With a small gasp of surprise, he landed against Lindsey. Like dominoes they went down, Lindsey across the bed, Jonas across her, knocking the breath from her lungs.

His face red, Jonas murmured, "I'm sorry."

From where her face was buried against his shoulder, Lindsey gave a muffled response.

"What? What did you say?" He drew back to look into her face.

"I said," she spoke clearly, "I'm not." She pulled her hands out from between them and placed them against the muscles of his chest.

The specter of Derek Lassiter loomed for a brief moment in her mind. Was she being a fool—again?

She stared deeply into Jonas's eyes, those beautiful turquoise eyes. How could she doubt him when he looked at her with the eyes that comforted her in her nightmares?

"Nothing else matters right now. Not your past—or mine. All that matters is this moment." Her green eyes glowed. "And us, together." Her lips rested against the side of his neck.

Jonas felt his heart race at her words. He threaded his fingers through her long, dark hair, and as her tongue slid up the strong muscles of his neck, he groaned, drew her head up and fastened his hot mouth over hers.

Their bodies rolled slowly, Lindsey coming up on top. Somehow Jonas managed to shed his trousers and divest Lindsey of her last remaining piece of clothing without loosening his mouth from hers. And then they were breast to breast, hip to hip, skin to skin.

His ardor was surprisingly, touchingly, restrained in the beginning, allowing Lindsey to lead the way. He gave what he gauged she wanted, holding his own needs in check, afraid of frightening her—of reminding her of Lassiter and his brutality.

But Lindsey was ferocious in her need of him. She taunted him with kisses, teased him with her hands and tantalized him with her tongue until he lost control. And then she really let him have it.

But Jonas was equal to the challenge she set him, and, true to his earlier promise, he managed to kiss every part of her body, titillating her in ways she had never imagined.

She writhed beneath him, begging for relief from the awful, wonderful yearnings he had aroused in her. But Jonas withheld fulfillment for a while longer, turned a deaf ear to her pleading, and found new ways to heighten the passion until they were both aching for release.

Finally, unable to suppress his own need a second longer, Jonas positioned Lindsey on her back and moved over her. He covered her body with his, pressed his hands over her breasts, her nipples between his fingers, and massaged gently in rhythm with their movement.

Lindsey lay drowning in wave after wave of pure delight, her senses succumbing to the mindlessness of sheer ecstasy as her body melded with his. They flew, they soared, they floated, they entered realms of passion she had only heard about and never truly believed in. But Jonas showed her the way. He took her by the hand, led her down the path, and then they entered the enchanted kingdom, too.

And when it was over and they lay with their bodies drenched in sweat, lungs laboring for air, their limbs still entwined, hovering on the point of mental as well as physical exhaustion, the luminescence lingered on.

Even as she moved away from Jonas and rolled herself in the sheet, even as remembered guilt over her friend's disappearance began, once more, to steal over her, the glow remained. All she had to do was to close her eyes and she could see Jonas above her, his eyes burning deep into her soul, feel his hands working their magic on her body, drawing her through the portal of this world and into the world only he could create for her, a world of sensual delight.

Mumbling an excuse, Lindsey wrapped the sheet like a sarong around her and hurried from the room. She was well aware that if she hadn't left right then, she would have begged him to make love to her again.

When she had herself firmly under control and could face him once more, she entered the room to find it empty. The bed was neatly made, the room empty of his presence.

Like a thief in the night, he'd gone from her, slipped away into the blackness, leaving no physical trace of his ever having been there. Yet he'd taken her most valuable possession. He'd left with her heart.

Chapter 10

"Lindsey?" There was no sense in reverting to the formal "Miss Hamilton" after what had transpired between them the night before.

"Jonas?"

She was surprised to hear from him. She glanced at the bedside clock. And so early, too. It wasn't yet eight in the morning. Not that she'd been asleep; she hadn't even dozed during the night. Thoughts of him and what they'd done, the step they'd taken, had plagued her through the long hours, along with thoughts of when she would see him again.

"Where are you?" she asked softly, unable to help the intimate note that crept into her voice. It was so easy to picture him lying in bed, nude beneath the sheet, the phone gripped in one strong hand.

"I'm at the office," he said, putting an abrupt end to her fantasies. "I'm making out a schedule of people I need to see today. I'm going to talk to Debra's boss and see if I can find anyone at her office who might be able to shed some light on her disappearance."

"I see."

"I called because I have an appointment to speak with your friend, Riddell's wife. He suggested I take you along— something about her being pregnant. I wondered if you would be free about eleven. That's when I have the appointment."

She felt disappointment like a bitter wind blow through her heart, but tried not to let it show in her voice. "Yes, of course, I'll go with you. Shall I meet you there?"

Didn't she want him—someone like him—showing up at her office? he wondered. Was she afraid it would give the place a bad name? This time he wouldn't give in to her.

"No," he answered firmly. "I'll come round and pick you up. See you about ten." He rang off before she could protest and heaved a heartfelt sigh of relief. That was one hurdle over for the morning.

Lindsey glanced at her watch, picked up her pencil and threw it down again. It was almost ten, and she hadn't gotten a thing done that needed doing. She'd spent the whole morning worrying about Debra and about her meeting with Jonas in—she glanced at her watch again—exactly eight minutes.

Would he be prompt? That was only one of the things she didn't know about him. And she hadn't forgotten Brian's mysterious allusions from the night before.

A low buzzer rang, and Lindsey answered it.

"You have a visitor, Miss Hamilton," Pam said over the intercom. "Shall I show him in?"

"Thank you, no, I'll be right out—"

The door across from her opened without warning, and Jonas's tall figure filled the space.

"I wanted to see where you work," he told her, looking around at the sumptuous surroundings, the real leather chairs, the impressionist paintings on the walls, the thick carpet underfoot.

Lindsey stood with her purse in her hand, feeling unaccountably defensive. He wasn't saying anything, but she could tell by the expression in his eyes that what he was thinking wasn't favorable.

But why should she feel defensive because she worked in elegant surroundings and had a bank account? Wasn't that what everyone strove for?

She moved around the desk and joined him at the door. "Have you seen enough?" she asked with her head held high. "Or would you like to look around some more, perhaps visit the executive lavatory? Better yet, I have a private one." She gestured back over her shoulder.

"I've seen enough," he told her abruptly and, turning on his heel, marched out.

In the car she began to give him directions to the Riddell house, and he informed her coolly that he knew where it was. Lindsey sat back in the seat and folded her hands in her lap. Okay, if that was how he wanted to play it, so be it. They would be strangers.

Twenty minutes later they were both seated in the comfortable living room belonging to Wayne Riddell and his wife.

"Would you like another cup of coffee?" Cheryl Riddell asked.

Jonas eyed her worriedly and refused. She looked as though she was ready to give birth at any moment.

"Cheryl, how have you been these past few weeks?" Lindsey asked with a smile. "I'm sorry I haven't been over lately, but I've been tied up with out-of-town trips, and then Debra—"

"I understand, honey." Cheryl patted the other woman's hand and smiled. The two women were seated beside each other on a small sofa placed before a roaring fire.

Jonas sat across from them in a thick overstuffed chair that was so comfortable he wished he could put his feet up and take a nap. He hadn't gotten much sleep last night after he'd left Lindsey's apartment. He felt like hell, and knew he looked it.

His eyes kept sliding in Lindsey's direction despite his attempts to keep them away. She certainly didn't look as though she had missed her sleep. Wasn't that supposed to be the sign of a clear conscience?

He wished he could say the same for himself. But his conscience was playing hell with him. He hadn't intended to see her again for a while. He could give her progress reports over the phone as well as in person. Yet here he was, and the more he looked at her, the more he wanted to.

"I really don't know what I can tell you about Debra that will help you find her," Cheryl said, including him in the conversation. "But if you want to ask me any questions—" she lifted her hands from her lap and shrugged "—go ahead."

Lindsey spoke immediately. "Did you by any chance talk to her on Monday? Or has anyone been around here asking about her before us? Has anyone called Wayne about her medicine before now?"

"Excuse me." Both pairs of feminine eyes darted to Jonas's stern face. "I believe I'm the one who came here to conduct the questioning, if you don't mind?" He directed the sarcastic question to Lindsey.

"I was only—"

"I know." He cut her short. "Trying to help."

His expression told her that he didn't need her help, and Lindsey stiffened in angry protest. She glanced at Cheryl and saw the look of concern on the other woman's face as she switched her glance from Jonas to Lindsey and back again. There was no sense in unduly upsetting her friend.

"If you'll excuse me." Lindsey stood and began to gather the coffee cups and saucers. "I'll just take these to the kitchen while the two of you talk."

She could hear the low murmur of their voices as she stood inside the closed kitchen door and fought back the tears, tears of anger and hurt.

He'd looked at her just now as though she were a stranger and spoken as though he wished she were anywhere else.

When he'd called that morning and asked her to accompany him, she'd thought perhaps it was an excuse for him to see her again—as though he needed one. But now she realized he'd asked her along only out of necessity, because Wayne had requested it. She felt like a fool.

She vowed silently that from now on she would concentrate on finding Debra and nothing else. She couldn't allow Jonas to keep crowding into her thoughts. She would have to make the effort and put him out of her mind *and* her heart.

"I'll come with you."

"No!" Lindsey turned slightly in the seat and shook her head. "No, it isn't necessary. I can find my way alone."

She had intended to ask him to take her back to her office directly after the visit to Cheryl Riddell, but somehow she had ended up going to lunch with him and then on to speak with Debra's boss. Now it was almost seven o'clock, and all she wanted was to be alone with her thoughts.

She was feeling depressed because they were no nearer to finding Debra than they had been, and still they'd heard nothing from the kidnappers. And even though Jonas hadn't said as much, she knew that no news in this case was not good news.

Debra had been on her mind to the exclusion of everything else since they'd left the Riddell house, and her worry had made her quiet and uncommunicative.

"Look." Jonas spoke abruptly into the silence. "I'm sorry I was so harsh with you earlier. But sometimes you—" He ran a hand through his hair in frustration. "Damn it! A man can lose his identity when he's around you."

Lindsey paused with her hand on the door handle. "I don't understand."

"You're a very self-assured lady. You charge ahead in whatever you're doing as though you know exactly where you're going and what the outcome is going to be before you get there." This was coming out all wrong, but he couldn't seem to stop the flow of words. "Not all of us have been raised to think we know what's right, all the time."

"Are you calling me arrogant?" she asked softly. "Are you saying that I think I know what's best for everyone whether it is or not? That I completely disregard other people's feelings and ideas as though they're of no importance compared to my own?"

"Not...exactly," he faltered. Was she angry? He couldn't tell from her profile, and her voice sounded neutral.

"Then what, exactly?" She threw the very same words he'd once used to her back at him.

"I—"

All at once her whole figure appeared to fall in on itself. "It doesn't matter," she whispered. "You're right."

She was out of the car and almost running, her heels clicking loudly on the concrete as she made for the elevator. He mustn't see her cry. He'd already seen her be sick, she couldn't suffer the ignominy of his seeing her cry, as well.

But tears clogged her throat and her hands shook so badly she had difficulty finding her key, and then she couldn't get it into the lock. All at once a strong hand closed over hers from behind and steadied it. The key slid smoothly into the lock and turned.

"Th-thank you," she murmured, keeping her face turned away from his.

The elevator doors opened, and she stepped inside, turned to lean against the wall and looked up. Jonas had followed her.

"W-what—"

He didn't say a thing, just moved in front of her as the doors whispered shut until she was pressed back against the wall. Her breath became trapped in her throat. Her eyes opened wide as she strained her head back to stare up at him.

His head descended slowly as though he was giving her, and himself, time to think twice about what was happening. When their lips were only an inch apart, he placed his hands against the wall on either side of her and let his full weight rest against hers.

Her legs turned to water, and a hot liquid feeling began to crawl through her lower body. She felt as though her clothes were steaming, and he hadn't even kissed her yet—but he was going to.

Lindsey rose onto her toes, as far as his body glued to hers would allow, and met his lips eagerly. Her arms encircled his waist beneath his jacket and pressed him into her. Her whole body melted against him just as her mouth melted against his mouth. She felt a sweet pain as her breasts were crushed against his broad chest.

One of his hands left the wall and found its way beneath her coat, under the jacket and blouse, to the warm pulsing flesh below. His fingers massaged her through the silk of her bra, and she tingled with an aliveness she only felt beneath his hands.

The small elevator became filled with the sounds of their heavy breathing, murmured sighs, long, drawn-out breaths. The air around them vibrated like a live thing with their need of each other, sweeping away her inhibitions.

Jonas couldn't seem to get enough of her. His mouth moved against her cheeks, her chin, down the sensitive cord of her neck. She moaned as he ran his tongue along her collarbone to the hollow between her breasts, and when he nipped the tender flesh there she thought she would die from sheer pleasure.

Lindsey pushed her arms up to the shoulders of his jacket and began to shove it off his shoulders. She wanted him, wanted him to make love to her right here, right now....

All at once Jonas backed off, disentangled her hands from his clothing, pressed them above her head and held them there while he kissed her thoroughly before backing away to lean against the opposite wall, his eyes on her face.

"Would you...do this?" he panted. "Would you make love with me, here, on the floor of this elevator?"

"Yes," Lindsey answered without hesitation.

The elevator slid to a smooth stop and the doors opened automatically.

A muscle worked in Jonas's jaw, and now it was he who turned aside so she couldn't read his expression. Without his having to say it, she knew that they wouldn't be making love that night. She sensed that something stood between them, something that held Jonas back.

It was the reason he'd left her bed so quickly last night without telling her, and it was the cause of the strange expressions she'd surprised on his face more than once since their first meeting, when he thought she wasn't looking.

Did it have anything to do with the past he had put behind him? Would he ever speak of it to her? Was this the time for her to ask him about it?

"Jonas, I—"

He lunged forward, caught her in his arms and captured her mouth hungrily. He offered her long, drugging kisses, drawing out her very soul, kissing her until she clung to him mindlessly, his to command.

And then, without warning, she was standing outside the elevator in the hallway and the doors were closing, taking him away.

She stood there in confusion, her head spinning, an emptiness stealing slowly over her.

Somehow, that last kiss had seemed too much like... goodbye.

"So, this is where you slipped off to."

Lindsey turned slowly to see Paul Fillmore standing in the doorway. They'd been introduced by Ryan Dennison before the charity dinner had begun. Paul was the reason for the dinner. The Dennisons were honoring him for his work with the city's homeless, and also for the delinquent youth program he had developed to get troubled teenagers off the streets and into schools and jobs.

When Ryan Dennison had called her at her office on Monday and invited her to the Saturday function she had initially declined. Her thoughts had been totally centered on Debra—and Jonas.

She had spoken with Jonas twice in the past few days, but both conversations had been very short, with nothing of a personal nature about them. He'd reported that he'd made little progress in finding Debra. He'd asked her questions about the people Debra knew and had associated with in the past few years. He'd told her he was in the process of tracking down old boyfriends and people she had worked with in the past, and then he'd rung off.

Every time the phone rang she jumped, her heart in her throat, and ran to answer it, hoping it was Jonas with news of Debra—only to be disappointed. At work she found it almost impossible to concentrate on her job.

By the end of the week Lindsey's spirits were at their lowest. Realizing that she had to do something to distract herself from her dark thoughts, she changed her mind about her original refusal to attend the charity dinner and called Ryan Dennison to see if the invitation was still open.

And so here she was. Dinner was over, with its speeches and toasts, and she had slipped off to find a quiet moment of privacy. It hadn't been as bad as she'd feared, being here alone, except for her thoughts of Debra. The only time she wasn't figuratively chewing her nails about her friend, strangely enough, was when she was with Jonas.

She'd seen Brian across the room and fended off a few pointed questions about why he was with someone else. Madge, Ryan's wife, had seated her beside the guest of honor during dinner. Paul Fillmore was an eligible bachelor, and Madge was always attempting to find Lindsey a suitable mate.

In this instance, Lindsey silently thanked the older woman. She and her dinner partner had talked during the meal and, much to her surprise, Lindsey discovered that the man was quiet and charming, not at all what she'd expected him to be. Most men with his wealth and standing were crass bores, concerned with two things—how fast they could get a woman into bed and telling her *all* about how brilliant they were.

Paul had been interested in neither of these things. He'd been polite and attentive. In fact, he'd spent much of dinner asking questions about her.

If she hadn't already met Jonas, Paul would have been someone she would have wanted to get to know on a more intimate level. But she *had* met Jonas....

The strains of a waltz drifted into the room from the open door, and Lindsey looked up in time to catch a curious expression on Paul's face. She gave a slight smile and said, "You're missing the festivities."

He shrugged charmingly, returned her smile and entered the room, closing the door softly behind him, then said, "I don't mind. I'd much rather stay here with you, if that's all right?"

"I'm afraid I'm not much of a party goer," she admitted ruefully.

"Neither am I," he answered, looking around at the wall-to-wall greenery. "Do you like plants?" he asked, coming to stand beside her.

"I love them, but I don't have any in my apartment. I feel as though any living thing should have someone around to care for it, nurture it with love—even plants," she told him in a burst of honesty that surprised her. "And I'm afraid I don't have much time for that," she ended, glancing up at him from the corner of her eyes and laughing a bit self-consciously. "I guess to some that might sound rather silly."

"Not at all," he replied quickly, his eyes on her face. "I thoroughly agree with you."

His attention shifted to the snow-covered scene visible outside the floor-length glass window.

"Everything—everyone—needs love, even those of us who have never known it, never given any special thought to needing it," he added pensively. "It isn't enough to simply give. There comes a time when we need to feel it returned...."

All at once he glanced down at the woman beside him and smiled a bit sheepishly. "Sorry, I do go on and on at times. Give me a soapbox."

"No, please." Lindsey touched his arm lightly. "I think you're right. I'm sure you must have had a great deal of experience with people needing love, working as you do with teenagers, even adults, who are out on the street alone. Sometimes their attitudes toward you must reflect their unhappy backgrounds. How do you handle that?" she asked curiously.

"Is it enough for you to simply help them? Or do you expect something in return?"

Lindsey was discovering that sometimes it was much easier to discuss personal subjects with a sympathetic stranger—even couched in terms of a hypothesis.

"I'm not certain I know what you're driving at, Lindsey. Do you mean, do I want their thanks? Or their respect?" He eyed her questioningly.

Lindsey shrugged. That wasn't exactly what she meant, but it was a start.

"Well, I must admit, when I first started I expected the people I helped to appreciate me." He laughed self-deprecatingly.

"It was a severe shock the first time I was told exactly what I could do with my good intentions. It set me back a bit, until I realized these people were used to being slapped down at every turn. And being from the street myself, I should have known that.

"They'd only seen the worst life had to offer. How could I expect them to thank me for a few hours of my time, some food, a few clothes, with them knowing that when I left their lives would go back to being the same as before? I had to prove to them that I wasn't there to play at helping them. I had to show them I was serious, that I'd stick with them to the sometimes bitter end."

Lindsey turned to face the window. She'd begun by thinking about her father, but now she was remembering Jonas.

Paul seemed to sense something of what she was feeling. "Now let me ask you something in return. Do *you* regret what *you're* feeling?"

"Oh! I didn't say—I didn't mean that I—" She was embarrassed all at once that he had realized she was discussing her own love life.

Paul laid a soothing hand on her shoulder. "We were speaking hypothetically, of course. But you have to ask yourself if your love is given only on the basis of receiving something in return, like an exchange of money for..." He hesitated, then looked down at the small pearl brooch she wore and touched it with a long finger. "Say this, for instance?"

Lindsey covered the brooch with one hand. It had been a gift from her father on her twenty-first birthday. They had been in Switzerland at the time, while she recuperated from her experience at Derek Lassiter's hands.

The brooch had been delivered to her at the sanatorium by a messenger, because her father was attending a business meeting several hundred miles away and couldn't bring it himself.

She felt the tiny pearls, twenty-one, one for each year of her life. Had her father really loved her? Had he known that she loved him? Or had he thought he had to buy her love with expensive gifts, like this one?

She would never know the answer to that question now. Perhaps it didn't really matter. For, despite everything, she had loved him because he had, after all, been her father.

"I see your point. Real love asks nothing in return."

In his own way, her father must have loved her. It might not have been another man's idea of love, but it had been his.

The door behind them suddenly swung open, and Ryan Dennison peered into the room. "So this is where you've been hiding, and with the guest of honor, too." He grinned mischievously. "Remember that dance you promised me?"

She crossed the room almost gaily and slipped her arm through his. "Take me away, sir, and dance me to the heights." Her laugh was happier than it had been all evening.

Ryan took her at her word and whirled her around the room, her skirts billowing around her, preparatory to dancing her out the door.

"Oops!" Lindsey lost hold of her small clutch bag, and it fell to the floor.

"Here, let me." Paul bent and swiftly retrieved it. "Perhaps you would like me to take it to the table with me and you can get it after your dance."

"Would you, Paul? Thanks."

Paul stood watching them dance across the floor for a moment before glancing down at the dainty sequin-and-pearl purse in his large hands. With a slight smile he closed the door and left the room.

"Are you certain you don't mind giving me a lift? I can call Mac." Lindsey slipped into the coat Paul was holding for her and looked up at him questioningly.

"I told you, I'd be pleased to give you a ride. And I'm going right by your apartment, so there's no need to bring your driver out into the cold."

Their goodbyes said, they hurried outside to Paul's metallic-blue Jaguar and drove off. They talked of many things on the ride, which took a little over an hour. By the time they reached her apartment, Lindsey felt as though she had known Paul all her life. And a small part of her wished things were different, or that Jonas were more like this man. But no, then Jonas wouldn't be—Jonas.

Lindsey directed Paul to the underground parking garage and allowed him to assist her from the low car. At the elevator she hesitated, then invited him up for coffee. She was surprised when he readily agreed, but glad at the same time. For a little while, he'd managed to take her mind off Jonas and her fears for Debra's safety, and she wasn't quite willing to let him go just yet.

As they stepped into the elevator, Lindsey caught her heel and would have pitched headlong to the concrete if Paul hadn't caught her against him. They both laughed self-consciously, and after a moment she stepped away from his chest.

So, Jonas thought as he stepped from the shadows, and who is this?

Against his better judgment, he'd been unable to prevent himself from dropping by her apartment that evening. He'd intended to use the excuse of checking with her to see if she had heard anything from the kidnappers—as though she wouldn't have called him immediately if she had—in order to gain entrance.

But in actual fact, he only wanted to see her. It had been a week since he'd seen her, and though he'd been eaten up with conflicting emotions, his need to speak a few words to her, hear her voice—had won over all his reasons for not doing so.

And here he stood, watching the doors close on another man. A man she was inviting up to her apartment, just as, another time, she had invited him.

Would this man—this stranger—take advantage of the situation?

Who was he? An old friend? An old lover? A new lover? Was he even now in the act of sliding her dress down over her creamy smooth shoulders?

Jonas stood for long moments beside the elevator doors, staring at nothing, and remembering.

All at once he slammed a fist against the wall beside the elevator, bringing the memories to a close. She was a free agent, just as he was. She could see whomever she liked, just as he could. It was none of his business who she brought home with her, just as—

The hell with that! He didn't want another woman; he wanted her. For his sins, he wanted only her. He had no idea how their relationship had come to that, but it had.

Knowing what he knew about women from his work, he should have been more wary. And then there was the fact that he didn't know Lindsey Hamilton at all. His knowledge of her past conflicted with what he'd learned about her these past weeks.

He knew she was capable of falling under the spell of a loser like Lassiter, and capable of being maneuvered by her tyrant of a father, but she was also capable of love. Just look at the way she thrust aside every obstacle in her quest to find her friend. No one, not the law, nor his brother, nor even himself, had been able to prevent her from forging ahead to prove that her friend had been kidnapped.

She was strong and determined, a good businesswoman. She could go after and get what she wanted, as she'd gone after him to get him on her side and on her friend's case.

But she was soft, too. He'd seen that side of her for himself. Soft and warm and vulnerable....

An enigma. Lindsey Hamilton was a total enigma to him. He didn't know what to expect from her from one minute to the next. Their brief telephone conversations this week hadn't been enough, but he'd held off. He kept telling himself that he was working for her. And he was a fool to get involved with a client.

But part of his mind was always on the woman who had hired him. She sounded distant on the telephone. Was she afraid he would try to presume on the fact that they'd made love? He could imagine the expression on her lovely face as she spoke to him—the same expression he'd seen on her face in the restaurant that day when she was dealing with the waiter, keeping him at arm's length.

He'd tried to tell himself that he wasn't ready to name what he was feeling for her, anyway, but . . .

Was fate paying him back for stepping on his brother's toes, for taking to bed the woman his brother had wanted?

No! That relationship and its ending had nothing to do with him. And she'd told him that they'd never been intimate. But had she lied?

He wasn't certain why it mattered so much to him, but it did. And now, here she was with another man. And from the looks of him, a man more in her class.

Maybe he should just go home, forget all about doing anything but his job. He was only her employee, nothing more; he had to keep that in mind. There was more than just the past between them. She was a millionaire, and he worked for peanuts.

He worked for her, but she wasn't paying him to be jealous.

Jonas turned away from the elevator, found his car and climbed inside. But he didn't start the engine. Who was the man with her? He looked like a man who had everything. Including the woman Jonas wanted? Who was he?

There was only one thing for it. Since he couldn't go upstairs, drag the man from her apartment—from her bed?— and beat him to a bloody pulp, he would do what other people paid him for: he would investigate.

Leaving his car, he found the Jaguar and squatted down behind it. From his pocket he withdrew a small notebook and pencil. It took only a few seconds to copy down the numbers.

Then he turned away, climbed into his own car, started it and drove away. This was Saturday night—or rather, early Sunday morning. By Monday evening he would know everything he wanted about the man who had been with Lindsey tonight. So why did he feel like such a lowdown sneak?

Jonas twisted on the bed. He was dreaming. He was running down a fog-enshrouded road in the dark. There were tall trees alongside, their bare branches like arms pointing toward the sky.

She was there, ahead in the night—Lindsey. He came close to her, reached for her white gown billowing in the wind. She turned to face him all at once, and instead of the green eyes and smiling lips, she wore a death's head mask. Without warning, Derek Lassiter jumped out at him from behind a tree.

"She's mine." He laughed. "She'll never forget me. She's mine—all mine—forever."

Jonas lunged at him, but he moved in slow motion. Finally he reached the other man and put his hands around his neck to throttle him. Then he looked up—into Hank's blue eyes bulging in the red face.

"Hank!" Jonas let him go, helped him to lean against the tree. "Hank, buddy, I'm sorry, I didn't know, I—"

But his friend only gave him a reproachful look and slowly faded away.

Jonas ran around the tree looking for him, calling his name, begging him to come back. "I should have followed you," he yelled. "I should have followed you." And in the distance, growing louder and louder, he could hear Lassiter laughing...laughing....

Jonas sat straight up in bed, the sound of Lassiter's laughter ringing in his ears. He shook his head to clear it, placed both hands over his ears to shut out the sound, and stared around him.

The ringing was not inside his head but coming from the phone sitting beside his bed. He reached for it.

"Yes?" His voice sounded muffled.

"Jonas? Is that you?"

"Lindsey?" He sat up alertly. "What's wrong?"

"I—it's crazy, but I have a note from Debra."

"She sent you a letter? What's the postmark?" Jonas asked quickly.

"No, no, you don't understand. Please, can you come over? I know it's early, but—"

"I'll be right there."

He was tossing the covers aside as he spoke; then his feet hit the floor. He didn't wait for Lindsey to ring off but dropped the phone back into its cradle and made a grab for his trousers. Everything else was forgotten in the excitement of the moment. They had a break in Debra's disappearance.

Lindsey was listening for the sound of the elevator through the open door to her apartment. It was forty-five minutes from the time she rang him until she heard the doors glide open. She ran unceremoniously from the room and into the hallway.

"Jonas! Thank God you're here."

She stopped before him, taking in the tousled dark blond waves and the heavy-lidded, sleepy look in the turquoise eyes. Her heartbeat accelerated alarmingly, and she looked hurriedly away.

"Here." She reached into the pocket of her yellow velour housecoat and handed him a small scrap of folded paper.

Jonas took a moment to read it before asking, "You're certain it's her handwriting?" He glanced up into her face. "There's no mistake?"

"It's hers." There was no excitement in her voice. "I'm positive. This proves she's all right, doesn't it?" She didn't wait for confirmation before adding, "I'm so relieved. I was more worried than I realized, until I got that."

"And are you going to do as she says?" he asked with his eyes on her face. She looked so good, even with her hair in a cloudy tangle about her face and the marks from her pillow still on her cheek.

"You mean, stop trying to find her—take you off the case?" she asked.

"Well," he said, glancing down at the paper in his hand, "it says here to sit tight and she'll be okay. In my book that means no cops, no private investigators."

"No," Lindsey answered in a determined voice. She shook her head and took the paper from him, then turned and walked into the apartment with him following close on her heels.

"Of course I'm not going to stop looking for her. She wants me to find her. This is something she was forced to write, like the note to the pharmacy."

There were things she didn't know about kidnappers, Jonas thought. Sometimes, immediately after making a victim write such a message, they killed the victim.

"Lindsey..." He touched her shoulder from behind. He was about to tell her not to get her hopes up when the telephone rang.

She whirled to face the instrument sitting on the hall table like a black-and-gold spider. Her eyes shot to Jonas's face; he was looking at the phone, too.

"Who could that be?" she asked all at once.

"There's only one way to find out." Jonas strode to the phone and picked it up, turned and held it out to her.

"H-hello," she murmured into the mouthpiece. Her eyes took on a sudden gleam, and then all at once went dim, like a light bulb going out. Jonas bent toward the receiver gripped tightly in her shaking hand, but could hear only her side of the conversation.

"What do you mean?" she asked, and then after a slight pause, "Yes, I got your note. Where are you? No, I—" She threw a sidelong glance in Jonas's direction. He was only inches away. "I'm alone. I can't believe it's you." She was clutching the phone in both hands now.

"Where are you?" she repeated after a moment. "Are you all right? Why are they holding you? What do they want? I haven't received a ransom demand.

"No! Don't hang up! Debra, don't hang up! Tell me where you are! I'll find you—" She was almost shouting into the receiver. "Do you hear me? I'll find you, Debra. I have someone looking for you—"

After a moment of silence she held the phone away from her ear and looked at it. "She's gone," she said dully. "She hung up on me."

Jonas took the phone from her and put it down. "Did she have the opportunity to give you a hint about where she's being held?"

"No." Lindsey shook her head, her hands twisting the belt of her robe. "She told me not to look for her." She glanced up at Jonas. "Why would she say that? She sounded upset when I said I had someone looking for her." She lifted her hands, letting the belt fall. "Why?"

"Perhaps the kidnappers were listening in, or maybe she managed to get away from them long enough to make the call.

"Which reminds me, where did you find the note? Was it delivered? I'd like to see the envelope it came in."

He was all detective now. He had to be, because that helpless, little-girl-lost look in Lindsey's green eyes was playing havoc with his senses, driving him to the point of wanting to forget everything else but taking her into his arms.

"It didn't come in an envelope. I found it this morning when I emptied out my purse." She went over to the coffee table and picked up a pearl-and-sequin evening bag, then held it out to him.

"How did it get in there?"

"I don't know. It wasn't in there when I left here last evening." She turned away and went to stand before a large window. "I didn't bother taking my things out until this morning."

"You went out last night?" he asked without expression, as though he hadn't seen her arrive home—and with another man.

"Yes, some old family friends invited me to a charity dinner, and I went. Brian was there," she added, wondering what it was about his voice that sounded different.

"I see. Did you go with him?"

"No." She fiddled with the lace curtain. "I went alone. Mac drove me."

"Was your purse in your possession, within your sight, all evening?" Jonas didn't pursue the question of how, or with whom, she had spent her time, nor how she had arrived home.

"No, of course it wasn't. It isn't very easy to dance carrying a bag. Not that I did all that much dancing," she added hurriedly, turning to face him.

But the glance he directed at her was one she recognized. Nothing of what he was feeling, if indeed he was feeling anything at all, showed on his face.

"How many people attended this affair?"

"I don't know. Fifty, perhaps a hundred."

"Of the city's elite, dressed in their finest to spend an evening writing checks for thousands of dollars—and for what?" he asked with contempt dripping from his voice. "To buy outlandish pictures painted by some rich woman's latest gigolo?"

"Not at all!" Lindsey answered angrily. "The dinner was to honor a man who helps get teens off the streets and back into schools or work programs where they belong. And he finds homes for the homeless. I'm certain Paul is no gigolo!" she ended indignantly.

"Paul?" He seemed to pounce on the name. "So you know the man?"

"Not really," she answered, feeling somehow as though she were in the wrong for having accepted a ride home with him. "I was introduced to him only last night, but he seems quite decent."

"Decent?" Jonas echoed sarcastically. "Is that the only word you'd use to describe him? What about handsome? Rich?"

Lindsey looked at him with narrowed eyes. There was more to this than she understood. "Do you know Paul?"

"What's his last name?" Jonas asked.

"Fillmore, Paul Fillmore."

"Never heard of him," he said with satisfaction.

"Why did you ask if he was handsome, or rich?"

Jonas stared at her from across the room.

"You followed me!" she accused in a disbelieving voice. "You spied on me!"

"I did no such thing!" he quickly denied.

"Then how do you know Paul is handsome and rich?" she asked, advancing slowly toward him.

"It's a safe guess under the circumstances, don't you think? From what you said, he's a real do-gooder, and that means he's got to have the dough to do good with—" He shrugged, but didn't quite meet her eyes.

"What about Debra?" she asked, stopping a few feet from where he stood. "What about the note and the phone call?"

"I can have the note analyzed by a friend of mine down at the police lab. Of course, our having handled it will make it more difficult to learn anything about the people who handled it before us."

"Yes, take it," Lindsey told him eagerly. "See what your friend can make of it."

She watched as he tucked the note away in his shirt pocket.

"Will your friend be able to get started on it today?" she asked, knowing he probably had other things to do on a Sunday morning besides spend it with her, but not wanting him to leave just yet.

Jonas rubbed a finger along his right cheek and kept his eyes on the floor. "No, he's off today. I'll take it to him in the morning. Then it depends on how busy he is." He moved toward the front door.

"Jonas!"

He halted, and after a slight pause turned around.

Now was the time to ask him about something Ryan had told her last night as they danced around the room.

"I—last night at the party—" She saw his face take on that rigid look she was coming to know. "I spoke with Ryan Dennison. He says you two are acquainted."

"Yeah," he answered cautiously. "So?"

"He mentioned something about your having been on the police force at one time." She didn't tell him that his brother had already told her that, or what else his brother had hinted at.

"That was a long time ago." He turned to face the door again.

"He said you left the force because you—" She saw his shoulders stiffen. She wished he would turn around so that she could see his expression.

"He called you a hothead. What does that mean? What *did* happen to make you leave the force? And why did you never mention to me that you had been a cop?"

"That's none of your business." He shot her a dark glance over his shoulder, while a voice inside his head yelled, *Fool! Tell her! Now is the time to get it all out into the open. Ask her what she remembers about eight years ago. Get the past cleared up between you.*

But he couldn't. Things had changed between them, and his last nightmare was too fresh in his mind. He felt too guilty for wanting her, because she had been involved with Hank's murderer. And then there was her father's part in it all. He couldn't talk about it. He wanted to forget it. And right at this moment, he wished he could walk out her door and forget all about her, too.

"It has nothing to do with my life now, or finding your friend. So stay out of it—stay out of what doesn't concern you. My business is my own. You hired me to find Debra, that's all."

He was angry with her again. But she couldn't let it go. "Jonas, please..." She took a step in his direction, one hand held out to him, but he couldn't see it. "I'm not asking out of curiosity."

"No? Then why? So you can compare me to your boyfriend, this *Paul* character, and see if I measure up?"

"I wasn't—I would never compare you— What do you mean, *boyfriend?* You *did* follow me!"

She was so angry that she wanted to scream. She had wanted a sign from him that he cared for her, just a little one, but *this*...*!* It was too much like what her father had put her through all her life right up until his death.

What was happening to her? Why was everything going so wrong?

Before she could say anything else, and without commenting on her final accusation, Jonas strode through the door, slamming it behind him.

Lindsey dropped onto the sofa and stared at the closed door. Now what? Would he call and let her know what he discovered about the note? Or would he make her call him?

Debra, where are you? I need to talk to you. It seems like you've always been there whenever I needed you. I need you now—oh, God, please be safe.

Chapter 11

Jonas tapped on the window and motioned toward the lone occupant of the room, a short, round, Oriental man. Robert Chin pushed himself away from the table where he was examining something under a microscope and hurried to open the door, beaming.

"So, Jonas, it is good to see you again." They shook hands. "But what are you doing here? No, do not tell me." He held up one hand, and his grin widened. "You have a favor to ask."

Jonas grinned back and nodded. "You know me too well, Chin. I have something I want you to take a very close look at. Unfortunately, it's been handled by me and one other person that I know of. It's the people I don't know about that I'm interested in."

He withdrew a long white envelope from an inside pocket and held it out to the other man. Chin placed a pair of clear plastic gloves on his hands before accepting it and removed the folded note from inside.

After a slight pause while he read it, he said, "I have other work that I am doing for Captain Dillon, a rush job. It may be a little while before I can get to this."

"Dillon," Jonas repeated in a hard voice.

"Yes." Chin moved back to the work he'd been doing before Jonas arrived. "He was on the force when you were here."

Robert Chin and Jonas had been friends from Jonas's early days as a rookie; Hank had introduced them.

"Yeah," Jonas answered, "he was here. He's one of the reasons I quit."

Charles Dillon had been the newly appointed captain of the division in which Hank was already working when Jonas was assigned there. He hadn't liked either of the two men and had made that perfectly clear from the first. He had taken great pleasure in accepting Jonas's badge the day he'd handed it in, and made no attempt to mask it.

Jonas glanced around the room. He saw a newspaper lying faceup on a table across from where Chin was working, walked over and picked it up.

A face that had become too familiar in the past forty-eight hours stared up at him. He began reading the article about Paul Fillmore, recapping the dinner held at the mayor's home on Saturday evening in the man's honor.

"You know him?" Chin asked, glancing up after he had adjusted the microscope.

Jonas darted an inquiring glance in his friend's direction. "Do you?"

"He helped my grandson out of some trouble a few months back. That one—" he nodded toward the picture of Fillmore "—is a very good man."

Jonas barely withheld a snort of contempt. "Is he?" he asked skeptically. "What kind of hard facts do you know about the man?"

"You want to hear a brief biography?" Chin laughed, his brown eyes flashing.

He had a mind like a computer, and without trying picked up information and stored it in his memory. He had both interesting and valuable knowledge about most of the people he had worked with or met at one time or another in his life. Jonas had learned that early in their acquaintance and Chin had become used to Jonas picking his brain whenever the need arose.

"I'd be interested to hear what you know about him."

"I know he came from a poor section of the Bronx and was in trouble as a boy. His mother and father deserted him when he was young, and he learned to steal whatever he needed to stay alive.

"By the time he was a teenager he was the head of his own gang. Somehow he attracted the eye of a man who worked with delinquent teens in the neighborhood. This man managed to get him straightened out before he ended up in prison. He helped get him into college, and Fillmore worked his way through, earning a business degree.

"At some point along the way he discovered he was good at playing the stock market, and by the time he finished college he was set. The word I hear is that he was a millionaire before the age of twenty-five. And now he spends all his time and a lot of his money to help the people in his old neighborhood and around the city."

"Sounds like a real paragon," Jonas commented dryly. "He married?"

"No, he is a most eligible bachelor. Many women have been connected with his name in the last few years, some famous, some not so famous." Chin shrugged. "He is much liked by the ladies, but it seems he enjoys his bachelor status."

Jonas stared at the grainy photograph in his hand. His charm seemed to have worked its magic on Lindsey. But there was something—something he noticed about the eyes. A look that said, "Don't take me at face value, because if you think I'm a pushover, you're wrong."

"You said you've met this guy?" Jonas asked.

"Yes, and I like him." Chin hesitated before adding, "But I think he is not the easygoing man he appears to be on the surface."

Jonas tended to agree, wondering what it was about Fillmore that stuck in his craw. He dismissed the idea that it was nothing more than jealousy. There was something else, something that nagged at the back of his mind....

"Chin, I really need to be going. Why don't you give me a call when you find something out?"

"Is it permitted to inquire what this case is you're working on?"

"A missing person case, a young woman. It's all mixed up with a theft of some antiques." Jonas shook his head. "My brother is working on the case from the theft angle, and even the police are stumped. This one's a real puzzler, Chin." He stared down at the newspaper in his hand with unfocused eyes.

"It is more to you than just another case," Chin murmured with uncanny insight.

"It's...important to me for several reasons," Jonas answered after a moment.

The other man nodded thoughtfully. "I will see what I can learn about the paper as quickly as possible."

"Thanks."

At the door Jonas paused to ask, "Do you mind if I take the paper along? I want to finish reading this article?"

"Go ahead, I'm through with it." Jonas was out the door before he could add, "It isn't mine, anyway." As he watched Jonas disappear, he finished with a wide grin. "It belongs to Captain Dillon."

Jonas trudged up the stairs to his office, slapping the folded newspaper against the side of his leg. There was something about Fillmore, something he wished he could remember, and he would think of what it was or be damned.

"Well, it's about time." Brian stood up from the stair he was sitting on, dusted off his trousers and met his brother at the door to his office.

"What are you doing here?" Jonas asked as he fitted the key in the lock. "Don't you ever work?"

He pushed the door open and strode inside, unfastening his jacket as he went. He wasn't in the mood to deal with Brian this morning. What he needed was some time alone to think. Taking a seat behind the desk, he laid the newspaper face down and glanced up inquiringly.

"Well, what do you want, Bri?"

"I came to ask you to reconsider your refusal to help me—"

"I told you," he interrupted. "I'm already on the case."

"Yeah, I know that, but if you find the stuff, you'll find the woman."

Brian began pacing up and down in front of Jonas's desk like a caged lion walking the perimeter of his prison.

"What I don't understand—" he stopped to face the other man "—is why, after what you told me the other day about your past association with Lindsey and her father, why the hell you want to do anything to help her."

"I—" Jonas started to make the quick retort that he didn't want to help *her,* then realized that would have been a lie and changed it to, "I want to find Debra. She's the innocent victim here."

"Don't make me laugh," Brian muttered contemptuously. "Innocent is not a word I would use to describe that little—"

"Look, I have a lot to do this morning," Jonas interrupted again. "I can't help you other than by letting you know as quickly as possible if I find any evidence of the missing items you're looking for—*when I find Debra.*"

He wished now that he'd kept his mouth shut about the past and not told his brother about it.

Brian stared into his brother's eyes. "My God, she's gotten to you, too, hasn't she? It isn't Debra who has you so fired up about this case. It's Lindsey. You're caught in the same trap I got caught in, aren't you?"

Jonas held his brother's eyes as he rose slowly to his feet and, fists knotted at his sides, leaned toward him.

"I don't know what you're talking about. But I suggest that you keep everything I said to you in this room in the strictest confidence. Is that clear?" he asked threateningly.

After a moment of tense silence Brian laughed nervously, but there was no amusement in the sound, only a kind of false bravado. "I should be mad at you—mad as hell—since it's my woman you're trying to pinch."

"I wasn't aware that she was your woman," Jonas answered, his face stiff.

"Hey, listen, I'm not angry." Brian raised his hands. "So just back off, okay?"

Besides, he knew what Jonas didn't. Unless he missed his guess, Lindsey would soon be in complete touch with all the facts about what had gone on eight years ago, and then this would all be academic.

Jonas relaxed a bit, but maintained his grim exterior. He didn't want to fight with his brother. They'd never been close, but at least there hadn't been this open hostility between them.

"I think there's something you should know about the *lady* in question." Brian couldn't let things go so easily. "Saturday night we both attended a dinner given for a rich type who thinks he's some kind of savior for the poor. It made me sick to watch everyone fawning over the creep. Including Lindsey, I might add." He watched his brother's face closely. "She left with him, too."

"Thanks for the information." Jonas dismissed him, turning away. "I have a lot of work to do, and since it's a Monday morning, I'm sure you do, too."

"You won't change your mind?"

"No," Jonas answered curtly.

"I have some information on the search for the missing antiques," Brian told him quickly. "It seems not all the servants are on vacation. There are two who can't be accounted for just yet, but it looks like both of them are still in the city."

"Is that so?" Jonas asked with interest. He hadn't been pursuing this case from the theft angle. Perhaps it was time to look at things differently.

"If you think she's any different now than she was eight years ago, forget it," Brian blurted out abruptly. "And don't think I'm saying this because I mind you poaching on my preserves. I just think you should know she's every bit as self-centered and conniving—"

"That's enough!" Jonas barked, whirling to face him.

Brian gave a start at the sharp command in his brother's voice and stomped to the door. "You're going to be sorry you ever met that woman—wait and see." With that parting shot he left the room.

Jonas almost called him back. He was, after all, his brother, but that didn't excuse his recent behavior. Apparently it didn't matter to him that Debra could be dead, or dying. All that mattered to Brian was what affected Brian.

Jonas went to look out his window. This was the same spot in which he had been standing the day Lindsey had come to see him—sent by the man below, angrily nosing his Corvette into the heavy traffic.

Before that it had been almost eight years, he reflected, since he'd seen her. And both times she'd entered his life she had in some way changed him forever. Had they now come full circle?

Perhaps that was what life really was, a series of circles, a lot of little ones within a larger, greater one.

He and Lindsey had made contact for a brief period in the past, and as a result he'd become a man without a future, his dreams in ashes at his feet. But eventually he'd come out of that a stronger man and had found his real niche in life.

And now they had come together once again, but this time he knew he would never be the same if she left him as quickly, as easily as she had eight years ago. This time the changes she had wrought in him demanded that she stay.

He was slowly recovering from the past. Now all he needed to be able to do was to forgive his own part in it.

Maybe soon he would be able to look forward to the future—and Lindsey.

Except there was Paul Fillmore to consider. Was it already too late?

If that was the case, then he knew he had no one to blame but himself. No man can live in the past, and he'd had plenty of opportunity to discuss the past with her, but he'd refused to.

The telephone rang, jarring him from his introspection. Jonas grabbed it quickly.

"Hello?"

"Jonas? This is Chin. I can tell you a little about that note you left with me. But it will not, I am afraid, be of much help.

"The paper was torn from a spiral notepad, the kind you can buy at any store. The ink came from a cheap pen sold in the same places. No clear prints—nothing, so far, to give us a clue about the person who wrote it. There are still a few more tests I can run on it."

"Thanks, Chin, I'd be grateful. Listen, about that guy Fillmore, you happen to know where he lives?"

"He has a very beautiful estate outside the city. It takes about an hour and a half to drive there. My grandson visited there with some other boys not long ago. To hear him tell it, the floors and walls were lined with gold.

"Apparently Mr. Fillmore collects paintings, and some of the rooms were decorated with expensive antiques. My grandson was shocked at the fact that furniture could be worth so much money. I believe his words were something to the effect that a guy could make a 'real haul' by cleaning out one room of Mr. Fillmore's home."

Jonas stood a little straighter, clasped the phone a little tighter. "Fillmore collects antiques? That's interesting," he muttered. "Very interesting. Can you give me that address?" he asked, reaching for a pencil and drawing a pad of paper across the desk toward him.

A few moments later Jonas grabbed his coat and shrugged into it. Paul Fillmore collected antiques, and he had spent considerable time with Lindsey at the party Saturday night. And with his own eyes Jonas had seen the man going into her apartment.

There was no question but that he had had the opportunity to place the note in Lindsey's purse without her observing it. But had he?

And why? Why would a man like Paul Fillmore resort to theft? He had more than enough money to buy whatever he wanted. And it seemed inconceivable that he would be a party to kidnapping—unless it was to cover up other nefarious activities, like collecting antique snuff boxes through theft?

As Jonas shoved the piece of paper with the Fillmore address into the pocket of his jeans, the phone rang. He hesitated, but slammed out of the office without stopping to answer it.

Lindsey listened to the phone ring six, seven, eight times. Jonas wasn't in his office, and he wasn't at home. She replaced the phone and sat with her cheek braced against her hand. Where was he?

What with her worry about Debra and the situation with Jonas, she had found it difficult to come up with a reason why she should get out of bed and face the world this morning.

And that was a first for her. Her work had filled her life for so long that nothing else, with the exception of her friendship with Debra, had been allowed to interfere.

Now, all at once, she found herself dissatisfied with everything about her life, her work, the places she went, the people she knew, even the clothes she wore and the style of her hair.

Her problems, she knew, all stemmed from the fact that she had never been allowed to be herself. Instead she'd always been an extension of her father. And Jonas had made her aware of that fact.

She was hardly what you would call deprived. She wore expensive makeup, had her hair done in one of the best salons and dressed impeccably. But she had never bought an outfit with the express purpose of attracting a man. She wouldn't know how. She didn't know what attracted men, outside of the obvious, of course.

But now she wanted to attract Jonas. For the first time in her life she wanted to be thought of as a woman, an attractive, desirable woman.

A warning buzzer somewhere in the back of her mind reminded her of the disaster she had precipitated the last time she'd given in to a desire to kick off the restraints imposed by her father and change her way of life.

But she ignored it. She wanted Jonas, wanted to know what it would be like to have someone to depend upon, and not always have to rely on herself. Wanted to know the contentment of falling asleep in his warm embrace every night and awakening each morning to the sight of his turquoise eyes and melting smile.

Lindsey glanced at the picture of the smiling, middle-aged woman on her desk. Her mother had understood how hard it was for her to stand up against her father. She had acted as a buffer between them. Perhaps if she hadn't died when she had, none of what followed shortly thereafter would have occurred.

The intercom buzzed, and she answered it reluctantly.

"Lindsey, the mayor and his wife are here to see you," Pam told her. "May I show them in?"

"Of course," she answered, standing and moving eagerly toward the door. They were just the couple who could cheer her up, if anyone could. And besides, there were a few questions she wanted to ask Ryan about Jonas, if she didn't lose her nerve first.

"Well, how do you like the food?" Ryan prodded.

Lindsey glanced up from her linguine in clam sauce and smiled. "You know I adore Italian food. And this is some of the best I've ever eaten."

She had been waiting for the opportunity to broach the subject of Jonas, but so far it hadn't appeared and lunch was nearing its end.

"Oh, no!" Madge's cry of horror drew all their eyes. She glanced down at the nickel-sized stain on the front of her dress. "I swear I'm getting clumsier every day." She folded her napkin and placed it on the table. "I'm off to the ladies' room."

Lindsey waited a moment after Madge had left the table before asking abruptly, "Ryan, do you know what made Jonas Kingston leave the police force?"

Ryan took a sip of wine, his eyes on her face, before answering. "So it's the brother you're interested in. I wondered what happened between you and Brian."

"I—"

"It's all right. I've known them both for a number of years, and Jonas is a fine man."

"You keep in touch with him?"

"Not often, and not personally for a while now, but I keep track of what he's up to."

"Did you know him when he was on the police force?"

Ryan eyed her closely. "I knew him then." There was a look in his faded blue eyes that she couldn't quite decipher.

"Well," she began impatiently, darting a glance toward the ladies' room, "are you going to tell me why he left the force or not?"

"Why do you want to know? Why now? How did you come to meet Jonas, anyway?"

"Debra is gone—missing. I can't find her."

"Missing!" Ryan repeated. "Since when? Why haven't you told me before now? I'll get the best men on the force onto it immediately."

"No, please." She touched his hand lightly. "Jonas is looking for her."

"Jonas, huh?" he asked thoughtfully. "He's been pretty successful—at least, as successful as he appears to want to be—since he went private. But I still don't see why you didn't contact me immediately when you discovered your friend was missing.''

"I know, Ryan, I know," she answered softly. "But I needed to do this on my own, without asking for favors." She didn't want to hurt his feelings, but she hoped he would understand that she couldn't be like her father, demanding everything as her due, especially favors from her friends.

Ryan understood, all right, and it made him love her even more. "I understand, my dear." He lifted her hand and patted it fondly. "Now, what is this about Jonas?"

"Something Brian alluded to, something that's been bothering me." She fiddled with her wineglass. "I don't know what to believe."

"But you *do* want to believe in Jonas?"

She met his eyes before replying softly, "Oh, yes."

"I suppose I should be surprised by your question, but I'm not. For a long time now I've wondered if you had any knowledge of, or any real part in, what happened eight years ago. And your question about Jonas proves to me that you didn't."

"I don't understand...." Lindsey frowned.

"Honey." He leaned forward and covered her hand lying on the table. "How much of what happened that summer when you were twenty do you remember?"

Lindsey drew her hand back immediately, her face going as pale as the white silk blouse she wore. "Why do you ask that?" she asked in a strangled whisper.

"Because I already know all about what took place—the parties, the drugs, the murder."

"No." Lindsey denied his words. "You can't...."

"Your father told me—"

"What did he tell you? That I was on drugs? Ryan, I thought you knew me better than that." There was no denying the deep hurt in her cloudy green eyes. "I was never on drugs. I admit to attending the parties, acting wild and being a poor judge of character in choosing my friends. But I was never on drugs," she insisted.

The older man sat watching her, knowing she was being sincere, and he wanted to kill the man who had been her father and his best friend for over forty years.

"So Horace lied to me, too," he muttered without surprise.

"What do you mean?"

"Honey, do you remember the night you—the night that man broke into your apartment and tried to . . . kill you?"

"Derek," she whispered so low he almost didn't hear. Her eyes were on her fingers twisted in the napkin on her lap. "Yes—or at least part of it. I remember him arriving at the apartment, threatening me with a knife, hitting me. She bit her lip to stop its trembling, glanced up at his face, then away. The memory was one that had caused her untold nightmares since that night. In her dreams Derek came after her, night after night.

"Do you remember regaining consciousness in the arms of a young policeman?" He watched her face keenly.

"No. . . ." She shook her head. "I don't remember much of anything at all about the time following Derek's forcing his way into my apartment."

She hesitated. "Well, some things, like the plane trip with father to Switzerland, but mostly it's blurry. The doctors said it was my way of shutting it all out, some kind of defense mechanism.

"And for a long time, that was exactly what I wanted to do—forget. Later, when I spoke with my father about it, he said it was best put behind me. He said he had taken care of everything."

"Did he say how he'd done that?" Ryan asked sharply.

"No."

"And you remember nothing about the policeman who was killed that night?"

"K-killed?" she repeated in a strangled voice.

"Yes." There was no way to soften the facts.

"Oh, my God," she whispered, her eyes wide with horror. "I have to get out of here."

Jumping to her feet in a panic, she rushed blindly from the table, knocking against other diners and their tables but not stopping.

"Lindsey, wait!" Ryan shouted, but she didn't hear, or else pretended not to. He glanced back over his shoulder, looking for his wife. Madge was on her way back to the table and saw Lindsey's precipitate flight.

"What happened?" she asked immediately, her eyes following Lindsey's path.

"I'll tell you later. Be a darling and take care of the bill. I have to find Lindsey."

Ryan quickly made his way outside. On the street, he glanced up and down, finally spotting her leaning against a building a little way off. He hurried toward her and wrapped her in his suit jacket.

"Come on, sweetheart, we have some talking to do."

Ryan led her to his car, knowing Madge would call herself a cab. They drove for a while without speaking until finally, on a tree-lined street in a quiet section of Manhattan, Ryan drew up to the curb and stopped.

"I think it's time you got the whole thing out into the open, so you can start to let it all go," he said in a gruff tone. He wished he could protect her from the past, but, unlike her father, he knew it had to be with truth, not lies.

After a while Lindsey began to speak.

"The summer I was twenty, just a few months after Mother died, Debra decided she needed some time alone. She went to Europe for three months and I . . . went wild. There was no one for me to talk to. Mother was gone, Debra was away. Father and I were left all alone in that great big house." She paused, swallowed tightly, her eyes burning at the memory of how alone she had felt.

"I had never been one of the 'in crowd,' never run with the rich younger generation, mostly because Father kept me on a very short leash." She licked dry lips and tucked a strand of hair behind her ear. She was coming to the part in her story that shamed her. "But that summer was different. That summer I felt—I felt as though I was smothering, as though I couldn't breathe, after a few minutes alone in Father's company.

"So I began to make excuses, at first, to keep away from him. Then, after a few weeks, I simply waited until he was gone one day and moved out and into an apartment of my own without his knowing about it.

"You see," she said, glancing at Ryan and then quickly away again, "I had met a man. Derek. I thought he loved me, that he cared about me as a person—what I liked, what I cared about, what I needed."

She shook her head. "I was the classic, poor little rich girl, being played for a fool. And Derek knew just how to feed my insecurities. He was an expert at it.

"But what I didn't know was that he didn't want to marry me for my money or anything like that. He only wanted to be seen with me, to be accepted by the others, so he could make money off the crowd.

"I didn't know it at the time, but he was supplying them with drugs. Oh, I knew they were using and I did nothing about it, but I didn't know Derek was their supplier, and I didn't use drugs myself.

"Not that he didn't try to get me hooked. That was when I discovered his real purpose in getting to know me. And that was when I finally woke up from my fairy-tale existence and told him to get out and never come back.

"He was so angry." She caught her breath at the memory. She had been certain at the time that he intended to kill her, but someone had arrived and interrupted him. She was hosting a party—one of the endless parties she had given and attended that summer—and he left.

"Two days later he came to my apartment and forced his way in. I—" Hot tears began to crowd her eyes and spill over onto her cheeks. She wiped them away with the backs of her hands. "I don't want to remember."

"I understand, honey." Ryan pulled her into his arms. "But it's best to remember and be free of the nightmare."

"All right. I'll try to tell it exactly as I remember it. It was late. I was in bed when he rang my buzzer. I wasn't asleep, so I got up. I should have used the peephole, but I didn't. When I saw who it was, I tried to push him out. He slammed the door back against me, knocking me to the floor, and then he was on top of me. He screamed at me—I guess he used his own stuff, because his eyes looked awful, and I knew he was going to kill me.

"He began to hit me. He knocked me out, and then I remember lying on my bed. There was a sharp pain in my arm. He had a needle, and he was laughing...."

There was silence in the car for a long while until she'd pulled herself together. And when she had, she turned to Ryan, and asked, "What does all this have to do with Jonas?"

"He was one of the two policemen who responded to a report of a disturbance in your building. His best friend and partner, Hank Wilson, was killed."

"By whom?" she asked through stiff lips. Could she have done something so horrible under the influence of drugs?

"Derek."

"Oh, God." It hadn't been her.

"But, Lindsey." Ryan took hold of her shoulders. "Listen to me. Your father did something almost as bad. He used his money and influence to get charges trumped up against Jonas, some of those being a question of who had actually...mistreated you and what had happened to the drugs they found that night in your apartment. It seems they disappeared."

"What?"

"It's true. He wanted your name dismissed from the case, as though you had never been on the scene. Jonas refused. He'd lost a partner, and he was afraid his friend's killer would go scot-free. And for all he knew, you were a part of the whole thing. You were high on drugs when he found you."

"But what happened?"

"Your father won. There were papers, signed by you, attesting to the fact that it was Jonas who had...slapped you around. It was a lie, we all knew it, but there was a new captain at headquarters, a man who owed your father a favor. He didn't like Jonas, and he said he'd see that Jonas went all the way up the river if he didn't back off.

"So Jonas gave in. He never really had a choice. Horace would have ruined him."

"But where was I? I don't remember signing any papers."

"Your father pleaded with the judge, said you'd had a nervous breakdown brought on by your mother's recent death and the unfortunate circumstances of this ... episode in your life. He said your mental instability had forced him to remove you from these surroundings and put you in a private sanatorium out of the country."

"He didn't—" she protested, not wanting to believe her father capable of such duplicity, but knowing it was true. It had to be, otherwise she would have a memory of what had occurred. Her own father had kept her drugged so she couldn't testify to what had really happened that night—what little knowledge she had of it.

"And was Derek found guilty?"

"No, he got off on a technicality."

"But I learned he was dead," she protested.

"He died later at the hands of his own people, for trying to steal from them."

"And Jonas? What happened to him?"

"He quit, just walked in the day after Derek Lassiter was released and handed in his badge. He could have stayed. When he finally agreed to stop pressuring to have your name added to the reports of that night, the threats made against him—and all the 'manufactured' charges—were dropped. But he refused to work for a system that was, in his mind, corrupt.

"No one heard from him for a while. He hit bottom for a while, but he came back and began working as a private detective."

"Poor Jonas," she muttered softly. "He must have been so hurt, so angry. He must have hated me." Her eyes shot to Ryan's face. "Does he know who I am? Does he realize I'm responsible for his friend's death?"

"How can you say that?" Ryan protested. "It was Derek, not you, who killed Hank that night. Hank followed Derek into Central Park."

"But, Ryan, Jonas must hate me! He can't have realized who I really am or he wouldn't have—" She broke off.

Would Jonas have made love to her, knowing her true identity? No, her heart cried, but her mind asked, would he?

Could he hate her so much, after all this time, that even though he hadn't sought her out, if she fell like a ripe plum into his lap, would he use the opportunity to get back at her?

Would he have made love to her, made her fall in love with him, purely for revenge?

Chapter 12

The drive to Paul Fillmore's home was both uncomfortable and time-consuming. The roads were clear of ice and snow, but traffic was heavy and road work caused additional delays. And Jonas's faithful heater gave up the ghost less than ten minutes outside the city.

It was one o'clock in the afternoon by the time he reached the Fillmore estate. Stone pillars faced the road. On either side a solid concrete wall rose at least eight feet high. It would be impossible to get even a glimpse of the house beyond its perimeter.

In any case, the house appeared to be set far back from the road; there wasn't a sign of it from what he could see. The tree-lined driveway leading to it curved away from the front gate, disappearing from sight.

There was only one thing for it: he would have to find a place to stash his car and walk the wall, looking for a way inside. He'd taken time to stop and gather a bit of information about the estate before leaving the city and knew it covered one hundred acres. That was a lot of walking.

He drove down the road about a quarter of a mile until he came to a dirt road, then turned onto it and found a spot where he could park among the trees and bushes. Even though the branches were stark and bare at the moment, there was enough cover to keep his car hidden from view should someone happen along.

After hanging a pair of binoculars around his neck and stuffing a spotting scope inside his jacket, Jonas began the trek through the underbrush and dead leaves in the direction of the Fillmore estate.

It took him just under an hour to hike through the skeletal trees to the wall enclosing Fillmore's house and grounds.

Jonas spent a few minutes looking for security devices like wires or electronic eyes, but he couldn't see any. He looked around and spotted some tall old sycamores and an elm close by. The elm looked to be about sixty or seventy feet tall. It was his best bet because the branches were wide enough to support his weight, and one even extended close to the top of the wall.

Fortunately, he was in pretty good shape, but he still found himself out of breath by the time he reached the strategically placed limb. He'd been fortunate in his choice; he could get a perfect shot of the house from his perch.

He could be in for a long wait. He wasn't even certain of what—if anything—he might find. He was only here on a hunch, nothing more. But all the facts seemed to fit together like the pieces of a puzzle to form one final picture: Paul Fillmore as a thief and kidnapper.

Fillmore had the means and opportunity. He traveled in the right circles to gain access to the victim's home, and it was likely he would have seen the items on display there. He'd also had the opportunity to place that note in Lindsey's handbag. All that was missing was a motive. Jonas hadn't come up with that as of yet, but he was working on it.

And then, of course, there was the matter of the description of the man at the pharmacy to consider. From what

Jonas had seen of him, as he entered Lindsey's elevator and from the newspaper picture, Fillmore was a good match.

If only he could get inside the house, have an opportunity to look around for himself. But he wasn't fooling himself. Just because he saw no signs of surveillance equipment, that didn't mean it wasn't there. He probably wouldn't get a yard inside the wall before he was surrounded by armed guards.

With the binoculars, he scanned the house. It was quite a place. The house was brick, with columns supporting a large front portico. At one side he could see a large greenhouse. And at the other end was a six-car garage.

A long black limousine was parked in the driveway just beyond one of the garage doors. The door next to that was open, and Jonas trained his binoculars on it. A metallic-blue Jaguar, exactly like the car he'd seen on Saturday, was parked inside.

Another building, which looked like a small château, was visible behind and to one side of the garage. Jonas figured it must be the servants' quarters.

Lucky servants, he was thinking, when he realized with a small shock that this was the kind of life-style Lindsey was used to. Suddenly the distance between them seemed much greater than it ever had before.

He would never be able to provide her with a life like this. And he had no intention of ever becoming a kept man. And that left them exactly where?

Jonas shoved the disquieting thought from his mind and continued to scan the area. There was an outdoor pool behind the house. In front, a circular driveway marked the end of the road that led in from the front gate. An elaborate fountain, surrounded by hedges and rosebushes, rested in the center of the circular driveway.

Movement drew his wandering attention directly to the side door of the house—the servants' entrance, he figured. A small, dark-skinned woman was leaving the house. She raised the third door on the garage and entered, and a few minutes later a cream-colored station wagon headed smoothly down the driveway to the gate, turning east on the main road.

The woman, he knew from the research he'd done before leaving the city, was Lucia Sirritis, Fillmore's housekeeper and cook. She and her husband, Miklos, ran the place; the only other servant in residence was a man named Nickolas Gianni, Fillmore's chauffeur.

Maybe he should follow the woman. No doubt she was going shopping, and this late in the day she could only be going to one of the two places that were located close by.

The thing was, by the time he got out of the tree and hiked back to his car, then drove to the first store, if he was wrong...

He looked back at the empty face of the house. It looked quiet, almost deserted. His decision was made. He would follow Lucia and see if he could perhaps buy a little information on Fillmore and any recent additions to his household.

Three hours later Jonas was back on his lofty perch, the infrared spotting scope to his eyes. His trip to town had been a real bust. Fillmore engendered a fierce loyalty in his household staff.

Lucia Sirritis had refused to allow herself to be either sweet-talked or bribed into disclosing anything about her employer. She had refused point-blank to have anything at all to do with him.

The only thing the little excursion had accomplished had been in allowing him to make a quick trip to the men's room. He'd also purchased a cup of hot coffee and given his tailbone a bit of a rest. Now, sipping the coffee, he looked up at the dark sky. It was only a little past six, and it was as black as pitch.

At a little after eight the station wagon made its way back up the road and stopped by the side door. The horn honked, and in a moment a small man, no taller than five foot two at the most, probably Miklos, the husband, hurried outside to assist Lucia. The woman left him to it and hurried inside the warm interior of the house.

When the car was empty, the man drove it into the garage and hurried into the house. Two down and one to go. He still hadn't caught a glimpse of the elusive chauffeur. Once he had, then he could leave the tree and get on with whatever he needed to do.

He'd just placed the scope to his eye, coffee in the other hand, when all at once the side door opened and a tall man, dressed in a black chauffeur's uniform, stepped into view.

Jonas caught his breath, then whispered explosively, "Bingo!"

The chauffeur limped hurriedly toward the waiting limousine, but before he could reach it the side door opened a second time and Paul Fillmore appeared. He headed swiftly toward the other man, agitation in every line of his lean body.

They conversed for a few minutes, the conversation obviously not to either man's liking. Then the chauffeur pivoted awkwardly on his heel, climbed into the limo and, tires squealing, raced down the driveway toward the main gate.

Fillmore stood looking after the black monster of a car, his hands on his hips, a worried frown on his face. He turned to look around him, and Jonas felt a slight shock. With the scope to his eye, it appeared as though Fillmore was looking directly at him.

After a moment Fillmore turned and went back inside. Jonas stared at the empty driveway. What had that been all about?

With a sudden flash of insight, he remembered the way the woman had hurried inside a few minutes earlier, when she'd returned from town—where she'd been approached by him.

All at once a series of questions began to pop into his mind. What if the whole thing was a setup? What if that conversation in the restaurant had been purposely staged so that Lindsey and her friend would overhear it? What if the kidnapping was the real purpose, in order to get Lindsey's attention?

No, that was crazy. Why would they want Lindsey's attention? To kidnap her, too? Or was it Lindsey they'd been after all along, and not her friend?

What if Brian was right? What if Debra wasn't the innocent victim she appeared to be? What if she was a part of it?

And where had the man in black taken off for in such a tearing hurry? Jonas's heart began to race as the questions crowded into his brain. He had to get back to town.

An inner sense was telling him that Lindsey was next on Fillmore's list of items to be filched.

And nothing else mattered but that he reach her in time.

By the time he reached the car, he'd calmed down a bit and was telling himself he was a fool and Lindsey was in no danger. Fillmore was a millionaire. He didn't need to kidnap people or steal antiques. The whole idea was ridiculous, unreal, as unreal as two women overhearing plans for a heist in a restaurant and one of them subsequently turning up missing.

No, he had to think calmly and rationally about this. He would simply go to Lindsey's apartment, tell her what he'd learned, lay it all out for her and see what she made of it.

Like hell! Fillmore was in this up to his eyebrows; he would stake his life on it—*or Lindsey's life?* Jonas rounded a curve doing sixty and pushed his foot to the floor. The man was guilty, but he wouldn't get Lindsey, not if Jonas got to her first—and he would. *He had to....*

Once he reached her and saw that she was safe then he would convince her of Fillmore's involvement. Together they should be able to figure a way to get inside the man's house and look for Debra.

Sensible thoughts, but all the same, his foot pushed down hard on the accelerator as he pulled onto the interstate and headed back toward the city.

Lindsey put down her pen and looked around her office. It was time to go home. She'd returned from her talk with Ryan with every intention of telling Pam to clear her calendar for the rest of the day, then leaving. She intended to take her courage in hand and corner Jonas, then question him about whether he knew who she was.

She had known she couldn't go through the rest of the day or the long, sleepless hours of the night wondering if he hated her. Wondering if his time with her had been devoted to the specific purpose of getting revenge for the death of his friend all those years ago, and for his own disgrace.

But common sense had prevailed, along with the fear of what his answer might be if she confronted him face-to-face, so she had called instead. And though she'd called every few minutes for the rest of the day, it was now almost ten o'clock at night and there was still no answer, at his office or his apartment.

Now it was time to leave; everyone else in the office had gone home a long time ago, but still she hesitated.

The long night was still ahead of her. She couldn't face it, not with so many unanswered questions on her mind, and not while she suspected Jonas of deceiving her for his own purposes.

Slipping into her coat, she made up her mind. She would go to his apartment and wait. She'd driven herself that morning, so she didn't have to worry about getting home or keeping Mac out to all hours of the night. She would wait— all night, if need be—for Jonas to come home.

She took the elevator to the first floor, waved goodbye to the security guard already on duty, and headed out to the garage. Unlike many people, she was unafraid to enter the parking garage alone. Keys in her hand, she descended the steps and made her way across the concrete floor, her heels clicking softly, then saw a long black limo parked near the exit ramp.

What was Mac doing here? She moved quickly toward the limo. Perhaps something was wrong! Perhaps Debra...

The thought was never finished. She was caught from behind, and something dark was thrown over her head. Then she was held against a hard chest, her arms pinned behind her, and walked slowly around the car to the other side.

At first, in a panic, she couldn't breathe for the covering over her face. And then she realized it was nothing more than a bit of silk, a scarf, perhaps. She struggled violently, twisting and turning, trying to get loose from her attacker's grip.

His touch was firm, but not rough, as he held her braced against the side of the car, wedged between his rock-hard body and the vehicle. Then, with another piece of what felt like the same material covering her face, he fastened her hands behind her back.

Lindsey tried to scream, but the sound only came out as a muffled grunt, so she used her feet and tried to kick him. She made contact at least once and had the satisfaction of hearing him grunt with pain before he managed to move out of range.

When her hands were secured to his satisfaction, he tied the scarf over her face and shoved her onto the front passenger seat. She could sense him next to her as he climbed in on the other side and started the engine.

He hadn't said a word during the whole of the proceedings. He had worked silently and efficiently, and it was that fact, more than anything else, that truly frightened her.

Her first thought had been of robbery, but now she suspected this was something else. All at once she became aware of the smell of smoke—cigar smoke—and she was reminded of the man she'd seen at Debra's apartment.

Would she soon be in her friend's presence? How strange. She and Jonas had been looking for Debra for days with no luck. And now here she was, she suspected, being taken to wherever her friend was being held.

She refused to think about what would happen to them once they were reunited—in the hands of their kidnappers.

Jonas drove faster than the law allowed and managed to cut a good chunk off the time it had taken him to reach the Fillmore mansion, but six blocks from Lindsey's apartment building he was pulled over by a traffic cop for running a red light.

He wanted to argue that the light had been yellow when he started across, but he knew that would only delay things, and he had to make certain Lindsey was all right.

The drive had given him time to think, and he had concluded that maybe Fillmore, with his street background, simply liked taking what wasn't his. Maybe he was the kind of man who got his kicks that way, even though he could buy whatever he wanted.

The police officer handed Jonas back his license, had him sign the ticket, tore it off and handed it to him. "Drive more carefully in future, sir. And have a good evening."

Jonas muttered, "Right," wadded the ticket up and stuffed it into his glove compartment.

Five minutes later he sped down the underground parking ramp and stopped by Lindsey's private elevator. As he fished his key out of his pocket, he noticed that Lindsey's car wasn't in its usual spot and wondered if she was out.

He almost ran from the elevator to pound on her door and ring the doorbell. After a few minutes, he was convinced she wasn't home.

The next best place to look for her was her office. He knew that sometimes she worked quite late. All during the drive there, he kept seeing the limo pulling hurriedly down the driveway of Fillmore's estate. Where had the chauffeur been off to in such a hurry?

Jonas drove down the twisting ramp to the parking area below the building. Right away he spotted Lindsey's car. With a feeling of deep relief, he realized she was still there.

He parked beside her car, climbed out and strode toward the back elevator entrance. Before he'd gone two steps, his foot came down on something hard. He stopped, looked at what he'd stepped on and bent over to pick it up.

A guard walked over just as Jonas was straightening up.

"Evening, sir. Can I help you?" the guard asked, barring entrance to the building.

"I'm looking for Miss Hamilton," Jonas replied.

"She's left for the evening, sir."

"Then what is her car doing here?"

The guard looked at the car and frowned. "I don't know, sir, I saw her leave the building a little while ago. Perhaps someone picked her up. Miss Hamilton has left her car here overnight before."

"You see anyone come for her?" Jonas asked sharply.

The other man shook his graying head. "No, sir, I didn't."

Jonas felt his hackles rise. "You mind if I take a look at Miss Hamilton's car?" he asked, already walking toward it without waiting for the other man's answers.

The guard followed him, and they both tried the doors. They were locked. Jonas glanced down at the object he'd picked up: a key ring with a large, colorful butterfly. He felt the world tremble beneath his feet. He tried one of the keys and, as he'd known it would, it fitted perfectly.

He was too late! They had gotten to her first. Lindsey was no doubt Paul Fillmore's prisoner at this very moment. He raced to his car, climbed inside and burned rubber on his way out.

It was almost midnight when Jonas found himself at the same spot where he'd caught his first glimpse of the dark man with the limp earlier that day. His only concern was for how to get inside the estate grounds without alerting anyone. There were no obvious guards, and no evidence that Fillmore employed guard dogs to patrol the grounds after dark.

If he could only be as certain that there weren't electrical sensors on the wall, or a laser alarm system. He knew there was only one way to find out.

He picked up a stick and waved it in the air a couple of feet from the wall. Nothing happened. So he stepped closer and touched the concrete wall with it, running it up and down the hard, uneven surface. And still there was no reaction. Dropping the stick, he climbed the tree he'd sat perched in for so long that day, climbed out on the branch near the wall and dropped softly to the ground below.

Something should have warned him that this was too easy. He hadn't taken more than five steps before he was surprised by two men carrying rifles. One of them had a limp.

Jonas did the only sensible thing under the circumstances and raised his arms.

Chapter 13

Still blindfolded, her hands fastened behind her back, Lindsey felt the car come to a halt. The ride had been long, and even though she was confident she would soon be seeing Debra, anxiety for their safety had filled her mind.

By the time her kidnapper led her from the car, her feet and legs had gone to sleep. For a moment she could hardly stand. He supported her, waiting patiently until she could walk before leading her up one step and through a door into a warm building. After a few moments the hand beneath her arm tightened, and she was brought up short. She heard a door being opened, and then she was pushed gently forward. The door closed behind, leaving her in the room, her face still covered and her hands tied behind her back.

What now? And where was Debra? A finger of fear trailed down her spine. Had she been wrong then in thinking this kidnapping had anything to do with her friend?

"I'm sorry about all this, Lin. If you'll turn around, I'll unfasten your hands."

Cool fingers moved against her skin, and in a moment she was free. But before she could raise her hands to the back of her head, those same fingers had deftly unknotted and removed the silk scarf from her face.

Lindsey turned slowly. "Debra—Debra! I'm so glad to see you safe and sound!" She grabbed her friend and hugged her tightly, then pushed her away to ask, "You *are* safe and sound, aren't you?"

Debra grinned and nodded, her own arms clutching Lindsey.

Lindsey couldn't speak again right away, because her throat was clogged with tears. She simply pulled Debra against her and silently held her close.

After a long moment they drew back, laughing and crying, gripping each other's hands.

"My God, I've been so worried," Lindsey said. Pulling a hand free, she wiped at her eyes. "I can't believe I'm here with you so suddenly after all this time, that you're here—" She broke off, then whispered, "Everything *is* all right, isn't it? I mean, why am I here? Why are you here? What's going on?"

All at once she sensed something in the atmosphere. Her friend was glad to see her, there was no doubting that, but she was different, and there was something about her eyes…

"Come on," Debra said, taking her hand and giving it a squeeze as she led her to a comfortable sofa. "Come sit beside me—" she patted the thick cushion "—and let me look at you. We have so much to catch up on."

Lindsey looked around at the book-lined walls, the marble fireplace, heavy oak desk and dark oak chair.

"Where are we, Deb? Whose house is this? And why are we here? What's going on?"

Debra was pouring coffee from a silver server on a low table and took her time before speaking.

"Wouldn't you like to hear what happened after you left the restaurant three weeks ago?" she asked by way of an answer.

Lindsey accepted a cup of coffee and took a sip. "Yes, of course I would."

Debra sat back against the cushions, curling her legs beneath her, and began to speak.

"After you'd gone, I looked for the men who'd been seated behind us. I know," she said, forestalling Lindsey's words about what a foolish thing she'd done, and continued. "I was all prepared to make up some excuse, but the table was empty.

"I was about to turn away when this man stepped up behind me." She put a hand to her throat in remembered fear. "I thought I'd had it, but he only reached around me and placed a tip on the table where he and his friend had been sitting earlier. He started to turn away without speaking, but I stopped him. I asked him if he was an actor—"

"Debra," Lindsey gasped, "you didn't."

"Yes." She grinned, her blue eyes sparkling with mischief in an expression Lindsey recognized. "I did. It was the only thing I could think of. He looked at me as though I'd crawled out of the woodwork and said, no, he sure as hell wasn't.

"So I asked, 'Then that wasn't a play you and your friend were rehearsing—'"

"Debra!" Lindsey breathed, aghast at her friend's temerity. "How could you let him know what you'd heard?"

Her friend shrugged, took a sip of her coffee and smiled. "What could he do to me in a restaurant full of people? Shoot me?"

"I don't know." Lindsey put her cup and saucer on the serving tray. "But how could you take such a risk?"

"I need to take a few risks, Lin. I've lived my whole life being careful." Debra put her own cup and saucer down beside Lindsey's and stood. "I don't want to live like that anymore."

"What happened then—with the man?" Lindsey prodded gently, wondering what had brought about her friend's sudden dissatisfaction with her life.

Debra had always been so cheerful. Lindsey had never suspected that the other woman felt this way. True, she was forever looking for excitement, but, Lindsey realized all at once, she had never really followed through and chased after it—before now.

Debra's voice drifted through Lindsey's introspection. "The guy looked at me for a moment with a blank expression, and then he grinned. He asked did I mean that bit about the theft, and I nodded. He said it had all been a joke, one he and his friend were planning to play on another friend. And that's all there was to it."

Debra turned and met Lindsey's glance. "You know what? I believed him. You were right when you said the whole thing sounded too fantastic to be real. So when he told me that—" she shrugged "—I believed it."

"And?" Lindsey asked, watching her friend's expression closely.

"I ended up as a guest here." Debra stood up and gestured at her luxurious surroundings. "Not bad, huh?"

"But what about the theft?" Lindsey climbed to her feet and moved to join the other woman. "Was—is the man a thief? He's certainly a kidnapper."

"Don't be so judgmental," Debra insisted sharply.

"Judgmental! Debra, I thought you were kidnapped. I certainly was. That isn't being judgmental—that's a fact!"

She was confused by Debra's attitude, and getting worried again. What made her friend so reluctant to face the real facts of their situation?

And what exactly *were* the facts of their situation? Debra certainly didn't seem upset at being here. If anything, she seemed happy.

Debra took Lindsey by the shoulders. "Look at me. Do I look as though I've been mistreated in any way?" She swept a hand around her. "Take a look at this room. Does it look like a prison cell?"

"But you do want to go home, don't you?" Lindsey asked in rough tones.

"I don't know," Debra answered honestly. And then, all at once, a secret smile turned up the corners of her wide mouth. "I have everything I want right here."

"I don't believe this." Lindsey pulled away from her friend in exasperation and paced the floor. Debra was different. And the difference continued to confuse Lindsey. What had caused the change?

"Debra, who owns this house?"

Before the other woman could answer, the door across the room was thrust suddenly open and a disheveled figure stumbled across the threshold and into the room. Both women turned abruptly, but it was Lindsey who found herself pinned by a pair of astonishingly beautiful turquoise eyes.

Forgetting her dignity, forgetting the half-truths that stood between them, she hurtled across the room, the cry, "Jonas!" bursting from her lips.

Jonas's arms closed strongly around her, and he held her pinned tightly to his chest. He bent his head and, eyes closed, rested his cheek against her soft hair. She was here, and she was safe.

He hadn't noticed that the room had another occupant. But as he opened his eyes and looked up, their glances met, and something of how they both felt about the woman in his embrace passed between them. He knew instantly who she was, and that they were going to be friends.

Lindsey didn't want to release her hold on Jonas's waist, but when he took her by the shoulders and drew back, she didn't resist. Their eyes locked, and she could feel all the words that remained unspoken between them in that glance.

"I don't want to sound nosy," Debra said from somewhere behind her, "but could I please be introduced?"

Lindsey moved to one side of Jonas, keeping a hand on his arm, and introduced the two.

"Debra Foley, this is Jonas..." She hesitated slightly before saying his last name. Debra would undoubtedly recognize it as Brian's, and she wondered what her friend would make of the way she had greeted him. "Kingston," she finished, her eyes on her friend's face.

"Jonas—Kingston?" Debra repeated with a slight questioning glance thrown at her best friend's face. "You have no idea how glad I am to meet you," she said with a smile.

"Jonas is a private detective. He's the man I hired to find you."

"Is he?" Debra asked softly, giving her friend a secret smile that asked, "And what else is he to you?" Stepping up, she took his hand and shook it slowly. "I'm *very* pleased to meet you."

Lindsey glanced at Jonas from the corner of her eye, wondering what his reaction would be to her friend's overly zealous greeting. She herself knew what Debra was implying, but then, he couldn't read her friend's mind as she could.

But Jonas only accepted the handshake and murmured a polite greeting in reply.

"I'm glad to find you both safe and sound," he said. "And now, would someone kindly tell me what in Sam Hill is going on here?"

Jonas looked at Lindsey, Lindsey looked at Debra, and Debra looked down at the floor. Before another word could be uttered, the door opened again, drawing all three pairs of eyes.

Paul Fillmore filled the space, gave each one a brief glance, then closed the door and strode into the room. Then he lifted his arms, and Debra flew straight into his embrace.

Over the top of her blond head, Paul grinned into Lindsey's astonished face.

"Will someone please explain what is happening here?" Jonas muttered angrily.

He didn't like what he was thinking right at this moment. He didn't like being played for a sucker by anyone, and he had hoped his earlier conclusions, teaming Debra up with Fillmore in bilking Lindsey, had been erroneous.

"Hello, Lindsey, it's good to see you again." Paul nodded politely in her direction, then added, "If you and Mr. Kingston would please be seated, I've taken the liberty of asking that fresh coffee and sandwiches be served. And then—'' he glanced directly at Jonas ''—I'll explain everything to everyone's satisfaction.''

There was a light knock on the door, and a tall man dressed all in black limped into the room pushing a serving cart. He set it before Paul and Debra, who had sat down side by side on a small love seat, and without acknowledging anyone else exited the room.

"Thank you, Nicky," Paul called to his retreating back.

Jonas watched with hard eyes as the man left the room. He didn't like having a gun stuck in his face, and this was the man who'd been on the other end of it.

Debra, appearing to be oblivious to the mixed thoughts and emotions around her, handed out coffee and sandwiches. And Paul watched her, bringing a blush to her cheeks when she glanced up and caught his intent gaze on her face.

Paul accepted only a cup of coffee, then waited until everyone was served and began to speak.

"As you both no doubt know—" he looked first at Lindsey and then at Jonas "—I have a certain knack for making money in the stock market. And I've used that gift to make me a rich man. Somewhere along the way, I discovered a love of art, especially antiques." His dark eyes began to glow, and he took a sip of coffee before returning his attention to his story. "I was attending a party before the holidays at the home of a man I know only slightly, through Mayor Dennison." He smiled slightly at Lindsey.

"This man, our host, had recently acquired a six-piece set of hand-carved, ivory snuff boxes, decorated with precious stones, dating from the early eighteenth century and said to have been given by Queen Anne as tokens of her esteem to various members of her court.

"On this particular evening we were all permitted the opportunity to view these examples of art at its finest. They were exquisite—"

He broke off for a moment, as though lost in the memory of their beauty, and then continued. "I spoke with the man privately, after the party, and inquired about purchasing them from him. He refused. I hadn't really expected anything else.

"Now, I know you're wondering what this long story has to do with your being my...guests. But my explanation isn't at an end.

"It seems that Nicky, who is a very good friend from the days of my youth, decided that he would acquire for me the antiques I had so admired, using his own, ah, unique talents."

"He pinched them," Jonas interjected abruptly.

Paul rested his dark glance on Jonas's tight face for a brief moment before answering. "Yes, Mr. Kingston, he pinched them."

"And now he's kidnapped two women." Jonas sat forward on the couch. "You can add two counts of kidnapping to grand larceny and see what you come up with. A fine friend you have there," he observed laconically.

A hard glitter entered Paul's eyes. "Perhaps if I explain a little about Nicky to you, you'll understand why he did what he did. You may not agree with it, but at least you'll understand it.

"He and I go back many years to the time my mother and father abandoned me in a dump in a very poor section of the Bronx. I was about twelve at the time, and Nicky still had one parent on the scene. I made my home off and on with them. His mother was a waitress who supplemented her wages with—other forms of employment." From the look in his eyes, his meaning was clear.

"Then, one day, she simply didn't come home after being gone all night. Neither one of us ever saw her again. So we made our way together. We were members of a street gang. There was no way we could have survived if we hadn't been.

"One night there was some trouble with a rival gang, and I kept Nicky from bleeding to death while the ambulance arrived." He shrugged broad shoulders. "He would have done the same for me. But he insists I saved his life and has been trying to find ways to repay me ever since.

"His plan was to present me with the snuff boxes as a gift. I would never have kept them, but I certainly wouldn't have turned him in to the police, either. One way or another, I would have seen that they were returned to their rightful owner.

"In any case, the antiquities were . . . pinched. He and another man we grew up with had the whole thing planned, were in fact meeting at the restaurant, where Debra and her friend happened to overhear their conversation, in order to smooth out any final flaws in their plans. And when Nicky discovered Debra had overheard their plot, he acted without thinking—foolishly—by kidnapping her to keep her quiet.

"I don't know what he thought he would do with her afterward. Maybe he hadn't thought that far ahead. But he brought her here. He kept her hidden in an upstairs bedroom for a few days before I found her. I can assure you—" he directed this to Lindsey "—she was given the best of care."

"I was never mistreated," Debra interjected. "Nicky brought me all kinds of good things to eat, and a color TV and a stereo. He treated me like a queen—"

"A captive queen," Jonas interjected.

"But I was never in any danger, not even from the first," she protested.

"What about the note, the phone call?" Lindsey asked. "How did you get the note into my purse?"

Debra looked at Paul.

"Paul?" Lindsey asked incredulously.

"Remember when you gave me your purse to hold while you danced with Ryan? It was a very simple matter to slip the note inside without anyone seeing," he confessed.

"And the phone call?" Lindsey asked, looking from her friend to Paul.

"We knew you had hired someone to find me." Debra spoke softly, shamefacedly. "Paul—we—thought if I called you and let you know I was fine, that I'd be released from captivity soon, that you'd be willing to wait, and that would give Nicky time to return the stolen property."

"So you've been in on it almost from the first?" Jonas asked in a hard voice, his question directed toward the other man.

Debra straightened quickly. "No, he hasn't," she answered for him. "By the time Paul found me, Nicky had already taken the antiques. Paul told him he had to put them back."

Paul patted her hand to calm her and took up the narrative. "I am not a thief, Mr. Kingston. Look around you. Do you really think I have to steal? I haven't had to steal to survive for a long time now, and that's the only reason I ever did. It was never something I enjoyed doing.

"But to continue with the explanations, after I discovered Debra and learned through her about Lindsey, we kept a watch on her. I'm sorry, Lindsey, that things have turned out this way, and that we met under these circumstances. I've admired you from afar for a long time."

He turned to smile briefly into Debra's eyes, and Lindsey, sitting directly across from them, shivered at the look that passed over his face as their glances met. It was an expression she would have given everything to see on Jonas's face, just once, when he looked at her.

"We knew you had gone to the police, Lindsey. But since Nicky had had Debra call her boss about her going to stay with a sick relative, we thought we would be safe until we could get the stolen items replaced and get out of the country for a while.

"Nicky almost gave the whole thing away when he arrived at Debra's apartment to get some of her things so she would be more comfortable—she had refused point-blank to accept anything from me—and almost stumbled across you leaving it. If he'd been a few minutes earlier, he would have entered the apartment while you were still inside.

"We didn't know about your having hired a detective to find Debra until almost too late. I couldn't employ anyone to follow you around, and I didn't want anyone else involved in this, so I tried to keep an eye on you myself. As you've guessed, I wasn't very successful.

"You know," Paul said, turning his attention to Jonas, "you almost had me at the pharmacy where I picked up Debra's prescription. When I looked back and saw the pharmacist frantically waving his arms at someone across the street, instinct took over and I resorted to a trick I learned as a youth. I ducked into a restaurant and went out the back door.

"I thought we were all perfectly safe until my housekeeper came home in a tizzy this evening, upset because someone had tried to bribe her into giving out information about me and my household.

"I realized that perhaps it was time to bring Lindsey here, so she could see that her friend was not in any danger. We hadn't planned on your being a guest, as well, but we found you, and as you can see, we never turn anyone away.

"The stolen property will be returned to its rightful owners just as soon as possible. Unfortunately, Mayor Dennison mentioned the situation to me, so the coast has not yet been clear. Since Nicky is the one who took it, he'll see that it gets back again," Paul assured everyone.

"But I cannot," he said as his jaw hardened, "I *will not* allow anyone—" his glance rested on Jonas's stern features "—to turn an old friend in to the police for a mistake he made on my behalf. The two of you will remain as my guests until this situation has been dealt with."

Paul rose. "Now, if you will come with me, Mr. Kingston, I'll show you to your room. Debra will take Lindsey to hers."

Jonas joined the other man at the door, hesitating long enough to dart a quick glance over his shoulder at Lindsey before following the other man from the room.

Debra turned to find Lindsey looking at her accusingly.

"You were a part of this almost from the beginning."

"I didn't mean to hurt you, Lin. You know your friendship has always been the most important thing in my life—"

"Until now," Lindsey finished for her. She had seen the interplay between her friend and Paul. It would have been impossible to misinterpret their feelings for each other.

"All this time, I've been worried sick, thinking you had been kidnapped, waiting for a ransom note, a phone call, and all in vain. I went to the police and practically abused them because they wouldn't send men out immediately to look for you."

Lindsey paced around the room, gesturing with her arms, striding back and forth as she spoke. "I even hired a private detective. I told Brian off—"

"You told off Brian? That's great!"

"Yes, it is." Lindsey paused in her tirade to smile. Then her eyes grew stormy again, and she asked, "How could you? How could you let me think the worst for all this time?"

"I'm sorry, really sorry, for all the unhappiness I caused you," Debra told her sincerely.

"I know, I know." Lindsey gave the shorter woman a hug. "I'm just glad you're all right. And I haven't missed how...close you and Paul appear to be."

Debra blushed. "It wasn't something I was expecting to happen. If you could have seen his face the day he unlocked the door and found me...!" Her blue eyes glittered with laughter. "I was standing on a chair beside the door with a lamp in my hands. I had decided enough was enough, and I was going to bash Nicky over the head and make my getaway in the best movie heroine tradition."

"But instead you stayed to fall in love," Lindsey finished for her.

"Yes."

"Have you and he discussed...everything?"

"If you're wondering about my epilepsy, it's all right. I told him about it up front. And he's the one who insisted on getting the medicine, taking the chance that someone might catch him. He even scolded me for going without it, for not saying anything about it sooner.

"He's not like any other man I've ever met, Lin. He's kind and gentle. I've never heard him raise his voice since I've been here. Not even when he called Nicky into the room, that day he found me, for an explanation about what I was doing there.

"And yet he's so strong, so masculine." She giggled like a teenager. "I approve of Jonas," she said, changing the subject. "He's a little worried about you right now, and not feeling very friendly toward Paul, but I can understand that."

"Worried about me?"

"Of course, silly. Didn't he practically deflate your lungs when he first entered the room?"

"I'm the one who ran to him—"

"And I'm the one who saw his face when he had you in his arms."

"He feels responsible for my safety."

"My Aunt Fanny!"

"Debra...."

"Come on, it's late, and I, for one, need my rest." Debra took Lindsey's arm and led her toward the door.

A few minutes later she left Lindsey with the words, "Don't let this one get away, Lin. I saw your future in his eyes."

Chapter 14

By the hands of the clock beside the bed, it was after midnight. Lindsey had been lying awake for the past two hours, the day's events running through her head. She should have been at peace. Debra had been found safe and sound, the stolen antiques were to be returned, and her best friend appeared to have found that rarest of all things, love.

The whole household had been busy for the past couple of days. Paul and Debra had decided to go to Europe. There had been a slight delay, because Debra was still listed officially as missing. A couple of calls had been necessary to assure the police department that the young woman was safe and sound. It had all been a huge misunderstanding, Lindsey had assured the gruff-voiced cop.

Debra was so excited, she had confided to Lindsey, that she could hardly remember her own name. She and Paul were making no immediate plans about marriage; they were going to play it by ear and simply let it happen at the right time and right place.

Lindsey found that romantic in the extreme. She envisioned them standing on the deck of a cruise ship, beneath the stars, making their vows. And a tiny voice inside whispered the question, *Don't you wish that you were on that deck, you and Jonas?*

The house was silent, until all at once the sound of a door closing somewhere along the corridor reached her ears. Jonas? Was he feeling as restless as she was tonight?

The two of them had been "guests" of Paul Fillmore for two days and three nights now. Very special guests, treated with the utmost care and consideration—but prisoners, nevertheless.

She hadn't seen much of Jonas, only spied him occasionally leaving a room, or walking on the grounds with Paul. The two men appeared to have reached some sort of an understanding, and they'd begun to appear, to Lindsey's surprise, almost friendly with each other.

The past two days had turned out to be strange but wonderful—strangely wonderful? She had known, at every hour of the day and night, that Jonas was somewhere beneath the same roof as herself, and had been filled with a sense of warmth and peace at the thought.

But, at the same time, she'd also known that this thing from her past, from their joint past, stood like a wall, separating them.

Once or twice, in the small hours of the night, she'd almost found the courage to go to him, confess the past and beg his forgiveness—his love?

But common sense had prevailed. He'd had plenty of opportunities to speak privately with her, and he'd made no attempt to seek her out.

Was that because he had nothing to say to her? Had he already said it all? Had she been right in thinking he'd only been after revenge?

Lindsey moved restlessly on the bed. She still hadn't told him what Ryan had revealed to her only a couple of days ago.

What if *he* didn't remember *her?* What if she was only imagining his remote behavior? What if she brought up the past and ruined everything for both of them?

But to keep silent would be lying by omission, and she couldn't do that. That was what her father had been guilty of doing. Hadn't he planned the whole thing, covered up his daughter's shame, *his shame,* by lying, pretending it had never happened, erasing any mention of her presence in the apartment?

Throwing the bed covers aside, Lindsey dropped her feet over the edge of the mattress and pushed them into her slippers. She couldn't do it. She couldn't leave things as they were. Even if Jonas had forgotten her true identity, she felt a need to confess.

Besides, even if he did remember and loved her despite it, she didn't want him to go through life harboring the thought somewhere in the back of his mind that she was a criminal, responsible for a man's death. She had to speak with him now. She couldn't wait a moment longer.

She grabbed the robe lying across the foot of the bed and quickly put it on. Her hand was on the doorknob, her resolve hardened to action, when she heard sounds from downstairs. She hesitated. It sounded as though the whole household was awake. Maybe this wasn't the right time to seek Jonas's company.

A slight sound from somewhere outside held her in place. She frowned, recognizing it all at once. A car engine. Was Nicky off on some mission again?

It didn't matter. She was going to speak to Jonas tonight, even if she had to wade through Miklos, Lucia, Paul and Debra to do it.

Jonas's room was around the corner from her own. Her footsteps were soundless on the thick carpet, every nerve in her body on alert. She felt as though she were doing something wrong, something she had to keep secret, in going to him this way. She knew the feeling was ridiculous, but nevertheless, she couldn't seem to shake it.

Outside his door, holding her breath, she raised one hand and knocked lightly, waited, then knocked again.

After several long moments, her heart beating double time, she grasped the doorknob determinedly and, pushing the door open a few inches, peeked inside.

A small reading lamp beside the bed was turned on. The bed was still neatly made, the room empty.

Jonas was gone!

Lindsey slipped inside the room, closed the door behind her and stood staring at the empty bed. Her mouth was dry, her hands shaking, and there was a sinking feeling in the pit of her stomach. There had to be some mistake. He couldn't have left—simply gone—and forgotten all about her.

And what about Paul and Debra? Nicky? Was Jonas going to turn the man in to the police? She'd thought he was going to cooperate with Paul in this and let them return the antiques.

The bathroom! That was it. Jonas must be taking a late bath. That always helped whenever she couldn't sleep. Until now, that was.

She quickly found the door to the bathroom and, mindful of what she might find, opened it with her eyes directed toward the floor.

"Jonas? Are you there?"

There was no answer. She allowed her eyes to move upward and found the room empty.

Where was he?

The car! Oh, Lord, please don't let him have left, she prayed as she hurried from the room. Her feet fairly flew as she rounded the corner, moved down the hall past her own room and headed for the stairs.

She knew his car had been brought to the house from its hiding place somewhere outside the main estate grounds. If it was missing, she didn't know what she would do. How could she betray her best friend and let Jonas go to the police? But how could she betray the man she loved—again?

She had just reached the front door when a strong arm whipped around her from behind.

With a sense of shock, Lindsey glanced up into twinkling blue-green eyes. "You're here," she breathed.

"And where else would I be?" he asked deeply.

"I thought you'd . . . gone," she admitted.

"No." He shook his head. "They have."

"They?"

"Paul and your friend and Nicky."

"Gone? Gone where?"

He shrugged, loosened his hold on her and stepped back. "I suppose they're on the way to the airport. They're leaving the country, remember?"

"But I don't understand," Lindsey protested. "I thought they were waiting until Nicky put back the antiques."

"That's true, they were, but with the police watching the house the way they are, it would be virtually impossible to get inside without detection.

"That's why I made a suggestion that your friend Paul was willing to go along with. I suggested an anonymous phone call to someone in the police department, telling them where they could find the missing items."

"Someone?" Lindsey asked, following his line of thought. "Or Brian?"

"He came to me, you know, wanting me to help him find the antiques—" He broke off and shook his head at her look of inquiry. "I told him no, but this way, at least, he'll get the credit for their return."

And that meant that the job of district attorney Brian coveted so highly would once more be firmly within his grasp. Jonas could at least give him that.

"Do you mind?" he asked, watching her expression closely.

Lindsey shook her head. She harbored no ill feelings toward Brian. The ill feeling had mostly been on his part.

"But what about Debra?" she asked, bringing the subject back to her friend. "I can't believe she didn't wait to say goodbye to me, or that she actually agreed to fly. She hates flying."

"She said she couldn't bear the tears—hers more than yours. And as for flying, I doubt she's noticing anything much beyond the fact that she's with Paul."

"Yes." Lindsey glanced away, knowing how she would feel if the circumstances were different and she were the one leaving the country with Jonas at her side. "I imagine you're right about that."

But she still felt a sharp jab of disappointment that her friend had left without saying goodbye. It would take a while for it to sink in that Debra would now put someone else above Lindsey.

She knew that was the way it should be. It would just take a little getting used to, that was all.

"Come on." Jonas took her arm. "Let's find somewhere comfortable. We need to talk."

Lindsey wondered if the ominous ring she heard in that last sentence had only been in her imagination, and hung back a little.

"Come with me." He pulled her along at his side.

"W-where are we g-going?"

"The greenhouse. I could use some fresh air, and it's too damn cold outside."

In a moment they were surrounded by sultry warmth.

"This is wonderful," Lindsey murmured, moving down a row of exotic-looking ferns. "I love plants. There's something special in knowing you have beautiful, living things actually growing in your home, sort of living with you, like part of the family—" She broke off and looked back at Jonas.

He was watching her closely.

"I'm sorry, I guess that sounds—"

"Don't apologize. I like how it sounds." He walked slowly toward her. "Paul said pretty much the same thing when he showed me this place. He said after his years of living in the concrete jungle he couldn't get enough of greenery. I've noticed you two share similar attitudes on several subjects. For a while I thought you and he..."

He tore his eyes from her face and looked around at the greenery surrounding them. It was almost like being in a jungle, deep in the heart of some South American country. There was a stillness, a sense of isolation.

"He and I?" Lindsey repeated his words. "We hardly know each other. We met only a few days ago."

"But you do have a lot in common." Jonas was concentrating on a broad-leafed plant to the right of him, the leaves thick and velvety to the touch.

"We know some of the same people," she conceded. "But we don't have all that much in common."

"You're both business people, millionaires."

"The business, the money, was my father's—"

That had been the wrong thing to say. She saw it immediately by the stiffening of his features. There was nothing for it. She'd wanted an opportunity to discuss the past with him. Well, here it was.

"Jonas, did you know my father?" she asked abruptly.

"I knew of him," he answered after a slight pause.

"When?"

"A long time ago." He brushed past her and started toward the connecting door that would take them into the main part of the house. Her hand on his shoulder stopped him.

"When?" she repeated softly.

"Let it go."

"I can't. It's standing between us."

"I don't know what you're talking about."

"Yes!" She shook his arm. "You do. I'm talking about one night's events and two men, one who would go to his death helping someone else, and one who would lose, forever, a part of himself because of that."

Jonas turned slowly to face her, deep sadness etched in the lines at the edges of his eyes.

"You do remember," he whispered without expression.

"Some of it. A little more since Ryan prodded my memory. I remember the terror, Derek's crazed eyes, the pain. I remember thinking, I'm going to die. I'm only twenty years old, and I'm about to die.

"All kinds of things went through my mind when I thought I was dying. I would never hold a child in my arms, my child. I'd never hear the sounds of an organ playing the wedding march at my own wedding. I'd never get to learn to scuba dive.''

She gave a small laugh with nothing of humor in it. ''I even wondered what the headlines would say about my death. No doubt something sensational like Socialite Found Slain in Drug Lord's Love Nest.''

Jonas clenched his jaw against angry, destructive words of his own. But he didn't have to voice them; they were there in his face.

''It would have been a lie,'' she murmured throatily. ''I didn't love Derek, and my apartment was no love nest.

''And I was not, voluntarily, under the influence of drugs that night.''

Jonas's glance wavered, but his body remained tense. He'd thought it wouldn't matter, but hearing her say it—the pictures her words brought to mind . . .

''No! Don't turn away from me. I'm telling you the truth. I was unconscious when he—'' She paused for strength. ''Injected me with the drugs.''

She moved closer, until her body was pressing along his rigid side. Perhaps the feel of her could get through to him where her words couldn't.

''I've had nightmares about that night ever since. It hasn't been until recently, along with some self-analysis, that I've discovered what those nightmares really stemmed from.

''They weren't caused only by the beating but also by a faint memory, a picture hidden deep in the recesses of my mind. A picture of turquoise eyes, kind eyes, eyes that were set in the face of my deliverer.'' She paused to let that sink in.

''Only they didn't deliver me from my pain. They plunged me back down into the midst of it.''

He whipped around to face her. ''I never touched you, except to help you!'' he protested strongly, drawing away from contact with her. Here they were, the old lies, the stories concocted by her father—at her instigation? Please, God, not that. He'd always hoped, despite all the evidence to the contrary, that somehow she'd had no knowledge of what her father had done.

"I know, I know," she whispered, moving close to him again. "I know you only wanted to help me. It was my twisted psyche blaming you for not staying with me, keeping me out of my father's hands."

"I don't understand."

"Neither did I, for a long time. My father kept me drugged after that night, kept me secreted in a sanatorium, locked up like a criminal, until he could ruin you and get me out of the country so I couldn't stop him."

"My God!"

Jonas turned so that their bodies made full contact and touched her cheek with shaking fingers, his eyes moving over her face feature by feature.

"What you must have gone through. And alone." His other hand turned her face up to his. "I promise I'll never leave you to face things alone, ever again."

"Do you mean that? You don't hate me?" she asked huskily. Her whole being awaited his answer.

"Hate you? How could I—when I love you so much?"

Lindsey's knees gave way, and she had to hold on to him to keep from falling. "You...love me?"

His answer was to sweep her into his arms and capture her lips beneath his in a kiss of longing and deep hunger.

Lindsey immediately fed that hunger, straining to meet his needs, drawing a response that startled them both. When the kiss ended, they drew a little apart, breathing heavily, staring at each other in mutual surprise.

The best Lindsey had hoped for by bringing up the past, and her knowledge of it, had been to clear the air between them and to get rid of any lingering misunderstandings.

She had hoped to find compassion and perhaps forgiveness in his eyes. She hadn't expected, hadn't even allowed herself to dream of finding, love.

Jonas's strong arms, still encircling her, drew her tightly against his chest. There had been too much talk already. He wanted to stop her from speaking again and breaking the spell being woven once more around them, wrapping them in a cocoon of enchantment. He didn't want to live in the past any longer. He wanted the present and—he hoped—a future filled with Lindsey and their love for each other.

"Jonas," Lindsey murmured, feeling her heart pound as his lips traveled slowly over her face, igniting small blazes with each soft kiss. She wanted nothing so much as to stand here and let him love her, but one thing still needed to be said between them.

Hearing the serious note in her voice and sensing the sudden restraint in her manner, Jonas withdrew, his eyes on her face. "What's wrong?"

This was going to be hard, but she had to say it. There had been so much subterfuge in the past that she wanted complete truth between them now.

"I—" She smoothed a nervous hand over the front of his jacket, her gaze faltering, then dropping to his chest. "I want you to know that despite everything—I loved my father." She felt him stiffen and pull back, the hands on her shoulders dropping away. Her eyes flew to meet his, and she felt something inside her clench at the distance she saw forming there.

"Please..." She tugged on the edges of his jacket, knowing what she risked losing with what she was about to say, but unable not to say it. "I'm so sorry about what happened to your friend, about his death. And for what happened to you, what my father did to you. But I have to be honest with you, I want there to be honesty between us—always.

"I don't know what I would have done back then, eight years ago. I was young, scared, I was very immature. I thought just being in my own place made me independent. But you know how that turned out."

"What are you saying?"

"I—" She wanted to look away, not to have to face him with what she was about to say. "I'm saying that if my father hadn't kept me drugged, if he had talked to me, he might have been able to convince me to do what he wanted—without the drugs."

He gripped her shoulders mercilessly. "You would have helped him to destroy me? You would have helped get the man who killed my best friend—a cop who was only there to help you—off scot-free?"

She could see the distance opening up between them like an impassable chasm. He didn't have to back away from her, didn't have to drop his hands as though her touch repelled him, for her to know she'd blown it with him.

"So your father and his precious position in society are more important to you than the truth? Money, power, position are more important to you than a man's life."

"No! You don't understand what I'm saying. I was only trying to be honest—"

"Honest! That's a laugh. It's not honesty we're talking about here. Neither you nor your father has ever known the meaning of the word."

He pushed past her, heading for the door.

"Jonas! I love you! And that's truth!"

She thought she saw him pause, but then the door was flying back on its hinges and his figure disappeared into the darkness beyond. Lindsey was left staring at emptiness, feeling it fill her heart—her soul—with blackness.

Her room overlooked the garage. She'd been standing at the window for hours, watching, waiting for the darkness to fade, for Jonas's car to back out of the garage and head down the driveway, but so far the sky was still pitch-black and the car remained parked where it was.

A large silver moon had risen, shedding its light on the world below. Lindsey stood there thinking about how, a long time ago, moonlight was said to bring bad luck to those who stood in its glow. Well, it was too late for her. Her bad luck had begun years ago and continued right up to the present.

"I always suspected you of being a witch, ever since the first time you looked at me with those green eyes of yours.

But I hadn't thought about your being a moon goddess in disguise.''

Lindsey held her breath, afraid to move in case it was a fantasy, in case Jonas's being in her room without her having heard him enter was a figment of her fondest imaginings.

He was behind her, close behind her, reaching out to her, his fingers spanning her waist, drawing her back against his warm, hard chest.

"I'm a fool," he breathed against her silky hair. "I'm hardheaded, stubborn and impossible, and sometimes it takes a really hard knock to get something through to me."

He turned her in his arms to face him. "The thought of losing you, of having you walk out of here, out of my life, was the knock I needed to make me see reason."

His hands smoothed her shoulders beneath her hair, moved up her neck, making her shiver, and then glided down to her waist and back, as though he couldn't get enough of touching her, of reassuring himself that she was real and not the imaginary goddess he'd proclaimed her to be.

"You were honest with me, so I'm going to try and be equally honest with you. I wasn't only angry with *you* a little while ago, but with myself, as well. I've felt guilty for a long time now because of Hank's death—because I didn't go after him soon enough, because it wasn't me lying on that path with my blood soaking the ground.

"But that isn't all of it. It was because I couldn't get you, and what I thought you'd done, out of my head." He stepped forward and clasped her body tightly to his. "But mostly," he whispered, his breath hot and uneven against her ear, "it was because I couldn't live with how I felt every time I thought about you, about the first time I saw you."

Lindsey buried her face against the muscles of his chest, her hands slipping about his waist. He'd been attracted to her even then? When he thought she was a criminal, a drug user, someone who associated freely with the likes of Derek Lassiter?

"I love you." She squeezed him to her, her face finding a loose button on his shirt, pressing her lips to the forceful uneven throb she felt there beneath tissue, bone and muscle.

"And I love you," he mouthed against her temple.

"Jonas," she began hesitantly, "about my money—"

"Money was never an issue between us, and it isn't now. It's your money. Do what you want with it."

He held her face between his hands and looked into her glowing green eyes. "All right?"

"Yes," she breathed, hardly daring to believe such happiness could be hers for the asking after so many years of misery. There was still Brian to contend with, but somehow it would all work out for the best. It had to. "You're wonderful."

"Not as wonderful as you." Jonas turned the words into a caress against her lips, making her forget everything but him.

All at once he bent and lifted her into the cradle of his arms, her diaphanous gown trailing out behind her as he carried her to the bed.

"What are you doing?"

He set her down gently, his body bent over hers, one knee on the bed beside her, his hands working swiftly to remove her gown.

"What do you think I'm doing?"

The gown glided over her head and and he threw it from him, leaned close and pressed his lips to the valley between her breasts, then rose to stand for a long moment looking down at her.

This time Lindsey made no move to cover herself, confident of his love for her, and hers for him. But by the time he'd looked his fill, it was all she could do to keep from throwing herself into his arms and begging him to make love to her.

Jonas, however, was busy removing his own clothing. And then, to her further surprise, he knelt instead of moving onto the bed beside her.

"There is one more thing I plan to do before the night is over." He smiled, a wicked twinkle in his beautiful blue-green eyes.

"And what is that?" She could hardly speak over the pounding of her heart.

One large hand pressed gently against the concave hollow of her belly. He rose on his haunches, bending toward her as he spoke, his eyes locked on hers.

"Make a start on that child—the one you want to feel so badly in your arms."

Lindsey's arms shot up, wrapped themselves around his shoulders and pulled, tumbling him onto the bed and atop her. After all, it didn't matter how their lovemaking got started, only that it did—and soon.

Epilogue

Debra and Paul were married in a small double-ring ceremony in Paris a month later. Lindsey and Jonas flew over for the ceremony. The only other person attending was the unlikely best man, Nicky, who wore his important position like a mantle.

Lindsey realized that she had never seen her friend's face glow so brightly as it did during the wedding ceremony. She was satisfied that at last her best friend, and her new friend, had found true happiness and would weather life's storms together—always together.

Three months later, in June, Lindsey and Jonas walked down the aisle. Ryan Dennison gave the bride away, and Brian was Jonas's best man.

Paul and Debra were in attendance, Debra as the matron of honor, and as happy as the bride herself in a brand-new maternity suit. She wasn't really far enough along in her pregnancy to need it, but she was so excited at the prospect of becoming a mother that she wanted everyone to share in her joy.

After the ceremony Brian immediately began handing out cigars and buttons with the slogan Brian's Against Lyin' printed on them. He reminded everyone that he was running for district attorney with the mayor's support. He also mentioned, whenever he could, that the happy couple owed everything to him, because he had introduced them.

But no one paid a lot of attention to him; everyone's eyes were on the bride and groom. And everyone was commenting on how happy, how radiant, the bride looked. Many were heard to speculate about what it was that gave her smile that soft, yet secretive look, and the general consensus was that it was, of course, the handsome groom.

And it was only the groom who shared the wonderful secret that made the bride's green eyes sparkle like fine emeralds. Because only the two of them shared the knowledge of the secret Lindsey carried, nestled warm and safe, growing, below her heart, something wonderful she and Jonas had created together with their first night of love.

And that was the real secret of what Lindsey knew.

* * * * *

Silhouette Sensation

COMING NEXT MONTH

UNFORGIVABLE
Joyce McGill

Pat Chase went home when her only living relative had a stroke, and found herself embroiled in a murder case. Pat's instincts as a journalist had her sifting clues and considering possibilities. But who would want to murder an old lady like Libby? And why?

Adam Wyatt wanted Pat's co-operation on the case; as the chief of police he was in charge of the investigation, but people were more likely to talk to Pat. *He* wanted to talk to Pat. He wanted to make love to Pat. . .

SOMEBODY'S LADY
Marilyn Pappano

Big city attorney Beth Gibson and smart, small-town lawyer Zachary Adams met in *Somebody's Baby*, and when Zach had a case he knew only a real hot-shot could win he immediately thought of Beth. He wanted to see her again, even though they were totally wrong for each other.

Zach had brought her an almost impossible case and then volunteered to help with it. Soon they were living together as well as working together and it was getting harder to remember how different they were, why they shouldn't be lovers. What would happen when the case was over?

Silhouette Sensation

COMING NEXT MONTH

TWILIGHT SHADOWS
Emilie Richards

Kelley Samuels was supposed to be a bridesmaid at her friend and partner's wedding, but she ended up diving to the floor as bursts of gunfire drowned out the music.

Any of the guests could have been the gunman's target, but with a long list of enemies and a young daughter to raise, Griff Bryant wasn't taking any chances. He was actually looking forward to having his body guarded by Kelley...

COMMAND PERFORMANCE
Nora Roberts

Cordina's Royal Family

It was at the request of His Royal Highness Alexander de Cordina that Eve Hamilton and her theatre company travelled to Cordina. The tiny principality still looked like a storybook place, but Eve knew that it had its villains and tragedies; she'd seen something of them seven years ago when Princess Gabriella had been kidnapped.

Alex was the heir but with Eve he felt like a man not a prince, just the sight of her made him ache. Was she the kind of woman who could take on the duties and responsibilities of a princess? Was she already involved with his brother?